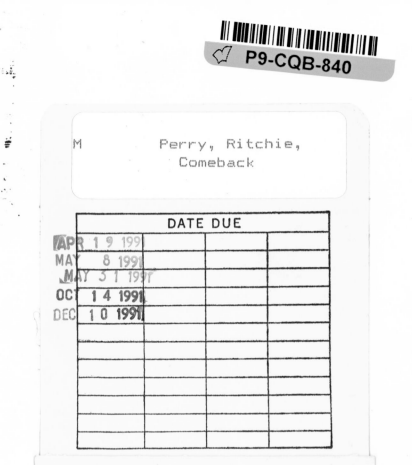

COMEBACK

By Ritchie Perry

Ritchie Perry

COMEBACK

A CRIME CLUB BOOK

DOUBLEDAY

New York   London   Toronto   Sydney   Auckland

A CRIME CLUB BOOK

PUBLISHED BY DOUBLEDAY
a division of Bantam Doubleday Dell Publishing Group, Inc.
666 Fifth Avenue, New York, New York 10103

DOUBLEDAY and the portrayal of a man
with a gun are trademarks of Doubleday,
a division of Bantam Doubleday Dell
Publishing Group, Inc.

Library of Congress Cataloging-in-Publication Data
Perry, Ritchie, 1942–
    Comeback / Ritchie Perry. — 1st ed.
      p. cm.
    "A Crime Club book."
    I. Title.
  PR6066.E72C66   1991
  823'.914—dc20   90-43774
                                           CIP

ISBN 0-385-41601-6

Printed in the United States of America
March 1991
10 9 8 7 6 5 4 3 2 1
First Edition

M

COMEBACK

ONE

Rocky stirred, slowly lifting his bearlike head. Although he had been asleep, the dog was alert now and, as he yawned hugely, his ears were pricked. Something was wrong and Rocky knew it. In the same way, instinct told him the danger wasn't pressing and Rocky took his time as he padded across to the window. For a dog his size, there was no need to put his paws on the sill. When he looked out through the net curtains, he could stand normally.

The two men were almost a hundred yards away, at the edge of the small copse of beech trees which marked the boundary of the farm. It was the faint sound of their voices which had first disturbed him and Rocky recognized neither of them. They weren't included among the select few his master had introduced to him as friends. In any case, their furtive movements were warning enough. They were intruders, a threat to his territory, and Rocky growled at the back of his throat. It was a low, hostile rumble which was barely audible.

Other dogs might have barked in an attempt to drive the strangers away but this wasn't part of Rocky's nature. He was an Anatolian shepherd. His breed's iron physique had been forged over the centuries in the Middle East, scaling boulder-strewn slopes, braving freezing river torrents or patrolling tirelessly ahead of grazing flocks. However, Rocky's ancestors had been no mere herders. They were the supreme guard dogs, afraid of nothing and imbued with a protective instinct which overrode any other consideration. Only the strongest of the breed had been allowed to survive, and with good reason. With its cropped ears and iron-spiked collar, a single Anatolian had been expected to deal with a full-grown wolf on its own. And Rocky was far bigger and far more powerful than his Turkish forefathers had ever been. Standing thirty-five inches at the shoulder and weighing 155 pounds, he could have disposed of a Doberman with a contemptuous flick of his massive jaws.

It was controlled power. Rocky belonged to a breed which was expected to think for itself, a trait which had been instilled over countless generations. He used his own judgement without needing any human handler to tell him what to do. Like the others of his kind, Rocky was prepared to die in defense of what was his and no amount of pain would ever be sufficient to make him abandon this duty. Only a command from his master could make him do this and, even then, not always. There might be occasions when the protective instinct could override his master's wishes.

For the moment, the house was Rocky's territory. It had been left in his care and he would defend it while there was breath in his body. This was his function, the sole reason for his existence. While they were standing at the edge of the copse, the two men posed no more than a peripheral threat and there was nothing for him to do. However, when Rocky settled down behind the sofa again, he didn't go back to sleep. He was waiting, head raised, ears pricked. His master was the only person he would allow across the threshold. If the men should come closer and attempt to enter the farmhouse, Rocky would attack as a matter of course. And he would attack to kill. It definitely wasn't part of an Anatolian's heritage to play games.

There were swarms of tiny black flies sharing the shade of the beech trees with them and Donnelly flapped a hand to clear them from his face. This was no more than a gesture. The flies merely dispersed for a few moments before they regrouped around his head. As if this wasn't bad enough, Donnelly felt uncomfortable in the suit, the unaccustomed tie tight around his neck. Underneath the jacket, he knew his shirt would be soaked with sweat. He could feel it sticking clammily to his armpits and back.

"Well?" he enquired softly.

"It's clear," MacFaddyn answered without removing the binoculars from his eyes.

Patrick MacFaddyn was taller and thinner than his companion, a sombre man who seldom smiled. At thirty-five he could have passed for ten years older, and he had looked little different when he had been in his twenties. This was nothing unusual in the part of Belfast where he had been brought up. There even the babies looked old by the time they had left their prams. After a last, slow sweep of the buildings below, MacFaddyn allowed the binoculars to hang by their strap while he took the radio from his pocket.

"Liam," he said quietly. "Are you still awake?"

"Just about."

"Is there anything to report?"

"You'd have heard from me if there was. So far I've seen one tractor, two rabbits and a pheasant."

Liam Ferguson was the lookout and driver. He was positioned almost half a mile away, where the track from the farm reached the road.

"We're going closer now," MacFaddyn told him. "I want to know the moment anything turns off the road."

"Don't worry. You will."

"Once Russell is on his way, get back to the car and stay there. You don't even get out to take a leak. We may need to leave in a hurry."

"That's understood."

The radio back in his pocket, MacFaddyn returned to the binoculars. Nothing had changed. Although the ivy-covered farmhouse looked peaceful enough in the bright sunlight, the Irishman couldn't still a faint prickle of unease. There was something wrong, something which was out of place.

"So we're doing it today," Donnelly said.

"God willing, yes."

"Why rush it? After three years, a day or two longer isn't going to make much difference."

Busy with the binoculars, MacFaddyn didn't bother to reply. His mind was already made up.

"We ought to keep Russell under surveillance for a few days," Donnelly persisted. "We ought to establish patterns. Then we could pick the time and the place."

"This is the time and the place." MacFaddyn had taken the binoculars from his eyes and was staring at his companion. There were occasions when Donnelly irritated him almost beyond endurance. "Tell me something, Martin. Did you ever meet Russell in the old days?"

"No," Donnelly admitted. "I was either in Derry or south of the border."

The older man nodded thoughtfully, as though this explained everything. MacFaddyn had known him, although Russell had been calling himself by another name at the time. Even now, after so many good men had died, MacFaddyn's hatred was tinged with grudging respect. God knew, the movement had embraced plenty of traitors in its time. There had always been the bastards who were ready to sell their fellows for a handful of silver, but Russell had been something else. No other outsider had ever managed to infiltrate the Provos so successfully. For his last two years, Russell had been operating at command level in Belfast. During this period, every last scrap of information he had gleaned must have been passed back to his masters in Whitehall. Thanks to bloody Russell, it had been one of the most disastrous periods in the movement's history. MacFaddyn wasn't quite sure how he could adequately describe the man to Donnelly.

"Are there times when I frighten you, Martin?" he asked.

Donnelly hesitated for a second, not certain how to respond. In the end he settled for honesty.

"Yes," he said. "A little."

"Well, Russell scares the hell out of me. He's the most dangerous bastard I'm ever likely to meet and that's saying something. We couldn't follow Russell for five minutes without him knowing we were there."

"He's really that good?"

By now MacFaddyn's mood had communicated itself to his companion. Donnelly found it difficult to accept that there might actually be somebody who frightened the man beside him. Fear wasn't something he had ever associated with MacFaddyn.

"You'd better believe it. That's why we take Russell cold, the moment he gets back to the farm. No talking, nothing. We don't give the bastard any chance at all."

"How do we handle it?"

Donnelly was sweating more than ever.

"You hide in the barn. I'll be in the house so we have him in a cross fire. You take your cue from me. The moment I start shooting, you join in. And you keep shooting until I tell you to stop."

"I get you."

"No you don't," MacFaddyn said.

There was no way to explain Russell adequately. He only hoped Donnelly didn't have to learn the truth the hard way.

Bronwyn was careful to keep her back to the bed as she dressed. Considering what they had just been doing together, Russell thought this smacked of closing the stable door long after the horse had bolted.

"Do you want a coffee, love?"

She was busy hooking up her bra and spoke over her shoulder.

"That sounds nice. I'll come through when it's ready."

Hands behind his head on the pillow, Russell watched as Bronwyn pulled on her tights. It always amazed him how awkward and uncoordinated most women were. Of course, Bronwyn wasn't exactly graceful at the best of times. No matter how conscientiously she dieted, she would never rid herself of the excess weight around her buttocks and thighs. She was a comfortable woman, not a beauty, but this didn't lessen her in Russell's mind. He supposed he had had his share of beautiful women and they weren't necessarily the ones he remembered best.

Once she had smoothed down her top and skirt, Bronwyn returned to the bed, the springs squeaking in mild protest as she seated herself on the edge. This was another small part of their ritual.

"Thank you, Alan," she said softly, bending down to kiss his forehead. "I enjoyed that."

The Welsh lilt was evident in her voice.

"It was good for me too."

"Was it really?"

Now Bronwyn was embarrassed. However much she might play the wanton in bed, the puritanism of her upbringing reasserted itself as soon as she had left it. Sex wasn't something nice girls talked about and Bronwyn was avoiding his eyes, preferring to toy with the puckered scar on Russell's left shoulder. She knew there was another, larger scar below his shoulder blade. This was where the bullet had existed.

"You know it was," Russell told her. "Your technique could do with some more work, but your interpretation was brilliant."

"Oh, Alan. Stop it."

Although she realized he was teasing her, Bronwyn couldn't stop the blush spreading from her cheeks to her neck. Russell smiled at her, then reached up to trap her hair, pulling her head down so he could kiss her properly. Despite the faint stirring in his groin, he made no attempt to detain her when she pushed him away.

"I'd better make the coffee," she said, rising to her feet. "Will you have something to eat as well?"

"Not today, thanks. I'll pick up a sandwich on the way back to the farm."

While Bronwyn busied herself in the kitchen, Russell stayed where he was. There was a reassuring familiarity about the bedroom. As always, the photograph of Bronwyn's late husband was face down on the dressing table. Russell was aware that it would be restored to its rightful position as soon as he had left. He also knew that her husband's clothes still hung neatly in the smaller of the two wardrobes. Russell found these reminders of John Price, deceased, another source of reassurance. While the shadowy influence remained, no demands were likely to be made of him.

It wasn't until MacFaddyn almost tripped over the yellow plastic bowl, half hidden in the grass beside the front door, that he finally identified the cause of his unease. Just in case there should be any doubt about it, DOG was inscribed on the side in large block capitals. MacFaddyn guessed that his subconscious must have registered the bowl without making the obvious association.

He hunkered down beside the bowl while he thought the problem through. Those few scraps of food remaining in the bowl were fresh. From the size of the bowl and what he knew of Russell, he could deduce that it was no lapdog. It would be a big brute and Russell would have imposed his own sense of discipline on the animal. It was also reasonable to assume that the dog wouldn't simply be at the farm to provide companionship. Russell was as close to self-sufficiency as anybody MacFaddyn had ever met.

No, MacFaddyn decided as he rose to his feet, it would definitely be a working dog. Russell would expect the beast to have some function beyond slavish devotion and there were no sheep to herd. It wasn't likely to be a gundog either—Russell was used to hunting far bigger prey than pheasant or rabbit. The animal was almost certainly a guard dog, but this caused MacFaddyn no real concern. However great his respect for Russell, he had no fear of dogs. They were essentially predictable creatures, lacking deceit or guile. The only point which did bother him was whether or not the dog was in the house. Although there had been no barking, this wasn't necessarily of any great significance. It would merely be a tribute to Russell's training.

MacFaddyn stepped up to the window closest to the door, careful not to leave footprints in the small flower bed. When he peered through the net curtains, he could distinguish the outlines of the furniture in the living room beyond. He could see nothing which resembled a dog. MacFaddyn tapped lightly on the windowpane and this provoked no response. He tapped again, loudly enough to be heard anywhere in the house, and there was still no movement. This was enough to satisfy him. No matter how well trained the dog might be, simple curiosity would have brought it to the window if it was in the house. The dog must have gone with Russell.

On his way round the side of the farmhouse to the barn, MacFaddyn was on the lookout for anything which might warn Russell of their presence. There was nothing. He spent another minute or so on a visual check of the barn and once again he was satisfied. Although he knew exactly where Donnelly was, it was impossible to see him from outside.

"There's one minor complication, Martin," he said. "Russell probably has a dog with him, but it doesn't change anything. If we have to take it out, we can do it once Russell is down."

"O.K.," Donnelly answered from inside the barn. "What happens if Russell heads for the barn before he goes to the house?"

The nervousness was evident in Donnelly's voice.

"You still take your cue from me." The patch of rutted, dried mud left MacFaddyn in no doubt as to where Russell normally parked. Whichever way he went, Russell would be out in the open. "It's the same if he brings anybody back with him. We deal with Russell first. Then we do the mopping-up."

Turning his back on the barn, MacFaddyn pulled the radio from his pocket. He wanted a final word with Liam before he went inside the house.

Lying on his rug behind the sofa, Rocky was totally alert. He had listened to the men's approach and their slow circuit of the house without moving. The only time he had stirred was when one of them had tapped on the window. Then Rocky had started to rise, but the movement had been arrested almost as soon as it had begun. Although the window would have been no barrier to him, training had won out over instinct. His master had closed the door when he had departed. This meant the house was his to guard, not the yard outside. The threshold was the dividing line and until this was breached there was nothing for him to do. Rocky yawned hugely and continued to monitor the slight sounds from outside. He was sure it wouldn't be long now.

The car park of The Ship was virtually empty when Russell arrived shortly after two. As most of the pub's lunchtime trade came from Chepstow, the main exodus would have been about a quarter of an hour earlier. Russell pulled his Range Rover in beside the landlord's folly, an old Buick which was Dennis's pride and joy. He seemed to spend more time polishing it than he did driving the vehicle on the road. Considering it guzzled almost a gallon of petrol before it reached the car-park exit, this probably made sound economic sense.

He found Dennis leaning on the counter in the public bar, checking form in *The Sporting Life*. The only other occupant of the bar was old Elwyn, who was sitting in his usual seat by the window. Russell had never discovered what line of work he had actually retired from, but since he had, Elwyn spent all his mornings and evenings in the pub. He was never totally incapable and never completely sober.

"I was beginning to think you wouldn't make it today, Alan," Dennis said by way of a greeting. "Have a good time in Abergavenny?"

"Not bad. Is that all the food you have left?"

There were only two rolls left in the display case. The lettuce in one was curling at the edges and the ham in the other had a decidedly aged look to it. Neither of them was doing a great deal to titillate Russell's appetite.

"I'm afraid so," Dennis told him. "I can get Gwen to rustle up something fresh if you like."

"No, leave the poor woman in peace. I'll risk the ham roll."

"That's brave of you. What do you want to drink?"

"I'll have a pint of Founder's, please. You'd better pull one for Elwyn as well while you're about it."

"That should make the miserable old bugger's afternoon. He's already had one pint bought for him today."

"Has somebody won the pools, then? Or is the beer sour?"

The landlord was laughing as he worked the pump. For reasons Russell hadn't bothered to explore, the old man wasn't popular with either customers or staff.

"There were outsiders in earlier," Dennis explained. If Russell hadn't known he was accepted now, he might have been insulted by the contempt in the publican's voice. "They didn't know any better. They were Irish."

He spoke as though this was sufficient to explain any vagary of human nature.

"Wearing Wellies, were they?"

"They didn't need to. For all their fancy suits, they were your genuine thick Micks. Why else would they sit with Elwyn there?"

"I'm going to sit with Elwyn," Russell pointed out.

"You have a reason, though." Dennis remained unruffled. "You're a bloody masochist."

After he had paid, Russell took the beers and the roll across to the table in the window bay. The old man acknowledged his arrival with a nod, taking a long drink from the fresh pint before he spoke.

"Been to Abergavenny, have you?"

"That's right."

"I bet it's not only the market you poke around in, then. You always look a new man when you get back. Got some little filly tucked away there, have you?"

Russell smiled and drank some of his own beer. They sat in silence while he was eating his roll, both of them gazing out of the window. Traffic on the road outside might be infrequent but there was a nice view, all grass and trees and hills. On sunny days like this, Russell found it soothing. If it was raining or overcast, he preferred to stay at the bar. Needless to say, in that part of Wales he spent far more lunchtimes in Dennis's company than he did in Elwyn's.

"I hear you've been socializing already," Russell said at last.

"Oh aye." Elwyn didn't sound any more impressed than the publican had been. "Bloody Irish, three of them. Called themselves farmers, looking for property in the area. They must have thought I came down with the last shower of rain. There wasn't one of them who'd know a harrow from a cow turd."

"What makes you so sure?"

"It was bloody obvious, man. They said what a nice little farm you had. Anybody with eyes in their heads can see it's a bloody disgrace."

To go with the insult, Elwyn bared his teeth in a delighted grin. There wasn't anybody in the area who took his farming very seriously, least of all Russell himself.

"Thanks for the compliment," he said, returning the smile.

"Think nothing of it, Alan. Farmer you're not but you're still not bad for a bloody Englishman. Fancy a quick game of dominoes?"

"Why not."

Although dominoes wasn't a game Russell particularly enjoyed, he reckoned he owed the old man a lot more than a few minutes of his time.

There were several things MacFaddyn found difficult to accept in the first few seconds after he had opened the farmhouse door. After this, he was far too busy fighting for his life to think about anything beyond survival. The dog had exploded out from behind the sofa the moment he stepped into the house. It had surged straight into the attack without warning or preamble, lips drawn back from its teeth in a soundless snarl. MacFaddyn's first fleeting impression was of a creature the size of a small horse and the damn thing moved so fast he had no chance to raise the gun in his hand. Then he no longer had a gun. It went flying as the weight and impetus of the dog knocked him clean off his feet, its teeth clamped around his forearm.

As soon as he felt the brute strength in the jaws, MacFaddyn had known what was bound to happen. Although he tried to compensate as he fell, there was very little he could do to save himself and he actually heard the sharp crack when his radius went. When the pressure was increased, the sound of loose bits of bone grating together in his shattered arm was equally audible. At the back of MacFaddyn's mind was the certain knowledge that, if he survived, he would have to learn to do a lot of things left-handed.

O.K., MacFaddyn told himself, fighting back the pain and nausea. Write off the right arm. Try to forget about it. Let the bastard creature mangle it as much as he wanted because at least it should keep him occupied. The spring-loaded knife was in his right-hand trouser pocket. It was awkward reaching across his body, especially with the dog half on top of him, but MacFaddyn had every incentive he could possibly need. He knew the knife was the only chance he had.

The handle was actually beneath MacFaddyn's questing fingers when, without warning, the dog released its hold. Not that this was any reprieve. Almost immediately the beast went for a new target, through fooling around and striking for the throat. The bearlike mask was so close MacFaddyn could see the tiny pieces of meat stuck between teeth stained with his own blood as he desperately wrenched his head to one side. This worked once, but there was no way to protect himself against the second lunge without bringing his left arm up in front of his throat, the knife temporarily forgotten. The best MacFaddyn could do was make sure the dog's teeth clamped down on his elbow this time, not the brittler bones of his forearm.

Although the pain was almost unbearable, it was a respite of sorts, an opportunity for MacFaddyn to take stock. There was no feeling at all below the elbow in his right arm, the lines of communication to his hand irrevocably severed. He had neither the leverage nor the target to make effective use of his feet or knees. No matter how he struggled, he didn't have the strength to push the animal away with one arm alone. The bastard creature was beating him out of sight and MacFaddyn knew it. Without help he was finished.

MacFaddyn's mouth was opening on a shout to Donnelly when the dog suddenly launched a new attack. Abandoning MacFaddyn's elbow, it lunged straight for his groin. The Irishman's reaction was immediate and involuntary, his left arm going down, his body twisting away. He was committed before he realized the beast was much smarter than he had thought. This was MacFaddyn's last coherent thought as the dog reversed its feint, its teeth ripping into his unprotected throat. It was less than a minute since MacFaddyn had entered the farmhouse.

The intruder was dead and Rocky stepped back, licking blood from his muzzle. There was no sense of triumph or relief. He had simply done what had to be done and in the dog's mind there had never been any doubt about the outcome. Unlike most other breeds, Anatolians had no fear of humans and dominance was as inherent to them as protectiveness. He would probably have attacked an elephant with the same blithe confidence with which he had attacked MacFaddyn, secure in the knowledge of his own superiority.

His existence was bound by a set of simple, primitive rules and this code remained under threat. Although the immediate danger had been faced, Rocky knew there was still work to be done. The door of the farmhouse was open now, the territory under his protection extended. Rocky stepped over the body, leaving one large paw print in the spreading pool of blood beside MacFaddyn's throat. In the doorway he stopped, testing the air with his nose. He knew there had been two men because he had lain and listened to them as they made their circuit of the house. This was why he went to the left, heading away from the barn as he followed the trail the men had left.

On his silent circuit Rocky stopped at every place where MacFaddyn and Donnelly had paused, testing the area thoroughly. To his sensitive nose, every smell had its own story. This was what prompted him to break away from the trail when he rounded the far side of the farmhouse. He had detected a fresher scent and Rocky's hackles rose as he turned towards the barn. Now he knew where the other intruder was. There was no doubt at all about what he had to do.

Running away had never been an option Russell had considered seriously. This was a purely practical decision which had nothing to do with pride or machismo. O.K., he had finally been flushed out. Whatever happened, he would never be able to spend another night at the farm. All the same, there was a very clear distinction between leaving and running. The chasing pack had to be slowed down. Russell had to buy himself the time to lose himself again. Besides, the Provo leaders certainly weren't fools. If he kept hitting them hard enough, they might eventually decide the hunt wasn't worth the price. Although Russell considered this most unlikely, it was the only hope he had.

There were doubts, of course. Three years was a long time and it wasn't at all like riding a bicycle. However well he remembered the moves, the fine cutting edge would have been blunted by lack of use. He was far more vulnerable now than he had been in Belfast when danger was something he had lived with through every minute of every day. It was something he had to keep firmly fixed in his mind. Overconfidence was one of the cardinal sins in the profession he had tried to leave behind him. It helped to breed carelessness, and carelessness was a guaranteed route into a pine box.

Binoculars would have been a help, but they weren't really necessary. Russell had always accepted the fact that this day would eventually come. From the start he had seen the farm as a place which might have to be defended. Most of the first week after he moved in had been spent in removing the cover from the immediate vicinity of the farmhouse. There had been deliberate oversights, of course. This way he could be sure of where any attack would start from. Now Russell took these danger points one by one, examining them in minute detail. There was nothing at all to alarm him.

His examination complete, Russell returned his attention to the house itself. Rocky's tawny body was still sprawled full length in the yard. He hadn't moved since Russell had first crawled over the skyline and he was probably dead. This was a thought which saddened Russell because Rocky had been everything he had ever wanted in a dog. Beyond Rocky, the door of the farmhouse stood open, but the shadows prevented him from seeing inside. Although it was impossible to tell, Russell guessed that his visitors must have left. In that case he would have to track them down before he left the area himself. They were far too close for comfort.

He had no real hopes when he whistled. It surprised Russell to discover how pleased he was when Rocky raised his head to look in his direction. Suddenly there was no longer any need for caution. The Anatolian would never have been sleeping if strangers were still around, and Russell rose to his feet before he whistled again. The sound had Rocky up and running, clearing the fence at the bottom of the hill without breaking stride. Russell started to walk down to meet him, only stopping to brace himself when they had almost met. Even at play, Rocky was never exactly gentle, and Russell staggered back a pace as the dog jumped at him in greeting, tail wagging frantically. With a front paw on either of his shoulders, Rocky stood higher than his master. This meant he had to bend down to nibble at Russell's neck. It was his individual way of saying hello.

"Get down, you hooligan," Russell said, pushing Rocky away and repulsing another attempt to jump up. "Stand still while I take a look at you."

Apart from the caked blood around his muzzle, there were other splashes on his neck and flanks. Russell checked Rocky thoroughly, looking for signs of injury, but there were none. The blood evidently wasn't the dog's and for the first time it occurred to him that some of the intruders might not have left. This was enough to quicken Russell's pace as he set off towards the house again, Rocky at his side. It was only when he reached the doorstep that he stopped.

"Did you do this?" he asked.

Rocky wagged his tail, pleased to see his master pleased, while Russell bent down over the body. He had recognized MacFaddyn at once and it chilled him slightly to realize how fortunate he had been. The Provos must really be bearing a grudge to risk MacFaddyn outside Ireland. The Bernadelli Model 80 on the floor beside him was one proof of the Irishman's standing. Only the cowboys needed to use cannons. The .22 was a professional's weapon.

He went through MacFaddyn's pockets quickly and efficiently, showing real interest only in the radio set to RECEIVE. He pocketed it, along with the automatic, and rose to his feet. As he did so, Rocky began to scratch at the door, his sign that he wanted to show Russell something. Usually it was an empty food or water bowl, but today he took Russell to the barn.

"Yes, you are a clever boy," Russell told the dog, scratching him behind his ear.

The second man was a stranger and the way he lay suggested Rocky had taken him from behind. The result had been equally final and Russell was impressed. He suspected that his mock fights with the dog would never be quite the same again.

The car was where Russell had expected to find it. The dark blue Granada had been driven far enough along the forestry track to be completely hidden from the road and it was empty. The lookout would be stationed somewhere with a clear view of the crossroads and he would be much harder to locate. Offhand, Russell could think of at least half a dozen places suitable for his purpose.

Although Russell could simply wait by the Granada, this could be a lengthy process. MacFaddyn and company would have no real idea of when he was likely to return to the farm. If necessary, they would have been prepared to wait all afternoon. Russell wasn't. Nor did tracking his quarry through the woods hold any great appeal for him. At best it would be time-consuming and Russell had a lot of things to do.

Once he had checked the vicinity of the Granada, Russell turned his attention to the car itself. There were no weapons concealed in the interior or the boot. He pocketed the keys which had been left in the ignition, wound down the driver's window and then moved off into the bushes beside the track. He even permitted himself the faintest glimmer of a smile as he pulled out MacFaddyn's radio. Simplicity had always appealed to him.

"This is Alan Russell," he said. "I don't know who you are and I don't particularly care. All you have to do is take a message back to Belfast for me. MacFaddyn and the man with him are both dead. Anybody else who comes looking for me is likely to end up the same. Bon voyage and think yourself lucky."

There was nothing more Russell had to say and he certainly wasn't interested in any possible reply. Now it was simply a matter of waiting.

It was almost five minutes before Russell heard the lookout, coming along the track at a dead run. His panic was obvious and so was his lack of experience. Russell allowed him to get into the Granada before he chose to reveal his presence. The lookout was wondering where he had left the car keys when the cool metal of the .22 touched him behind the right ear.

"Surprise, surprise," Russell said.

The expression on the lookout's face suggested it was anything but a pleasant one.

"That's barbed wire." There was incredulity in the young Irishman's voice. "You can't use that."

There was no point in answering him. Russell had left his prisoner in the house with Rocky while he had gone to the barn. As far as he could tell, the man hadn't moved a muscle while he was away. This was hardly surprising. MacFaddyn's body, which was only a few feet away, was a potent reminder of what Rocky could do.

"It'll rip me to pieces."

Now the youngster's voice was a whine.

"That all depends on you." If Russell sounded disinterested, this was the way he felt. "You should be all right provided you don't move."

Before he finished, Russell had managed to prick himself a couple of times on the sharp barbs. There were also several drops of blood on the lookout's neck. The wire had served its purpose, though. Any attempt to free his hands or feet and the man would rip out his own throat. As Russell pointed out, the choice was his.

Now that his prisoner was secure, Russell was free to use the telephone. It took him nearly five minutes to be put through to Dietrich. There had been a time not so long ago when the mere mention of Russell's name would have been sufficient to obtain an immediate connection.

"How are you, dear boy?"

It was a poor line and Dietrich's voice was distorted.

"Bearing up, but this isn't a social call. It's time for me to move on again."

"You always have had gypsy blood."

"Sure." Russell was in no mood for verbal games. "The thing is, I'll need the use of a safe house while I'm sorting myself out."

"Consider yourself my guest, dear boy. Epping is vacant at the moment, if it's not too upmarket for your taste."

"That will do fine. Warn the warden to expect me sometime this evening."

"I will. Are there any little problems I ought to know about?"

"That's the other reason I rang. You'll need to send a team to the farm. There's some clearing-up to be done."

"How many bodies?"

"Two. Patrick MacFaddyn and one unknown."

"We'd heard a whisper that MacFaddyn might be on the mainland." For the first time Dietrich sounded really interested. "It will be nice to cross his name off the list. Was he troublesome?"

"Not really. He died thinking it was a dog's life."

"If that's one of your little jokes, Alan, it passed way over my head. I didn't understand it at all."

"You will," Russell promised. "Incidentally, I'm leaving you another unknown in prime condition. I thought somebody might like to talk to him."

"You always were thoughtful."

"Consideration is my middle name. Do me a favour and get the Belsen unit to ask him how I was tracked down. I don't have the time to find out myself."

Or the inclination, if he was honest.

"It's as good as done, dear boy. Is that all?"

"For the moment."

"In that case, goodbye for now. I may pop over to Epping in a day or two for a chat."

"Don't bother. I don't want the nightmares to start again."

As he hung up, Russell could hear Dietrich laughing. Personally, he wasn't at all amused. He knew this move was simply an expedient, not any kind of a permanent answer. He had no ambitions to spend the rest of his life one step ahead of vengeful Provo gunmen. What he needed was a completely new identity in another country. Unfortunately, this took money, far more than Russell could lay his hands on. It was something for him to think about as he gathered together the few bits and pieces he would be taking with him.

TWO

Light was finally beginning to seep through the thin curtains. It would be dawn soon, the start of the most momentous day in Raul's life. The thought excited him but he honestly didn't think there was any apprehension. From the moment the plan had been presented to him, Raul had accepted the fact that things might well go wrong. It was quite possible that he might die. Even worse, the rest of his manhood might be wasted away in a cell in Viana. Against this, there was the certain knowledge that the next few hours would change his life forever. This was something for him to savour in the semidarkness. Most of the previous twenty-five years had been spent in a depressing progression from one rut to another. Now he was about to take his destiny into his own hands.

The prospect exhilarated him. It filled Raul with an all-pervading excitement which had found physical expression in the erection which was pushing up at the sheets. He had seldom felt quite so potent and his arousal had little direct connection with the woman sleeping peacefully beside him. He would take her again soon, but Maria was no more than a symbol. She was the last link between what had gone before and what lay ahead. Severing this link would give him nothing except pleasure.

It was funny, Raul reflected. Platitudes and lies seemed to be the staple diet of childhood. "Education is the way to better yourself," his parents had told him. "Hard work brings its own rewards," the teachers had said. So Raul had worked hard, studying while his friends were out enjoying themselves. And what had happened? His parents, the same couple who had praised education so highly, had informed him they couldn't afford the fees at the university. The family needed another breadwinner and Raul was elected. So Raul had unloaded lorries, taking orders from that bastard Herrera who had never opened a book in his life and who probably couldn't count how many fingers he had on each hand. Not that he needed to when his uncle was an assemblyman. Spreading Herrera's nose over his fat, complacent face had been the last act of Raul's working life. It had also been the one which gave him most satisfaction.

The hell with them all, Raul thought. Even your friends lied to you.

Turning towards Maria, Raul pressed himself against her. She shifted slightly to permit easier access, but Raul was too aroused to have any patience with foreplay. Maria muttered something which might have been a protest, but Raul ignored her. She started to say something but this was the last thing Raul wanted, and he attacked her body with a ferocity Maria hadn't known he possessed.

Eyes tightly closed, Raul was completely lost in the intensity of his own pleasure. Although most of his friends saw virginity as the greatest prize, they were fools. Raul knew better. Deflowering some young girl couldn't even begin to compare with taking a woman for the very last time. Nothing could possibly match the excitement he was experiencing now, knowing that after him Maria would never, ever have another lover.

At the last census, the population of Viana had been 31,896, although there were several thousand more people clustered along the coast on either side of the capital. Small as it was, Viana was by far the largest community of which Paolo had any experience. His entire life had been spent on Madura and the prospect of leaving the island frightened him. Almost thirty years previously, way back before independence, his father had spent six months working in Portugal. The size and magnificence of Lisbon had been, and remained, a recurrent theme in his conversation. As a child Paolo had never been able to make a clear distinction between his father's reminiscences and his tales of dragons and giants. He wasn't entirely sure that the distinction was any clearer now.

Paolo was honest enough to admit to himself that he had never possessed any spirit of adventure. His ambitions had never extended beyond the confines of the island. Why he had ever agreed to this crazy scheme was beyond him. It certainly hadn't been the money. Perhaps it was because he had thought it was mere talk, another one of the fantasies he had grown up with. By the time Paolo had realized it was really going to happen, it had been far too late to back out. However frightened he might be by what he was doing now, Raul frightened him far, far more. As Paolo's mother had once said in an unguarded moment, Raul had death in his eyes.

He had reached the corner at the bottom of the Duque de Avila, so lost in his thoughts that he didn't notice the van until it had pulled level with him. Old Salazar must have coasted down the hill to save petrol. This was precisely the sort of thing he would do. His stinginess was a local byword and his reputation was well deserved.

"You're up early, young fellow."

Salazar's smile was all gums. He never wore his false teeth before midday.

"I couldn't sleep." Paolo knew he sounded nervous. He was sure he must have guilt stamped all over him. "I thought I'd go for a walk."

"Hop in." The old man was indicating the seat beside him. "You can do something useful instead."

"No, thanks. It's too early to hump boxes."

"I'll pay you."

"Not enough to make up for stinking of fish all day."

Salazar laughed. Nothing ever seemed to upset him. It was one of his most irritating characteristics.

"Suit yourself," he said. "There are plenty of others who'll jump at the chance."

The van pulled away as Salazar took his foot off the brake. Paolo watched the vehicle until it was out of sight, heading down towards the harbour. The chance encounter had upset him. Although he knew it wasn't of any real significance, he could feel the nervous perspiration on his brow as he turned onto the 16 de Julho. Now one of the great storm drains which bisected Viana was on his right. Today there was no more than a muddy trickle of water some fifteen metres below him. Back in 1974, though, the drains had overflowed. The level of the floodwaters could still be seen on a few of the houses on the far side of the road, a brown stain reaching almost a metre above the level of the pavement.

Checking his watch, Paolo saw it was almost twenty past five and he quickened his pace. The silence was beginning to unnerve him as much as the chance meeting with Salazar had done. The streets were completely deserted, not even a stray dog in sight. Paolo experienced a sudden craving for human company and there was a distinct sense of relief when he saw Cesar waiting in front of the Igreja de Carmel. If Cesar was at all nervous, it didn't show. He was considerably older than any of the others, in his mid-thirties, but it was only Paolo he treated with easy condescension.

"You're late," Cesar said. "I was beginning to think you might have chickened out."

"You know me better than that."

"What you mean is you're shit-scared of what Raul might do to you if you let him down."

Cesar had fallen in beside Paolo. Instinctively, they were both keeping their voices low. It was as though they thought anything louder than a whisper might disturb the people sleeping in the houses on either side of the road.

"I notice Raul kept the best job for himself."

"What else was he supposed to do?" Cesar's tone was derisive. "I'm no beauty and you've never managed to get yourself laid yet."

"You don't know that."

Paolo was suddenly defensive.

"Come on, Paolo. It's stamped all over you. You've never managed to get your leg over in your life."

The remark was accurate enough to make Paolo blush, but Cesar didn't appear to notice. Besides, the post office was ahead of them, its neo-Gothic façade dominating the Praça do Comércio. The time for banter was past. This is where it really starts, Paolo thought to himself, beginning to sweat again although the morning was still cool. In a few seconds they would be committed, his very last chance to back out gone. He glanced sideways at his companion, wondering whether Cesar really was as nonchalant as he appeared. He would have liked to see some small sign of stress.

The two men turned into the alleyway beside the post office, then turned again into the street behind it. Now there were no houses to overlook them. On the far side of the road there was only the high, blank wall at the rear of Lojas Americanas. This did nothing to make Paolo feel more secure.

The big wooden gates leading into the yard behind the post office were firmly padlocked. For a moment the two men stood and examined the barrier, Paolo glad that he wasn't the one who had to climb over them. Although he could probably have managed, he wasn't at all athletic. Cesar, by contrast, was like a cat. The gates would pose no problem to him at all.

"Here," said Cesar. "You'd better take this now."

The 7.65 mm Savage was heavy in Paolo's hand, looking cold and deadly in the early morning light. While they had been practising up in the mountains, blazing away at bottles and trees, it had all seemed like a game. Now reality was with him. Paolo knew that the Savage's twin was in Cesar's pocket. If things went wrong, they might soon be using the guns against human targets.

"Just whistle if anybody comes along," Cesar instructed. "I won't be a moment."

Then Cesar was gone, scaling the gates in one fluid, continuous movement before he dropped lightly to the ground on the far side. It was a second or two before Paolo realized he was still holding the gun in his hand. He quickly stuffed the automatic into the waistband of his trousers, buttoning his jacket to conceal it. This was so uncomfortable that he removed it again after a few moments. He felt much more at ease when it was in one of the zip-up pockets of his jacket.

The seconds dragged by with leaden slowness. If anybody should come by, Paolo had no real idea what to say. What possible reason could he give for hanging around the back of the post office at such an ungodly hour? Come to that, how the hell was he supposed to whistle when his lips were so dry? The sudden sound of the post office clock striking the half hour made him start. Come on, Cesar, he said to himself. What's taking you so bloody long?

Paolo tensed again as he heard the noise of an engine coming towards the Praça but the lorry turned off into one of the side streets. It probably belonged to another of the fish merchants. He would be going down to the harbour to sort through the early morning catch.

"Is it still clear?"

Although Cesar's whispered query made Paolo jump, he recovered quickly.

"Yes," he whispered back. "You're all right."

Seconds later Cesar was back beside him, his smile broader than ever. Without consultation, they started walking, both of them eager to put distance between themselves and the post office. It wasn't until they had crossed the Comércio that Paolo trusted himself to speak. By then his breathing had just about returned to normal.

"How did it go?" he enquired, trying to sound casual.

"Easy." When Cesar patted his pocket, Paolo could hear the metallic clink of the rotor arms. "Postal deliveries will be slightly delayed today."

Although Cesar sounded pleased, the success of their mission did little to make Paolo feel any better. The first hurdle might have been negotiated but many others lay ahead. All of them were infinitely more hazardous.

Even in the dim light of the shed, the van looked what it was, a botch-up. The lettering was all right—they had made a proper stencil for that —but the rest was a disgrace. They hadn't had any of the correct equipment, not even the right paint. In Fernando's professional opinion, the van couldn't stand up to anything more than the most cursory of examinations. And the uniforms were even worse. They might just pass at a distance, but close to they would immediately be revealed for the poor imitations they were. Not that Fernando really cared. It was all a gamble anyway. If he lost, he would be dead or in prison. If he won, he would be rich. There were no in-betweens, something Fernando had accepted from the start. The potential rewards made the risks worthwhile, espe- cially as this was probably the only shortcut to wealth which would come his way.

One of the hinges on the shed door was broken and he had to heave it open, blinking as the early morning sun temporarily dazzled him. Pulling on the thin cotton gloves, Fernando went back to the van, sitting behind the wheel while he ran through his mental checklist for the final time. If anything did go wrong, he was determined it wouldn't be the result of any mistakes he had made. Satisfied that nothing had been forgotten, Fernando backed carefully out of the shed, swinging left onto the narrow road. The die had been thrown. Now everything was in the lap of the gods.

The shower only added to Raul's sense of well-being. He would have liked to spend longer with the cold water drumming on his body but there were preparations to be made. Turning off the water, Raul stepped out of the stall and padded back into the maid's room. He barely glanced at the woman sprawled obscenely on the bed as he briskly towelled himself and then dressed.

When he checked his watch, Raul discovered he could have spent longer under the shower after all. He still had ten minutes before he needed to move and he lit a Dom Pedro, inhaling the acrid smoke deep into his lungs. The presence of Maria's mutilated body disturbed him not at all. In Raul's mind she had already been consigned to history. It was the future which interested him now.

The pickup point was on the corner of Laranjas and Uvas. "Fruits' Corner" the local wags called it, though this was more a reference to the Zephyr Bar than to the street names. Fernando wasn't entirely con- vinced that the Zephyr's reputation was deserved. His work had taken him there on several occasions and everything had seemed normal enough. None of the men in the bar had been sporting limp wrists, leather or lipstick.

Now there was no Cesar or Paolo on the corner. Fernando swore under his breath and started a leisurely circuit of the block, following the one-way system through the narrow, cobbled streets of the Old Town. He was used to being out this early and he had always considered that this was when the town was at its best. Not that this was saying a lot. Capital city or not, Viana was irredeemably provincial. Ever since pu- berty Fernando had dreamed of escape, away from Viana and away from Madura. He needed space, not a stinking island thirty miles long by twenty wide. Brazil was Fernando's personal grail, his land of opportu- nity. Rio de Janeiro, São Paulo, Pôrto Alegre, Belo Horizonte. Just saying the names to himself made Fernando excited. Brazil was the reason he was taking the gamble. Brazil was where his share of the money would take him.

When Fernando started down the Uvas for the second time, he could see the two figures standing on the corner at the bottom of the street. Even at a distance it was evident how tensed up Paolo was. If there had been a machine for measuring anxiety, Paolo would have sent the indicator rocketing off the scale. The thought made Fernando smile. For the life of him, he couldn't understand why Raul had included Paolo in his plans. Or how Paolo had allowed himself to be persuaded.

Fernando only stopped long enough for the two men to clamber into the back of the van. Then he was off again, following the road which skirted the harbour. Once he reached the Pátria, he was able to pick up a bit of speed. Less than a mile long, the section along the front was still the longest stretch of straight, flat road on the island. All too soon Fernando had to drop a gear as the road began to spiral up out of Viana, heading towards the surrounding hills. The highest of them were shrouded with clouds of mist which wouldn't be burned away until the sun was fully up.

By now the town was slowly coming to life, preparing for another day. Although Fernando still had the road to himself, he passed several pedestrians, all of them walking towards the town. Fernando knew most of them would be hotel staff, catering to the whims of the foreign tourists who came flocking to Madura each year. When he had been younger, Fernando had never understood why anybody would waste good money coming to the island when they didn't have to. Now he was old enough to appreciate that his own attitude might have been different if he had only had to stay a fortnight instead of facing a life sentence.

The van was out of Viana, still climbing on the Pinas road, when Fernando heard the tapping on the metal bulkhead behind him. He had to drive another half mile before the road widened sufficiently for him to park. Although he still hadn't seen any other traffic, this was no time to be taking unnecessary risks.

It only took a few seconds for Cesar to join him in the front. The big man might look slightly ill at ease in the unaccustomed post office uniform, but his habitual smile was firmly in place. It was a smile which Fernando had never really trusted. Presumably Cesar had similar reservations about Fernando. While the two of them had never quarrelled, they preferred to keep each other at a distance.

"The van is bloody terrible," Cesar commented, banging the door closed behind him. "It looks as though a kid painted it."

"Thanks a bundle."

"That's all right." Cesar was immune to sarcasm. "Mind you, it's such a bloody useless postal service, people won't expect anything better."

"How's Paolo bearing up?"

"He's shitting bricks as usual. I'm surprised he didn't have to change his underwear when he put on the uniform."

"Will he be all right?"

"I should imagine so. He's so scared of Raul, he wouldn't dare let him down."

"Aren't you scared of Raul?"

Fernando was genuinely curious.

"At times."

"That makes three of us then."

"I thought he was supposed to be your friend."

"He is. That doesn't stop me from realizing he's a certifiable maniac."

This was a subject both of them had skirted around before and neither of them wanted to probe any deeper. There had been a strangeness about Raul for as long as Fernando had known him. Even as a kid, he had sometimes behaved as though he came from another planet. Raul had always wanted to be the leader of the pack, his friends of the moment tagging along behind. And if they hadn't wanted to follow, this was their choice. Rather than compromise, Raul had always been perfectly content to go his own way alone. For Fernando, he had an almost mesmeric quality. Raul's very unpredictability had attracted him like a magnet. This was why Fernando had stayed the course while most of Raul's other friends had fallen by the wayside.

"Paolo was complaining about Raul keeping the plum job for himself," Cesar said.

"I'm not so sure about that. The maid looked pretty gross to me."

"I've known worse."

"You would have. Taste isn't exactly your strong point."

Cesar grinned, not at all offended. There might not have been many beautiful women in his life but, to Cesar's mind, the quantity more than compensated for any lack of quality.

"What do you think of Senhora White?" he asked. "That's one very classy woman."

"I prefer to think about all her husband's money. Besides, she's about twenty years too old."

"Don't you believe it, Fernando. Women are like good wine. They mature with age."

"You've been reading your book of clichés again. That's a bullshit excuse for ugly bastards like you who can't pull the young stuff anymore."

"Maybe it is," Cesar admitted, laughing out loud. "Mind you, I'd still jump her bones given half a chance."

"I'd forget it," Fernando warned him. "Rape isn't included on the agenda."

"Who said anything about rape? After a few days in my company she'll be begging for my body."

"Some chance. One look at you and she'll be asking for a vibrator."

Cesar laughed again, keeping the thought which was lurking at the back of his mind to himself. There was always the chance that hubby wouldn't cough up the money. If this happened, he wasn't going to end up with nothing at all to show for his efforts. Cesar had always had a yen for one of those snooty Anglo women with their superior airs.

The villa had originally been built for Raimundo Dias in the late 1940s. He was one of Salazar's cronies who had made a fortune during the war selling the same information to the Allies and the Nazis. After independence from Portugal, however, even Dias's wealth hadn't been sufficient to make him welcome in Madura any longer. He had been forced to leave the island in a hurry and for several years the villa had stood empty.

Then White Industries had moved into Madura. There had been a kind of commercial vacuum in the aftermath of the break with Portugal. This was precisely the kind of situation Derek White had been exploiting since he was in his late twenties. The fish cannery and the food-processing plant were simply the bait he had dangled in front of the island authorities. However vital they might be to the fledgling Maduran government, their combined profits for a century would have been no more than small change to a businessman of White's stature. It had been the shipping contracts he was really after. As a result of the package he had negotiated, almost seventy-five percent of Maduran trade with the outside world was carried aboard his ships. It was the White Line tankers which had the exclusive contract with the island's only oil terminal at Catoro do Castelo. Without anybody apart from Derek White really appreciating what was happening, Madura had passed into a new kind of economic bondage.

Purchasing the villa had been no more than a gesture. On those rare occasions when he did visit the island, Derek White always stayed at the Viana Sheraton. Although senior executives in White Industries were sometimes rewarded with a week or two at the villa as a tax-free perk, for most of the time it had stayed empty.

It was only in the past five or six years that Deborah White had begun to use the villa as a home. For the first couple of years it was simply a place for her to escape the worst of the English winter and the pressures of a marriage which was foundering without trace. Gradually, like so many other foreign visitors, she had fallen in love with the island. The mild climate, with no extremes of temperature, seemed to be reflected in the character of the Madurans themselves. She was accepted without being overwhelmed. Although everybody knew about the White millions, Deborah was judged on her own merits. People liked or disliked her as a person in her own right, not because she was Derek White's wife. She found this suited her very well.

Without any conscious decision on her behalf, the villa had turned into the place Deborah thought of as home. One or two months every year became six months and then nine months without her really thinking about it. In a way this mirrored the steady downward spiral of her marriage. To all intents and purposes, she and Derek were separated. Apart from the occasional function where a united front was necessary, they lived their own lives. Deborah knew she had been a grave disappointment to her husband and this no longer bothered her. Derek's constant infidelity more than balanced any deficiencies on her part.

For most of the time she was alone at the villa with Maria, her maid. When she was young, Deborah had had artistic pretensions and she had reverted to these now. Most of her days were spent on the verandah, trying to capture the essence of the surrounding mountains on canvas. Her lack of success to date made her very glad that marriage to Derek had removed any need to put these pretensions to the test. All the same, she enjoyed her painting, and if she felt the need of company, it was readily available. She received far more invitations than she could possibly accept.

Occasionally, as now, her son Rodney came to stay, usually with some strumpet or other in tow. Fond as she was of him, Deborah had long since realized that Rodney had inherited all his father's lack of taste. And this year's folly was the worst so far. She looked like a whore and she behaved like one. The previous night she had made so much noise rutting with Rodney that Deborah had nearly gone down the corridor to throw a bucket of cold water over them. Janine was probably the kind of woman Derek should have married. He would never have been able to accuse her of frigidity.

Deborah wondered about this now, her eyes open beneath the sleep shades while she listened to Maria coming up the stairs. She didn't think she was frigid. Given the right partner, she was sure she could respond, but as Derek had been her only lover, she didn't know. Perhaps it was time for her to experiment before it was too late. She could hire herself a gigolo or two and help the island's unemployment problem.

She was smiling to herself as the bedroom door opened and she rapidly composed her features. Instead of coming across to put the breakfast tray on the bedside table as usual, the servant remained just inside the door.

"It's all right, Maria," Deborah said. "I'm awake."

"I'm afraid Maria is indisposed today, madam. Breakfast will be a little late."

Even before she pulled the shades from her eyes and saw the young man standing by the door, Deborah knew what was going to happen. She was going to be raped. It was a punishment for her thoughts about gigolos. Although she was terrified, her brain was still working with a kind of icy detachment.

"What do you want?" she asked, realizing the stupidity of the question as she spoke.

"We'll come to that in a moment." There was a mocking half-smile on the man's lips. "What I don't want is to have to use this."

It was only now that Deborah noticed the gun he was holding. It was sufficient to make her abandon any thoughts of shouting for help. Being hurt herself was preferable to exposing Rodney to danger.

"All right." Her voice was less firm now. "I'll be sensible."

"Excellent. It probably won't be nearly as bad as you think." The same mocking tone was in the man's voice. "Just get out of bed and take off your nightdress."

To Deborah, it seemed as though some other person was going through the motions. It wasn't she who scrambled awkwardly out of bed. Nor was it she who pulled the nightdress up over her head. She would have turned her back or tried to cover herself with her hands, not stood with her arms at her sides while she exposed her nakedness to a total stranger. But the blush was definitely all hers. Deborah could feel it spread from her face to her neck as the man ran his eyes down her body, lingering on the small, still firm breasts and the triangle of hair between her legs.

Then he started towards her and Deborah closed her eyes. She had already decided that she would endure whatever it was she had to endure. She would do nothing to provoke him to violence. Although Deborah knew this was the only sensible thing for her to do, breathing normally had suddenly become very difficult. Her flesh was cringing in anticipation.

To her surprise, the intruder walked straight past her and opened the wardrobe door. When she heard him rummaging around inside, her eyes snapped open again and she watched the man quickly sorting through the hangers. Still uncomprehending, she saw him remove a red sweater, a tweed skirt and a quilted jacket. He tossed all of these onto the bed.

"Your underwear and any clothes you take are your own choice," he said, "but you'll definitely need these. It can get chilly at night where we're going."

"Going? What do you mean?"

"You're being kidnapped," Raul explained gently, "but there's no need to worry. You'll have your son and his girlfriend for company."

It was only now that Deborah White began to be very frightened indeed.

THREE

It afforded Superintendent Lopes a certain satisfaction to watch Miguel Targa throwing up all over his neatly polished shoes. Chief of bloody police, he thought disgustedly. Although Lopes could appreciate the need for checks and balances, it still offended his pride to have a civilian as figurehead for the department. Having a civilian like Targa only made it worse. However good a politician he might be, Targa would still have problems finding his arse with both hands and a flashlight.

"I should have warned you it was a bit messy, sir."

Lopes spoke without a great deal of sympathy but the chief was too busy retching to notice. It was doubtful whether he even heard what the superintendent said. In any case, "a bit messy" was something of an understatement. The maid hadn't simply been killed. She had been slaughtered like an animal. The sight of her had been enough to turn Lopes's stomach as well and he hadn't spent any longer in the bedroom than was strictly necessary. He certainly didn't envy old Dr. Oliveira his job. Or the photographer and forensic unit, come to that. The killing had been the work of a maniac. This was a thought which Lopes found chilling.

"I'm sorry about that, Lopes." Although Targa was still a trifle green about the gills, he seemed to have regained control of his stomach. He was dabbing at his lips with a crisp linen handkerchief. "I'm not used to seeing bodies."

"I know, sir."

If Targa noticed an edge to the superintendent's voice, he chose to ignore it.

"Who's that?"

He was nodding in the direction of the elderly man who was sitting on a wall a few metres away flanked by two uniformed policemen. As the man was holding his head in his hands, it was impossible to see his face.

"That's Vitorino Ribeiro," Lopes answered. "He's gardener-cum-handyman for Senhora White and he found the body. He also happens to be the dead woman's father."

"I see." Now that he had recovered, Targa's normal pomposity was beginning to reassert itself. "I understand that most murders are committed by members of the immediate family."

Sure, Lopes thought sourly. The poor old bastard came up here, hacked his daughter into little pieces and then cut the lawn before he phoned the police. There's obviously no need to look any further.

"There's more to it than murder," Lopes said out loud. "A lot more. Senhora White and her houseguests appear to have been kidnapped. We found this pinned to her bedroom door."

Targa took the note in its plastic envelope from the superintendent and read it through quickly. By the time he had finished, he was looking decidedly ill again.

"How many are missing?" he asked.

"Three," Lopes told him. "Senhora White, her son and his girlfriend. All of them are British passport holders."

"Were there any indications of a struggle inside the main house?"

"None at all. I'd say they were all taken by surprise while they were still in bed."

"How about this Maduran Liberation Army?" Targa was tapping the note. "What do we know about them?"

"Sod all," Lopes answered succinctly. "The only army I know of on the island is the National Guard."

And that's a bloody joke, he could have added. The functions of the two hundred men in the island's security force were largely ceremonial. Although they were armed, Lopes shuddered to think what might happen if they were ever asked to fire their weapons in anger. As the National Guard was one of Targa's pet projects, this was an opinion he preferred to keep to himself.

"I see," Targa said. "I think the best thing for me to do is to return to Viana and try to contact Senhor White. He'll have to be informed of what's happened as soon as possible. Meanwhile, I want you to concentrate all available resources on this investigation. The faster it's cleared up, the better for all concerned."

"All right, sir."

Pompous little prick, Lopes thought as he watched Targa head back towards his official limousine. All the same, he knew the chief of police was correct. It would be best for Targa if the mess was sorted out quickly because he could then claim all the credit. And it would be best for Lopes too. If he failed to come up with something double quick, it would be his arse that was in a sling.

For somebody who hated flying as much as he did, he seemed to spend a hell of a lot of his life in aeroplanes. The company jet made things easier, of course, but Derek White couldn't pretend he was having fun. The Hanson negotiations were at a critical stage and he should have been in London, not flying to Madura. Wasting his time would have been how he summed up most of his relationship with Deborah. Even now that they lived apart, she still retained the capacity to mess him around.

When the cabin door opened, White jerked his attention away from the banks of cloud outside. Despite the bloody silly name, Petula was always worth looking at, the kind of honey blonde wet dreams were made of. Body apart, she had the naughty little girl look which White found increasingly attractive as he grew older. Youth and a hint of depravity were all he asked of his women nowadays.

"Adrian says we'll be landing at Viana airport in fifteen minutes, Mr. White." The stewardess had one thigh lightly brushing against his arm and he could feel the heat radiating from her. "Is there anything you want before we arrive?"

Too damn right there is, White thought, and Petula knew it, the same way he knew she was his for the asking. But he wouldn't ask. Screw an employee and you were asking to be screwed yourself.

"I'm fine, thanks," he told her. "Just check that the car is waiting and that they're ready to do a quick refuelling. I need to be back in London this evening."

"Yes, Mr. White."

Petula returned to the flight deck and White went back to looking at the clouds. He supposed he should have been worried about Deborah and Rodney, but he was honest enough to admit that his dominant sentiment was one of annoyance. He had never been one for looking back. They were no longer part of his life and he felt no particular responsibility for them. The allowances he made them were more than generous enough for them to lead their own lives. All he asked in return was that they leave him alone. Getting themselves kidnapped wasn't part of this bargain.

The island was in sight now as the Lear dropped below the clouds and White sank back in his seat, shutting his eyes. He kept them tightly closed until the plane was down and had finished taxiing. Only then did he relax, feeling the tension start to drain out of him. Even so, it was another couple of minutes before his hands had stopped trembling. It was always the same since the accident going into O'Hare six years previously.

The crew knew all about his foible and he was left well alone until the limousine was beside the Lear. By then White was back to normal. With any luck he could sort out the kidnapping and be on his way back in time for dinner in London.

"You say you've found the bogus post office van?"

"That's right, sir," Lopes answered. "It was in the woods just outside Avila. The kidnappers would have had another vehicle waiting for them there."

"So they were heading into Viana itself."

"They might have been."

Lopes was deliberately noncommittal, although he suspected that Viana was the last place the kidnappers would be. They would be up in the mountains somewhere, miles from anywhere. However, this wasn't an opinion he was prepared to volunteer. When he was dealing with a slippery bastard like Targa, he preferred to keep his cards close to his chest.

"What about the van itself?"

"It was registered to Evaristo Antunes. He reported it stolen in Avila almost four weeks ago. He's being questioned now but I doubt whether he had any part in the kidnapping."

"Let me get this straight, Lopes." Targa was leaning forward in his chair. "Some members of the Liberation Army immobilized the post office fleet while others used a stolen van for the actual kidnapping?"

"It seems that way, sir."

"Were there any sightings before or after the kidnapping?"

"That's something we're checking now."

"How about fingerprints?"

"It's all in hand."

As per usual, Targa was beginning to get up Lopes's nose. This wasn't simply because the police chief had missed the pun. The basis of Lopes's resentment was purely professional because the fat idiot didn't have the slightest idea how to conduct a proper police investigation. To hear him speak, though, you'd think he was the one with thirty-five years' experience.

"Fine." Targa remained oblivious to the superintendent's contempt. "What else do we have so far?"

"Well, old Oliveira has established that the maid had sex immediately before she was killed."

"You mean she was raped?"

"No." Lopes made this categoric. "All the evidence points to the perpetrator having spent the entire night with her. So far we've only managed to interview one of Maria Ribeiro's close friends—she's the maid at the pinhal house just down the road. According to her, Maria had a new boyfriend who was the love of her life. Unfortunately, she wasn't able to give us a name or a description. Nor could Senhor Ribeiro when we questioned him."

"Make sure you follow up on it, Lopes. It could be important."

"Yes, sir. I will."

Silly sod, Lopes thought. Of course it was important. So far it was the only thing approaching a real lead that they had. He was saved from any more half-baked advice by the buzzing of the intercom on the chief of police's desk.

"Senhor White has arrived, sir."

"Show him straight in," Targa instructed his secretary. "I'll see him now."

Lopes interpreted this as the signal for him to leave. However, Targa waved him back into his seat.

"You'd better stay, Superintendent," he said. "I may need you."

Sure, Lopes thought. If White begins cutting up nasty, Targa will need somebody to carry the can.

As it turned out, White didn't cut up nasty at all. In fact, he impressed Lopes, which was most unusual. The superintendent had adopted cynicism as a way of life.

The Englishman and Targa already knew each other to the extent that they had met at a couple of cocktail parties. After Lopes had been introduced, the chief of police used his atrocious English to deliver a long spiel about how upset the kidnapping made him. Although he didn't actually yawn, White sat through it all with the expression of somebody who had been bullshitted plenty of times before. He also gave the impression that he didn't find the kidnapping nearly as tragic as Targa imagined.

Once Targa had finished, Lopes used his much better English to outline the events of the morning. White listened attentively, the only questions he asked pertinent and to the point. However, it was when he was shown a photocopy of the ransom demand that White really impressed Lopes. There were any number of responses that White could have made but the one he chose was totally unexpected. It also caught Targa on the hop, which was worth bonus points as far as Lopes was concerned.

"What's the official Maduran policy with regard to terrorism and kidnapping?" he asked.

"I'm not sure I follow you."

Targa had been thrown completely off balance and Lopes was mentally applauding. He didn't think he liked White very much, but he wouldn't have missed him for the world.

"I would have thought it was obvious." White spoke as though he was addressing a small child. Lopes thought this displayed a remarkably accurate assessment of Targa's IQ. "Does your government give in to terrorists, or does it refuse to have any dealings with them? Are kidnappers paid their ransoms or does the government refuse to authorize them?"

For once in his life Targa was at a complete loss for words. This was a sweet moment for Lopes. The only reason he bailed his superior out was that he was fascinated to hear what White would say next.

"I don't think there is an official policy," he said. "Until today, we've been fortunate. There have been no terrorist acts on Maduran soil and no kidnappings. I suspect policy is likely to be formulated as we go along."

"I see. In that case, I'd better make my own position perfectly clear. White Industries does have a policy, which is known to all of our senior executives. Under no circumstances will any ransom be paid. I regard this as a form of protection for them. Once a company has given in to terrorism, all of its employees are up for grabs."

"But these aren't executives, Mr. White," Lopes pointed out. "It's your wife and son."

"The principle remains exactly the same. Any form of compromise with terrorism merely serves as an encouragement. It has to be resisted no matter who may be involved."

White spoke as though he had learned the lines by rote.

"I hear that you and your wife are separated."

"That's perfectly true." Lopes had been quite prepared for White to take offense but he simply smiled. "My wife and I can't abide one another and my son hasn't spoken to me for two years. I wouldn't pay ten dollars for the pair of them, let alone a million. However, my personal prejudices don't affect the underlying principle. My attitude would be the same whoever was involved."

There was the unmistakable ring of truth to his words and Lopes could sympathize with the Englishman's sentiments. However, there were practicalities to be considered. As Targa seemed to have withdrawn temporarily from the conversation, the ball was still in Lopes's court.

"Principles apart, Mr. White, you presumably don't want any harm to come to your wife and son. You wouldn't want them to finish up like the maid."

"Of course not."

White was shocked at the very thought.

"In that case, we can't afford any outright rejection of the kidnappers' demands. We need to buy ourselves time."

"So lie to the bastards." White had it all straight in his own mind. "Pretend you're negotiating while you track them down. It's a small island, so it shouldn't take you long."

"Hopefully not, Mr. White, but take a look out of the window." Lopes was indicating the mountains which surrounded Viana on three sides. "Ninety percent of the island is a jumble of volcanic cones like those. If Madura was ironed out flat, it would become a very large island indeed. There are still villages in the interior which can't be reached by road. There are large areas which are completely uninhabited. I'd be a fool to promise a speedy conclusion to this affair. When the kidnappers do contact us again, we'll need something to negotiate with."

White shrugged his shoulders.

"Surely that's built into the ransom demand itself. Raising a million dollars might not be too much of a problem, but a fifty percent wage increase for workers at the cannery and the packing plant is so much pie in the sky. Both places barely break even as it is. Any increase in the wages bill of that magnitude would simply price them out of the market."

"That allows some room for manoeuvre."

"There's more." Now there was a half-smile on White's face. "If things do get sticky, you can always say I'm prepared to sell both factories to the Maduran government. If the kidnappers really are nationalists, that should sweeten them a little. You should be able to spin out the negotiations almost indefinitely."

It was also a neat way for White to get himself off the hook, but for the moment Lopes was satisfied. Although there were a lot of questions he needed to ask about Mrs. White and her son, this could best be done later, when Targa wasn't around.

"Will you be staying on Madura long, Mr. White?" Targa asked.

"No. I have to be back in London tonight. If you do need me personally I'm always near a telephone. John Telford can represent me here."

Telford was manager of the cannery.

"There may be no need." Now Targa was attempting to emanate optimism. "Although the island's police force is small, we're very efficient. We may have recovered your wife and son before you land in London."

"Let's hope so."

The industrialist managed to sound suitably sceptical.

"One final point, Mr. White," Targa continued, unabashed. "Can you tell us anything about your son's houseguest? Her name is Janine Haywood."

There was no mistaking the surprise on White's face. He was about to reply immediately but he restrained himself until he had examined the photograph in the passport Targa had handed him. When he did look up again, there was a grim smile on his face.

"Gentlemen," he said. "I think we've just been wasting our time. If I were you, I'd contact the British Ambassador at once. And President Amado come to that."

"What do you mean?"

Even before White answered, Lopes was sure that a bad day was about to become worse. He didn't realize how much worse until the Englishman had finished explaining.

FOUR

Southwold was one of Russell's favourite places. If the town was an anachronism, so in a way was he. The all-pervading gentility, spiced with a healthy dash of eccentricity, was something he found soothing. It amused Russell to see the adult members of the local model yacht club playing unashamedly with their toy boats. When he looked up at the neat white bell tents of the Scout camp by the water tower and heard the buglar playing reveille, it comforted him to know that all was still well with the Raj. He enjoyed pubs like the Sole Bay, where even the local artisans were prepared to discuss subjects ranging from anthropomorphism to Zoroaster. Then there was Adnam's brewery, the commercial heart of the town, which seemed to be as interested in preserving the past as it was in making the best-tasting beer in the country. It was as if the stately, lumbering dray horses set the pace for the entire community. It had been a moment of special delight when Russell realized that the immaculate row of terraced houses which he had walked past a dozen times was actually the false façade of the brewery. Although Southwold might not be any permanent answer to his problems, he couldn't think of anywhere better to be while he was sorting himself out.

Rocky relished the sea air too. Russell had rented a cottage on Ferry Road, down by the riding school where the young ladies from St. Felix's learned all about mastering dumb animals. In later years they would undoubtedly apply many of the same techniques to their husbands and lovers. The horses themselves held no interest for Rocky once he had accepted that they were no threat, but he regarded the dunes across the road as his special preserve. Although established patterns were always dangerous, Russell relaxed sufficiently to allow Rocky's early morning galumph among the gorse bushes to become a ritual. The dog took such pleasure in these outings, enthusiastically following every scent he cut, that Russell didn't have the heart to deprive him. Later on in the day, when there were other people around, it wouldn't have been the same.

The first cloud on the horizon appeared during one of these pre-breakfast jaunts. Russell had finished the outward leg, at the Warbleswick end of the dunes, and was turning for home when he saw the red Cavalier draw up outside his cottage. There was one man inside, young, fair-haired and casually dressed in shirt and jeans. Russell had never seen him before. Through his binoculars, he watched the stranger cross the road and knock at the door of the cottage. When there was no reply, the man tried the unlocked door and went inside. A couple of minutes later he reappeared and returned to his car.

As he showed no inclination to drive off, Russell whistled to Rocky, who had been endeavouring to join a rabbit in its burrow, and began to walk back. Although he kept to the seaward side of the dunes, where he was out of sight, he was unhurried and without apprehension. Apart from the simple fact of being there, none of the stranger's actions had suggested any kind of a threat.

Where the short grass of the path gave way to sand, Russell leashed Rocky and climbed the dunes. This brought him to a point directly above the Cavalier. The man inside was slumped down in the driver's seat, apparently asleep. Bending down, Russell scooped up a handful of sand and tossed it in the window. Some of it went in the man's half-open mouth and he sat up with a start, spitting out the gritty granules.

"That could have been a grenade," Russell said, still standing at the top of the dune.

"In Southwold?" Although he was talking to Russell, he was looking at Rocky. "Is that a dog or a small horse you're holding?"

"He's a dog. What were you doing in my house?"

"Looking for you. I have a message from Dietrich."

"Next time you wait until you're invited in."

Russell started down the slope, walking past the Cavalier and across the road to the cottage. Once he was inside, he closed the door behind him before he went through to the kitchen. He already had the kettle on when he heard the knock at the door.

"Come in," he called. "The door is unlocked."

Rocky's growl was almost simultaneous with the sound of the door opening.

"For Christ's sake, Russell." There was a note of panic in the man's voice. "Call Baskerville off."

Russell went to lean in the kitchen doorway while he surveyed the tableau in the hall. Dietrich's envoy was standing just inside the half-open door, one hand still on the knob. Rocky was in front of him, teeth bared in a snarl which left no doubt at all about how he felt. It was enough to freeze anybody to the spot.

"What's your name?" Russell asked.

"Bewick. Mike Bewick."

His eyes didn't leave Rocky for an instant.

"Well, Mike Bewick, this is how Rocky behaves with visitors when he's heard me tell them to come inside. The trouble is, I didn't open the door for you. He won't allow you any further into the house unless I tell him to."

"So tell him. Please."

"In a moment. I want you to think about what might have happened if Rocky had been here when you let yourself in earlier."

"O.K., O.K. I've thought and I was a very silly boy. Now will you call the bloody thing off?"

There was a certain reluctance on Rocky's part when Russell called him, but he came. Russell fondled the dog's ears while Bewick followed instructions and went through into the living room to sit down. After Russell had introduced him as a friend, Rocky gave the visitor a perfunctory sniff, then ambled off to lie down in the hall.

"Is he all right now?" Bewick asked.

"Sure. You're accepted as long as you don't try to come into the house while I'm not here."

"Thank God for that. Is he really as fierce as he looks?"

"You'd better believe it. What do you want to drink? Tea or coffee?"

"Coffee will do fine."

"Toast as well? I'm making some for myself."

"Why not."

Once breakfast was ready, Russell brought it through into the living room. He ate his toast smothered with thick, chunky marmalade from the local delicatessen and Bewick followed his example. Although neither man spoke much, it was a period of appraisal.

"Aren't you going to ask me why I'm here?" Bewick said at last, licking a stray crumb from his top lip.

Russell shrugged.

"Dietrich sent you. He either has information for me or he needs my help. I'd guess at the latter. That probably means I won't be interested."

His answer produced a smile from Bewick.

"Dietrich said you'd play the reluctant virgin."

"I don't play at anything."

"Maybe not. The question is, will you come up to London with me?"

"No."

Russell made this unequivocal.

"That's what Dietrich expected. The alternative is for him to buy you lunch at the Swan. How does that sound?"

"As though Dietrich must need me very badly."

"I wouldn't know." Although Bewick was almost certainly lying, he carried it off well. "Is lunch all right with you?"

"I'm not wealthy enough to refuse free meals."

"Fine. Shall we say one o'clock in the bar?"

"That suits me. All I have to do is dust off my jacket and tie."

"Fine," Bewick repeated, rising to his feet. "I'd better get hustling then. Thanks for breakfast."

Then he enquired, "Why don't you have a telephone installed? It would make it much easier for people to contact you."

"That's the whole point. I prefer to be left alone."

"You and Greta Garbo both. I'll see you at lunch."

Russell watched Bewick to his car before closing the front door. It occurred to him that it might not have been such a bad thing to be forced out of the department when he was. He didn't seem to have a great deal in common with the new generation of operatives.

It was market day in Southwold. This didn't amount to much, no more than a few stalls clustered together outside the Swan, but it did mean there were a lot of people about. Although the electric kettle he was examining with such apparent interest looked like any other member of its clan, it afforded him a reason for being there. It was the large, bald-headed man standing at the secondhand bookstall who really interested him. He was an alien in Southwold, neither resident nor tourist.

His opportunity came when the man moved around the bookstall, presenting his back to the hardware shop. Russell put down the kettle, left the shop and crossed the road, approaching the man from behind.

The first two fingers of his right hand were rigid as he stabbed them into the man's back.

"Bang, bang," he said. "You're dead."

For a moment Peter Ellis tensed. Then he relaxed and turned round, a smile on his lips.

"I suppose you think that's bloody funny, Alan."

"It did strike me as being vaguely amusing," Russell admitted. "Besides, you obviously need sharpening up. A few years ago I wouldn't have got within twenty yards of you."

"A few years ago you wouldn't have tried anything as corny as that kettle routine," Ellis retorted. "That's the only reason I took pity on you."

Russell dipped his head in acknowledgement. It would take a very good man indeed to catch Peter unawares. He was Dietrich's chauffeur-cum-minder, had been for ten years, and he took his work seriously. Even while they were talking, his eyes were constantly on the move, monitoring the people in the market square. Back in London he had his own self-contained flat in Dietrich's house. As far as Russell knew, the bodyguard had no private life of his own.

"Where is the old boy?" he asked.

"Inside the hotel waiting for you."

"What exactly is he doing down here? It must be something important for him to venture this far from base."

"I wouldn't know." Like Bewick before him, Peter was probably lying. "Mr. Dietrich enjoys the occasional trip into rural parts. Deep down I think he hankers to be a country squire."

"Sure. I can see him flogging the peasantry and deflowering the young maidens."

"He's likely to flog you if you don't get a move on, Alan. You know what he's like about punctuality."

Everybody at the department did. Dietrich was a great believer in good habits, an attitude which Russell wholeheartedly endorsed. Any kind of sloppiness was a weakness.

He left Peter at the bookstall and went into the hotel. The first person he saw in the bar was Bewick, sitting on a stool on his own. His eyes passed over Russell without a flicker of recognition and Russell went along with the game. Dietrich's was a scalp which would be prized by every terrorist organization operating in the U.K. He enjoyed better protection than the average member of the Cabinet and he was considerably more valuable to the country than most of them. In Russell's book this would have included the Prime Minister, but he would have been the first to admit that he was prejudiced.

Dietrich himself was at a table in the corner, sipping a sherry and gazing forlornly at the almost empty platter of cashew nuts in front of him. The linen suit he was wearing made him look particularly gross and the Sandhurst tie did nothing to compensate. To Russell's certain knowledge, Dietrich had never held any rank in any of the armed services.

"Alan, my dear boy." Dietrich had levered all of his eighteen stone into an upright position and was pumping Russell's hand enthusiastically. "How are you keeping?"

"I survive," Russell answered, rescuing his hand. "Do you want another drink?"

"Now that you mention it, I think I could manage another schooner of the extra dry. And I don't think nibbling another nut or two would spoil my appetite."

Nothing could possibly do that because Dietrich was a glutton. He ate and drank so prodigiously, it was a wonder he didn't weigh twice as much. Russell bought Dietrich his drink and a pint of Adnam's for himself, then returned to the table.

"You must need me very badly," he said without preamble.

"I do, dear boy. I really do."

"If I say yes, it's going to cost you."

"That's only the mercenary in you speaking, Alan. Whatever's happened to patriotism and love of country?"

"They're luxuries I can't afford any longer. I far prefer hard cash."

There had been a time when Russell was a patriot and he didn't think it was his fault he had changed. It was his country which had betrayed him, not the other way around.

"Well, dear boy," Dietrich said dismissively. "Let's leave sordid little matters of finance until later. First of all, I've brought something for you to read."

The report was in an ordinary clip folder and there wasn't much of it. After Russell had read it through, he returned it to Dietrich.

"There's nothing there for me," he said. "What have you missed out?"

"Only the important parts." It was all business now. Dietrich was through playing the buffoon. "We'll get to them in a moment. To begin with, I'd simply like your impressions of the report as it stands."

"What the hell can I say?" Russell was perplexed. "As it stands, it shouldn't concern the department at all. It's strictly amateur night."

"Why do you think that?"

The answer was obvious. Dietrich was merely seeking confirmation of something he already knew.

"Where do you want me to begin?" Russell asked with a shrug. "The whole kidnapping was far too elaborate. There were far too many different elements which might have gone wrong. Professionals would simply have driven up to the villa and snatched the White woman and her son. With no security, they were such soft targets there was no need for anything more. Butchering the maid doesn't make sense either. God knows, there are enough terrorists who are psychopaths but none of them would do that. It's counterproductive."

"All right, Alan." Dietrich wasn't arguing with him. "Let's add another element. What would you say if I told you Rodney White's girlfriend was Janine Haywood."

"I'd say, who the hell is she?"

"You're obviously not reading the right gossip columns, dear boy. Janine Haywood is the Prime Minister's stepdaughter."

For a moment Russell was silent. When he did speak, he was smiling.

"Now I'd say that my price has just gone up. Way, way up."

Dietrich knew exactly why the man across the table from him was smiling. After what the Prime Minister had done to him, Russell wouldn't cross the road to piss on her if she was on fire.

A great deal had been made of the dirty war in Northern Ireland. However, Russell himself had never been entirely convinced that it was a war at all. Although battle lines had been drawn and people were certainly being killed, there was no clear moral distinction between the factions. Not one of them had right on its side. They were all tarred with varying degrees of wrongness. Russell had seen the situation in the province as a barbaric tribal conflict which had no place in the twentieth century. Ulster was the perfect example of bigotry and prejudice in action.

Nor had Russell possessed many illusions about his own role. He didn't see either himself or his superiors in London as knights on white chargers. It was a fact of life that you couldn't infiltrate any terrorist organization without behaving like a terrorist yourself. Russell had cheated and lied and murdered with the worst of them. He was amongst animals and, to protect himself, he had behaved like an animal himself. This was the way he had progressed upwards through the ranks. The sole justification for what he had been forced to do was that he had saved a lot of lives. His warnings had thwarted terrorist attacks. His information had removed some of the worst animals from the streets.

Six years he had spent in Northern Ireland. For all Russell knew, he would have been there still if it hadn't been his turn to be betrayed. And, as was so often the case, betrayal had come from the most unlikely source. One sentence was all it had taken. A few ill-chosen words during the Prime Minister's question time in the Commons had been sufficient to destroy the entire edifice he and Dietrich had so painstakingly built together.

"We have men infiltrated into the highest echelons of the Provisional's command structure," the stupid bitch had said in that plummy voice of hers, and suddenly Russell's life had been on the line. Although he had always known it was inevitable, he had never expected it to be like this. He was being thrown to the lions so the PM could escape from an awkward corner. This had been sufficient to destroy what few illusions Russell had had left.

To give him his due, Dietrich had reacted immediately, before the Provos had had an opportunity to respond to the Parliamentary gaffe. Russell himself had been prepared to hang on a while and bluff it through, but Dietrich had refused to countenance this. Instead, he had pulled Russell out of Belfast inside twenty-four hours. Within another week, after a full debriefing, Russell had been in Madura, able to relax for the first time in six years. It was during the three months he was on the island that he had decided his future. Dietrich, of course, had wanted him to stay with the department. Now his cover was blown, Russell was finished as a field operative for the foreseeable future. The Provos would have circulated his description to every major terrorist organization around the world. However, there had been an administrative post waiting for him if he wanted it. Russell hadn't wanted. He had lost his motivation. He was too disillusioned and too resentful to continue any longer.

Of course, Russell had never believed that resigning from the department would be an end to it. You never completely escaped from the half-world he had inhabited for so long. This was why MacFaddyn and company had turned up at the farmhouse in Wales. It was why Dietrich was sitting in the cottage at Southwold now. Money was the only way to freedom, lots and lots of money. It was like escape velocity for rockets. In Russell's mind there was a definite amount which would enable him to pull free from the mess which had been his previous life. And now it seemed as though it might be within his grasp.

"Why me?" he asked.

"You know why."

Dietrich's bulk filled the armchair opposite to overflowing. Although the patio doors were open to allow in the breeze, he was sweating heavily. Considering how much he had eaten for lunch, this was understandable.

"If I knew, I wouldn't have asked."

"You were the best, Alan. The very best. There was nobody to replace you when you left."

"Maybe not." False pride was as much of a sin as pride and Russell was well aware of his own abilities. "But these aren't terrorists. It's purely investigative work."

"I'm not so sure, dear boy. They claim to be terrorists and that's why the PM came to me. Until we have definite proof to the contrary, we have to treat them as such. Besides, there are the political implications to consider. Have you given any thought to those?"

"Some. I'm wondering if the kidnappers know whom it is they've kidnapped."

"So am I." Dietrich used his handkerchief to mop his face. "In view of the ransom demand, I'm assuming they don't. If I'm right, they certainly won't hear anything from the media—we've clamped down here and in Madura. Of course, that doesn't mean the girl won't let it slip herself. Or one of the Whites for that matter."

"You always did like to look on the bright side," Russell told him. "How about the worst possible scenario? How about if those clowns know exactly whom they've kidnapped? What if they're already negotiating to sell her to the IRA or Qaddafi?"

"Don't, Alan." When Dietrich shuddered, his entire body quivered like a badly set blancmange. "It hardly bears thinking about but that's why I need somebody with your experience. Besides, you spent three months on Madura. That makes you the only person in the department with any local knowledge worth talking about."

"I'm not with the department any longer."

"My slip, dear boy." The words were no more than a formality. "There's another thing in your favour as well. I believe you already know Superintendent Lopes."

"That's right. We were in an SAS course together. I looked him up again while I was in Madura."

"Excellent. Lopes is in charge of the investigation. You see, Alan, everything points to you. There are even one or two special considerations which are right up your street."

"Special considerations" was one of Dietrich's pet euphemisms. The phrase always sent a slight chill up Russell's back.

"What exactly are these considerations?" he asked.

"All in good time, Alan. We can discuss them once you've made up your mind about the job."

For a second or two Russell was silent. Not that there was really anything for him to consider. Providing the price was right, he had always known he would be going to Madura. He didn't have a great deal more choice than Dietrich.

"One hundred and twenty-five thousand pounds," he said finally.

Dietrich pulled a face.

"That really is a bit steep, dear boy. You know the departmental budget can't possibly stretch to that. I was thinking in terms of temporarily reinstating you on the departmental payroll."

"Bullshit. The hundred and twenty-five thousand is up front, with another hundred and twenty-five on completion. That's my price and I'm not haggling. And before you give me any more crap about the departmental budget, we both know the PM will be financing this out of Special Funds."

"It's a lot of money, Alan."

"You're still getting me cheap. 'Special considerations,' you said. I could make a hell of a sight more as a contract killer."

Although Dietrich argued a bit more, this was purely for form's sake. They both knew the bargain was sealed. Once it was all settled, Russell went through to the kitchen to make a cup of tea. He even celebrated by digging out a packet of the chocolate biscuits which were one of his few vices.

"I'd better make one thing perfectly clear from the start," Dietrich told him. "Our revered Premier doesn't give a tinker's toss about her step-daughter."

"Whatever happened to caring parents and husbands?"

Derek White's attitude towards his wife and son had been contained in the report.

"Never having indulged in either occupation, dear boy, I wouldn't know." Dietrich was a confirmed bachelor. To the best of Russell's knowledge, he had never been involved in any meaningful relationship, heterosexual or otherwise. "When she favoured me with one of her little monologues yesterday, the PM implied that dear Janine was nothing more than an embarrassment to her. For once I tend to sympathize with the lady. The girl is an out-and-out tramp. Ever since puberty she's been opening her legs to just about any male who came near her. There's been one abortion and at least one treatment for a venereal infection. There have also been a couple of instances of drug abuse which Special Branch have managed to smooth over without any publicity."

"She sounds quite the little charmer."

"She is, Alan. Take my word for it. What I'm saying is that as a person Janine Haywood is of no consequence at all. She's totally useless as an emotional lever on the PM. As a symbol, though, it's a very different matter. For a start, there's the precedent. You know how the terrorist organizations work as well as I do—they follow the latest fashion. With a few minor exceptions, until now they've left the families of politicians alone. Any publicity about the Haywood girl and that would all change. Everybody would jump on the bandwagon and you know what that would entail."

Russell nodded without speaking. The security problems would be immense. Resources were spread thin enough as it was, simply providing basic cover for VIPs themselves. Throwing a net around their entire families would be well-nigh impossible.

"That's in the long term, of course," Dietrich continued. "In the short term it would be equally disastrous. Just think of all the mileage the SLA got from the Hearst girl. Miss Haywood is far better material. You put your finger on the main problem earlier, Alan. While she's on Madura, the situation can be contained. If the kidnappers do realize whom they've snatched, I shudder to think of the consequences. Do you see what I mean?"

"I think I have the picture."

The shit hitting the fan wouldn't come into it. Part of Russell's work had been to put himself inside the terrorist mind and he knew Janine Haywood was an almost priceless asset. If it was properly handled, whoever had her could grab every headline across the world for weeks. Play the sex and drug angles right, throw in a few juicy, intimate details about her stepmother's private life, and the PM could kiss her political career goodbye. Quite possibly, the government would go down with her. Although Russell didn't necessarily consider this to be a bad thing, he could understand Dietrich's concern. He was also beginning to think he should have asked for more than a quarter of a million. He was sure the market could bear it.

"Speed is of the absolute essence, Alan. The Madurans will be handling the routine investigative work and you'll have total access to their files. Use them. Take all the shortcuts the police can't. Do whatever you think is necessary, legal or otherwise, and I'll keep the authorities off your back. Just find the bastards. Once the kidnappers establish contact, we'll buy you as much time as possible, but you don't need to bother about that side of it. You find Janine Haywood."

"I'll do my best. How about those special considerations you mentioned?"

"You can read between the lines as well as I can. The PM didn't have to spell it out for me."

"Maybe not, but there is one big difference. I can't afford for there to be any mistake."

"All right, Alan, if that's the way you want it. Both the PM and I feel it would be best if the kidnappers didn't stand trial. In fact, it would probably be best if they weren't even interrogated by the Maduran police."

"Just so long as I know. What about Janine Haywood?"

For a long moment the two men simply looked at each other. Then Dietrich made a slight inclination of his head.

"Her too," he said.

"Does that come from the PM?"

"Not in so many words but the implication was plain."

Although Dietrich didn't choose to elaborate, Russell didn't press him. His line of reasoning was easy enough to follow.

"One final thing," Dietrich said. "Mike Bewick will be going to Madura with you."

"I'd rather work alone."

"I know, Alan, but this time it can't be avoided. Since you resigned, you don't have any official standing. I need to send at least one fully paid-up representative of the department. Besides, you'll have overall control of the operation. Bewick will be another pair of legs for you to use as you think best."

"All right."

Leaning forward, Russell helped himself to the last of the chocolate biscuits. It was settled and there was nothing more for either of them to say.

"You'll learn a lot from Russell," Dietrich said.

"So everybody keeps telling me."

Bewick was driving Dietrich back to London while Ellis brought the Cavalier. He was also slightly miffed. Ever since he had transferred to the antiterrorist squad from Special Branch, he had been hearing the same note of near-reverence whenever anybody mentioned Russell's name. O.K., the man must be good. Very, very good indeed if his track record was anything to go by, but Bewick didn't want to live in anybody's shadow. Like those of most legends, he suspected that Russell's abilities had been exaggerated in the telling.

"He's the best, Michael." Now Dietrich was at it. "I doubt whether the department will see his like again."

"Perhaps I ought to take notes while I'm with him."

This time Bewick was unable to keep the resentment out of his voice. It made Dietrich look up sharply.

"You could do a lot worse," he said. "Think of working with him as a privilege. And remember one thing, Michael. Russell has my complete confidence. He's the man in charge. If he tells you to do something, you do it without question. There will probably be times when you don't understand what he's doing—there have been times when I didn't—but that doesn't make any difference. You're a tool for Russell to use as he thinks fit. He won't mollycoddle you and he won't tolerate any mistakes."

"I understand, sir."

The rebuke had come across loud and clear and it had merely added fuel to Bewick's resentment. For a while he drove in silence but he knew he had to ask the question. He had tried it on other people in the department without ever receiving a satisfactory answer.

"What is it that makes Russell so special?"

"I honestly don't know, dear boy." It was almost as though Dietrich had expected to be asked this. "Part of it is that he's a natural. Other people have to be trained for the work, but I sometimes think Russell was born knowing more than any instructor. Going by the book is an irrelevance to him because he operates at an intuitive level. I've often suspected he has a terrorist mentality himself. And then I thank my lucky stars he chose to come down on our side of the fence. Heaven help the world if he hadn't."

Although Bewick didn't comment, Dietrich was aware that this had been no real answer. There were so many different facets to Russell's character that it was well-nigh impossible to encapsulate him in words. Of course, not all these facets were wholly admirable, and it was this mixture which had made him so good at his work. There was a ruthlessness to him which chilled even Dietrich at times. If something was necessary, Russell would do it, untroubled by moral qualms. This was why there had been no question of sending anybody else to Madura. It promised to be very messy indeed before it was finished. Dietrich's own instructions had virtually guaranteed this.

"When will we be leaving, sir?" Bewick asked, the question cutting across Dietrich's chain of thought.

"Early tomorrow morning," he answered. "The RAF are laying on a VC-10 for you and Russell."

"Isn't it amazing how all the stops are pulled out when the Prime Minister's kith and kin are involved."

Bewick was smiling into the mirror.

"It's the way of the world, dear boy. There's no sense in seeking power unless you're prepared to abuse it."

There were occasions when the ways of the world worried Dietrich a great deal. Although he hadn't mentioned his reservations to either Russell or Bewick, he didn't like the feel of this Madura business at all. There were far too many coincidences involved. No matter how hard he tried, he couldn't entirely convince himself that a bunch of amateurs could have stumbled across the Prime Minister's stepdaughter by chance. Then there was the way the job was tailor-made for one man and one man alone. It was as though some malign influence was pulling strings he knew nothing about, leading Russell and himself into a carefully baited trap.

When the telephone rang, Dennison was watching Samantha Fox on *The Wogan Show*. This seemed sufficient reason for remaining where he was and leaving his wife to answer it. Although the Fox girl didn't inspire any specific feelings of lust, she was easy enough on the eye. Besides, she interested him. As an accountant, money was his business and he was constantly fascinated by the variety of ways it could be accumulated. A pleasant smile and outsize boobs were just one shortcut to a fortune.

"James," his wife called. "It's for you."

He had known it would be. Putting his whisky on the table beside him, Dennison heaved himself out of the armchair and went out into the hall. Marjorie was holding the receiver out to him, one finger keeping the secrecy button depressed.

"Who is it?" he asked.

"He wouldn't tell me. He did say it was urgent, though."

Dennison grunted and took the phone from his wife. He waited until she had returned to the kitchen before he spoke.

"James Dennison speaking."

"Good evening, Mr. Dennison." The voice wasn't one he recognized although the Irish accent was unmistakable. "I have a message for your friends in Belfast."

It was as though somebody had thrown a bucket of ice-cold water over Dennison.

"Who are you?" he demanded hoarsely.

"That isn't important."

"It is to me. I'm afraid you must have the wrong Dennison."

After he had replaced the receiver, Dennison remained where he was. His heart seemed to be beating faster than it should and his hands were trembling. For the moment, he wasn't sure what to do. The sudden ringing of the phone beside him made him jump. It also removed the need for a decision.

"Listen, Mr. Dennison," the same voice said. "There isn't any mistake. If I meant you any harm, I wouldn't be talking to you. I'd have contacted the police. All I want is for you to relay a message."

"Why me?"

"Because you're clean, Mr. Dennison. At least, you are for the moment. Do you have a pencil and paper ready?"

"Wait a minute." The threat had been implicit and it was very real. "O.K. You can go ahead."

"The message is for Patrick Grogan."

"I don't know him."

"You know people who do. Tell them that there's been a terrorist kidnapping in Madura. Have you got that?"

"Yes."

It was all meaningless to Dennison apart from the word "kidnapping." He was more convinced than ever that this wasn't something he wanted any part of.

"Dietrich's department are handling it. That's D-i-e-t-r-i-c-h. Alan Russell is being sent to Madura tomorrow. That's most important."

"I've got it."

The caller wasn't taking anything on trust. He made Dennison repeat the brief message back to him before he was satisfied.

"That's fine, Mr. Dennison. You're to relay the message to Belfast straightaway—it's of the utmost urgency. Any delay and a lot of people are going to be very upset. Very upset indeed. Good night, Mr. Dennison."

When he put the phone down, Dennison could see the damp print of his hand on the plastic of the receiver. Although his connection with Belfast was purely financial, it was supposed to be secret. In fact, Dennison had insisted on adequate safeguards befor ehe had accepted the commission. They obviously hadn't been good enough.

"Marjorie," he shouted. "We're almost out of soda. I'm just going to the off-licence to buy some."

"All right, dear, but don't be too long. Dinner will be ready in twenty minutes."

This would allow him plenty of time. The next phone call wasn't one he wanted to make from home.

FIVE

Raul had been right. There were no roadblocks on the road to Viana, at least not on the Barcelos side. Nor were there any signs of increased police activity. If things were different on the far side of the capital, nearer to the Whites' villa, Cesar had no intention of going there to find out. Simply being in Viana had him on edge. He would do what he had to and no more. Cesar knew he wouldn't feel really comfortable again until he was safely back in the mountains.

The rendezvous was in the Tropical, on the Avenida do Infante, and Cesar was a quarter of an hour early. Although it was a hot day, he took a table inside where he was close enough to the window to keep an eye on the street and deep enough in the shadow to be invisible to anybody outside. This was the kind of precaution he had been taking for as long as he could remember. It was also one of the reasons why there was no file under his name at police headquarters. Cesar had been involved in petty crime since before he had left school and he had never seriously considered finding permanent employment. Living by his wits had always seemed more preferable to him than hard work. For Cesar, the only difference between the kidnapping and what had gone before was one of degree. And, of course, a corresponding escalation in the danger. It was this which made him nervous. Most of his life had been one kind of gamble or another. However, he had never before risked quite so much on one throw.

Although it was late in the season, the Avenida do Infante was still crowded with tourists. The Hotel Quinta do Sol was only just up the street and the Artecouro leather shop was virtually opposite. A couple of hundred metres away, on the Rua Favila, the open-air market was in full swing. All of these were magnets for visitors to the island. And where they went there were the inevitable hangers-on.

For as long as Cesar could remember, the tables outside the Tropical had been a favourite assembly point for the young men of the capital. It was an established fact that all Northern European and American women were whores, prepared to spread their legs at the first possible opportunity. On straitlaced Madura, where girls of good family could still marry without ever having been kissed, they were a valuable safety valve for the young men. Contempt might be mixed with their lust, but event them from seizing the opportunities. It was a game ~~~en played himself, although he had left the younger tourists ~~d preferred the more mature tourist women, the widows ~~es who had the money to subsidize their temporary lovers. There ~~~~ ~~lways been a very practical side to Cesar's nature.

The uniformed policeman was an intrusion. Sipping at his drink, Cesar watched him walking slowly towards the Tropical. At the door, the policeman stopped, pausing to scan the customers inside. Then he came in, making his way to the bar. Although he walked right by Cesar's table, he paid him no particular attention.

Cesar waited until the policeman was talking to the barman, his back turned, before he rose to his feet and walked briskly to the toilets at the rear. He barely had time to finish urinating before he heard the door open again behind him. When he turned around, the policeman was standing just inside the toilet.

"What the hell was Raul playing at?" Fernando demanded without preamble. "He didn't say he was going to kill her."

"Kill who?"

"The maid, idiot. Raul butchered her before we snatched the others."

This was the first Cesar had heard of the killing. There were no newspaper deliveries up in the mountains and Raul certainly hadn't mentioned it. Unlike Fernando, Cesar wasn't particularly surprised or upset. He had always known that Raul was crazy.

"He must have done it to protect himself," Cesar said. "She would have been able to identify him."

"What about us, Cesar? We didn't agree to any killing. If we're caught, we'll be facing murder charges as well as Raul."

Cesar nearly shrugged but he managed to stop himself. There was no death penalty on Madura. If things did go wrong, an extra charge or two would make no difference. The kidnapping alone was sufficient to guarantee that the authorities would lock them up and throw away the keys.

"I'll talk to Raul about it."

"Talk to him about it." Fernando's vehemence was rather unnerving. "You're not listening to me, Cesar. Raul carved the poor girl into little pieces. Everybody at headquarters is saying it was the work of a madman."

"For God's sake, keep your voice down." Cesar was glancing anxiously towards the door. They had already taken longer than was safe. "Look, Fernando, it's done. There's nothing we can do to bring the maid back to life. All we can do is make sure we don't get caught. I need to know what progress the police are making."

For a moment it seemed as though Fernando wasn't prepared to let the matter drop. He had to make a visible effort to control himself.

"O.K." The anger was still there in his voice. "So far Lopes doesn't

appear to have any worthwhile leads. He's worked out that the Whites
are being held somewhere in the mountains, but that's as far as he's
got."

"How close are you to the action?"

Fernando shrugged.

"Lopes doesn't take me into his confidence, if that's what you mean,
but I'm on the kidnap squad along with almost everybody else on the
force. I should hear pretty quickly if anything does turn up. At the
moment we're simply going through the motions and following routine."

"That's good."

Although he had never really liked or trusted Raul, Cesar believed in
giving credit where it was due. Involving Fernando in the kidnap had
been a stroke of pure genius.

"There is one thing we hadn't bargained for," Fernando went on.
"The government has asked London for help. Presumably it's because
Derek White has been pulling strings. Anyway, a couple of antiterrorist
specialists should be flying in today."

"Let's hope they find themselves some terrorists then." Cesar was
feeling good. "You'd better get going now. We don't want people wondering what we're doing in here."

"You haven't told me how things are going at your end."

"There's no sweat. Everything is under control."

"How about the boat?"

"I'll be arranging that as soon as you've gone. Go on. Bugger off and
stay lucky."

After Fernando had left, Cesar stayed for another minute before he
went back into the café himself. The other customers were still far too
busy ogling the female tourists in the street to pay him any particular
attention. Cesar decided to treat himself to another drink before he went
about his business.

The cellar was five paces long by three wide. The only furniture was a
straw mattress against the rough rock of the wall and illumination came
from a small hole in the roof which also allowed in the rain. Although
the opening was no more than five feet above Janine's outstretched arms,
it could have been on the moon for all the use it was to her. Even if she
could have reached it, she would never have been able to squeeze
through.

She had had plenty of time to wonder about the purpose of the cellar
and the two like it where Mrs. White and Rodney were incarcerated. So
far she had failed to come up with a satisfactory explanation. Although
there had to be some reason for hacking into the solid rock, Janine
didn't know enough about the island to understand why. The cellars
could have been intended for storing wine, but why dig three of them

when one large cellar would make far more sense? Besides, Janine was pretty sure they were too high up in the mountains for grapes to grow.

Not that this was important anyway. What she had to do was find a way out. At first, when the armed men had burst into the bedroom at the villa, Janine had been very frightened indeed. The fear had stayed with her all the while they had been in the vans and continued while they were being marched into the mountains. After she had been bundled into the cellar, Janine had finally given way, crying for the first time in years.

Since then, however, fright had gradually been replaced by boredom. Although she was treated well enough, being cooped up on her own fed Janine's claustrophobic tendencies. An hour of exercise in the morning and another hour in the afternoon simply wasn't enough. Janine had already decided that she wasn't prepared to wait around until Derek White coughed up the ransom. She was used to being in control of her own destiny. Looking after number one was her way of life.

So was realism, and she had no illusions about staging the Great Escape. The opening in the roof of the cellar was out of her reach and far too small. There was no way past the locked door. Besides, even if she did get away, Janine had no idea where to go. After they had left the second van, they had walked for almost three hours, following narrow, rocky paths with never a proper road in sight. When she had been outside during the exercise periods, she had seen no signs of other habitation. There were only trees, mountains and more trees. The prospect of being lost in the back of beyond frightened Janine far more than staying with her kidnappers.

However, she did have some things in her favour. For a start, the kidnappers didn't seem to have any idea who she was. In the beginning, Janine had been convinced that she must be the target, but the way she was treated had soon made her change her mind. The kidnappers had been after Rodney and his mother. Janine was simply somebody who had happened to be at the villa at the time. Long may it stay that way, she thought. If the kidnappers ever discovered who darling stepmummy was, there would be all manner of complications. As long as she remained the Whites' houseguest, she wasn't of any particular importance.

Her main cause for optimism, though, was that all the kidnappers were male. Janine had been manipulating men ever since puberty. Virginity had become history by the age of thirteen and she had spent the night of her fifteenth birthday in bed with a cabinet minister. Of course, Michael hadn't actually been a minister then, any more than the bitch had been PM, but he had been well on the way. It still amused her to watch Michael's pompous little speeches on television. It was difficult to relate this public image to the sweaty, guilt-ridden buffoon she could remember kneeling beside her bed. Michael was just one of the men who would pay her a small fortune not to write her memoirs. Someday, when the juices ran dry, she was going to become very rich by not being an author.

This was for the future. Without any immodesty, Janine knew her looks were holding up pretty well. Certainly, there had never been any shortage of suitors. And once she had a man between her legs, he was there for as long as she wanted. Nobody had to tell Janine that she was a great lay. Even in her teens, Janine had taken to sex like a duck to water and it remained her main hobby and pleasure. Janine supposed it was her career as well. Although she had never accepted hard cash for her services, she had managed to live well without ever working. Perhaps she would marry a lonely old millionaire in a few years and then publish her memoirs just for the hell of it. Janine knew her stepmother would never, ever forgive her if she did. This was all the incentive she needed.

First she had to extricate herself from the present mess. And if a bit of judicious screwing was likely to help, so be it. Originally there had been four kidnappers, but only three of them had accompanied the prisoners into the mountains. Ever since her initial panic had died down, Janine had been watching them and observing their reactions to her. The only one she could really fancy called himself Raul. There was a dark intensity about him which appealed and he looked to have a good body as well. It was his air of brooding menace which excited Janine most. At another time in another place, she might have set out her stall for him, if only to discover if he was as dangerous as she sensed. For her present purposes, Raul was useless. She might be able to seduce him but she would never be able to control him. Janine could recognize a kindred spirit when she saw one. Young as he was, Raul was somebody who was accustomed to bending others to his will.

The man with the pockmarked face would be much easier. On a couple of occasions Janine had caught him examining her with unconcealed interest, something she had automatically played up to. He was the soft target, the one who would be only too happy to have his brains screwed out. Janine's only reservation was that Cesar looked the most experienced of the three. He was obviously somebody who had spread himself around. It might take time for her to break through the veneer of cynicism, and time was something she didn't have.

Sooner or later the ransom was going to be paid and Janine intended to be long gone by then. Once the money was handed over, she and the Whites ceased to be a potential source of revenue. At a stroke they would become potentially dangerous witnesses instead. Both Raul and Cesar looked perfectly capable of taking the appropriate action.

This was why Janine wanted to get out fast and why she would go for Paolo. He was shy and obviously inexperienced with women. He even blushed and avoided Janine's eye when she looked at him. Janine knew she might have to virtually rape him to get anything started but, once she had, Paolo would be hers. She would be able to mould him as she saw fit. Janine was still planning her strategy when she drifted off to sleep.

The Rua do Gorgulho wasn't somewhere Pilar went very often. No respectable girl in Viana did. Although there was very little prostitution on the island, what little there was had been concentrated in the bars along the Gorgulho for as long as anybody could remember. Sailors the world over had the same needs and the Maduran government had adopted a pragmatic approach to the problem. Cater to the seamen's needs in the port area and they weren't likely to spread their semen further afield. Register and license the girls working on the Gorgulho and you could regularly check them for venereal disease. This was an arrangement which suited everybody. The sailors were kept entertained, the prostitutes could earn their money without any hassle and so could the police. It was in the best interests of the bar owners and pimps along the Gorgulho to keep their own houses in order.

Despite the street's unsavoury reputation, Pilar was more intrigued than apprehensive. The very notion of making your living from sex both repelled and fascinated her. How could a woman open her body to a succession of strangers for money? What special tricks did they have to learn? Was there any pleasure in it? Pilar was no virgin, but she had been in love with the one man who had bedded her and he had been in love with her. At least, so she had thought at the time. Raimundo had been the man Pilar had intended to marry and since his death she had never seriously considered having sex with another. Yet these women were doing it more times in a single day than she had in her entire life. And they were doing it day after day.

By rights, their profession should have left some mark on their faces, but Pilar couldn't see it. Although the women along the Gorgulho used more makeup and wore more revealing clothes, these were the only real differences Pilar could spot. There were one or two older, more raddled women, but they were swamped by the young ones. In ordinary clothes there would have been no way of telling what they did for a living. This was something which Pilar considered to be most unfair.

The São Pedro was the most popular of the bars along the Gorgulho and it was already packed. For a moment, Pilar paused just inside the door, allowing her eyes to adjust to the dim light and her ears to the volume of noise. At the table nearest to her was a group of foreign sailors. One of them, a pimply youth with greasy, blond hair, reached across to grab hold of her arm.

"Come and sit here, love," he said in English, having to shout to make himself heard above the blare of the jukebox. "I'll look after you."

"No, thank you," Pilar answered in the same language.

When she attempted to free her arm, the sailor tightened his grip, pulling her towards him.

"Come on, love. There's no need to be standoffish. I've got plenty of money."

Suddenly Pilar was frightened. The sailor's hand was like a vice around her wrist and, to her eyes, his smiling face seemed full of menace. The flushed, semidrunken faces of his companions, mouths open as they shouted encouragement, were equally frightening. Pilar had no idea how to behave. It was as though she had been pitchforked headlong into a waking nightmare.

Fortunately, help was near to hand. Pilar wasn't entirely sure where her benefactor had come from, but he was there by her side, a big, fat man with his stomach hanging down over the belt of his trousers.

"All right, boys," he said. "You've had your fun. You can leave the lady alone now. She's with me."

"Bloody typical," one of the men at the table commented. "Patricio keeps all the prime stuff for himself."

The grip on Pilar's arm hadn't slackened. There was a sheen of sweat on the young sailor's face and his smile had become fixed. He was still trying to pull Pilar down onto his lap.

"One little kiss isn't going to hurt," he said.

For such a bulky man, Patricio moved surprisingly fast. A large hand dropped onto the sailor's arm and Pilar was suddenly free again. She took a nervous step backwards as Patricio squeezed harder. This was enough to produce a gasp of pain from the sailor.

"I told you to leave the lady alone, sonny." Patricio's voice was soft but clearly audible. "Do you understand?"

"I understand. For God's sake, let go of my arm."

There was no vestige of a smile left on the sailor's face. He was in pain and it showed.

"This is my place," Patricio went on in the same tone. "I make all the rules. If you don't like them, you go out of the door and you never come back."

"It's all right, Pat," one of the other sailors said. "Craig will behave himself from now on."

"Make sure he does."

With one last squeeze, which produced another yelp of pain, Patricio released the young sailor and turned to Pilar. He was one of the biggest men she had ever met and seemed to tower over her. Pilar shuddered to think how much he must weigh.

"You're that bastard Cesar's sister, aren't you?"

Patricio had reverted to Portuguese.

"That's right."

"I thought so. I caught your act at the Ipanema one night. You were very good."

"Thank you."

The response was purely automatic. Pilar still felt rather like a fish out of water.

"Come on up to the bar. You look as though you could do with a stiff drink."

Although the bar was crowded, a space cleared for them as if by magic. Patricio obviously ruled the establishment with an iron fist. For the first time since she had stepped into the São Pedro, Pilar began to feel at ease. As Patricio had promised, the whisky helped as well.

"What sort of trouble has Cesar landed himself in this time?" Patricio enquired. "It must be bad if he sent you down here on your own."

"I don't think there is any trouble."

"Rubbish." When Patricio smiled he revealed a sizable gap in his front teeth. "Cesar's whole life consists of rushing headlong from one mess to another."

There was no denying the truth of this. Ever since their parents had died in the typhoid epidemic, Pilar had done her best to look after her brother, but this hadn't been easy. There had always been a wild streak in Cesar, even as a child, and he had preferred to go his own way. After a while Pilar had discovered that life was much easier if she didn't pry too closely into what he did. Nevertheless, she wasn't blind. Pilar had long since realized that her brother would never qualify as a model citizen.

"I came here on a business matter," Pilar explained, pushing such thoughts to the back of her mind. "Cesar asked me to speak to a Senhor Anderson for him."

"James isn't here at the moment, I'm afraid. It's a bit early in the day for him to surface. I can pass on a message, though."

"I'd rather you arranged a meeting for me. It's to do with hiring his boat."

Patricio nodded. This was the only reason anybody ever wanted to see Anderson. He was an American who had moved to Madura from Florida a few years previously. Since then he had never been short of work and, to Patricio's certain knowledge, had never carried a legitimate cargo. Anderson's boat, *Amico,* was the only one on the island which could both reach the African mainland and outrun any patrol boats it encountered.

"He should be in later this evening," Patricio said. "I'll get him to phone you at the Ipanema."

"That will be fine."

"Do you want another drink before you leave?"

The owner of the bar was indicating Pilar's empty glass.

"I'd better not. I have a rehearsal in half an hour."

"In that case I'll escort you to the end of the street."

Despite Pilar's protests, Patricio insisted. The Gorgulho was no place for respectable women, especially when they were as attractive as Cesar's sister. If he had been a few years younger and a hundred pounds lighter, Patricio might have tried for her himself.

SIX

Although the island's only airport was little more than ten miles from Viana, the drive in the police car lasted long enough for Russell to confirm something he already knew. He liked Madura a lot. The island was a place where he could have happily seen out his retirement if the circumstances had been right. Unfortunately they weren't; Dietrich had seen to that. Whatever the outcome, Russell knew this would be his last visit to the island. People were almost certainly going to die. Quite possibly they would die at his hands and killings inevitably meant enemies and resentments. Madura would be somewhere else he could add to the list of places where he wasn't welcome.

The road into the island's capital hugged the coast, twisting and turning with the shoreline. To the left was the sea, usually some distance below at the bottom of sheer cliffs. To the right, smallholding succeeded smallholding, the carefully tended terraces clinging precariously to the steep hillsides. They were a part of the ribbon of development which continued all the way round the island. Over eighty-five percent of the population of Madura lived within a couple of kilometres of the sea. Most of the remainder was crowded into the few river valleys. By far the greater part of the mountainous interior was uninhabited and uncultivated, with only the odd isolated village here and there. For such a small island, an awful lot of Madura was effectively inaccessible. In Russell's professional opinion, the island could almost have been specifically designed for terrorists, kidnappers and the like.

"How high do the mountains reach?"

Bewick, who had never been to Madura before, had been peering up at the highlands, where the entire centre of the island was obscured by a bank of cloud.

"The Pico de São Jorge is the highest point. It's just under eight thousand feet."

"That's high."

"It's only the tip of the iceberg," Russell told him. "Most of the mountain is under the sea. Madura is simply the summit of an underwater range. The average height of the island must be well over three thousand feet."

"I'd have brought my crampons and ice pick if I'd known. What's the transport situation in the interior?"

"Poor to nonexistent. Two roads completely cross the island and several others go a few miles inland. Apart from them, you walk. There's one village in the centre which is almost two days' travel from Viana. By air it would take about thirty seconds."

"Jesus Christ. What are the bananas like?"

Bewick was referring to the groves of banana trees which surrounded most of the houses they were passing.

"Unripe by the look of them. Mind you, when they are ready, you realize what rubbish we eat at home. Over here, they wouldn't feed them to the pigs."

It wasn't until they were in the outskirts of Viana itself that Bewick spoke again.

"Do you have any ideas about how we handle the kidnapping?" he asked.

"Some," Russell answered.

Thanks a bundle, Bewick thought to himself, turning back to the view. It was nice to be kept fully informed.

Superintendent Lopes was waiting for them in his office at police head-quarters. He and Russell greeted each other like long-lost brothers while Bewick had to make do with a polite handshake. More than ever, he was feeling like a spare prick at a whorehouse.

"We'll talk later, Alan," Lopes was saying in his excellent English. "We'd better get Targa out of the way first. You haven't met our revered chief of police before, have you?"

"I don't think I've had the pleasure."

"Pleasure doesn't have anything to do with it, Alan. The man is a complete arsehole. And that's probably an insult to arseholes."

"So you two are a real team. Like Batman and Robin."

Bewick had thought it was about time he contributed something to the conversation. His remark produced a snort of disgust from the su-perintendent.

"I'll tell you what our relationship consists of," Lopes said. "Long monologues from Targa while I try not to throw up. He might be chief of police but the thing to remember about Targa is that he's a politician first and a policeman one hundred and ninety-seventh. What he knows about handling an investigation could be written on the head of a pin. And there'd be plenty of room to spare. Targa probably needs help to find the zip on his fly."

"I can hardly wait to meet him," Russell commented drily.

"I'll buy you a stiff drink afterwards to help you recover. All you have to remember when you're with Targa is to nod every thirty seconds and try not to be too obvious when you yawn."

"Do we get provided with brown paper bags, just in case?" Bewick enquired.

For a moment Lopes didn't understand. Then he laughed.

"Perhaps I've been exaggerating a little," he admitted. "Targa isn't quite that bad."

Provided you don't have to work for the bastard, he thought to himself as he ushered the two Englishmen to the door.

Despite Lopes's gloomy predictions, the chief of police only kept them for half an hour. As the superintendent suggested on the way out, perhaps Targa was in a hurry to give his mistress a quick one before he returned home to the bosom of his family.

Lopes used his own car, a big Datsun with a dent in the back bumper, to transport Russell and Bewick to the Hotel Méridien, where they were staying. After the porters had taken their suitcases to their rooms, the three men assembled in Russell's quarters. With them they had the bottle of Macallan's that Lopes had ordered from room service.

"Tell me something, Roberto," Russell said once they were settled. "Targa fed us a lot of bull about what an honour and a privilege it was to have our assistance. How do you feel?"

"I thought you'd realized by now. The chief and I speak with one voice."

"I'm being serious," Russell persisted. "After all, it is your case. I'd like to know how you feel about having us foisted on you. Is there any resentment?"

"None at all." Lopes was looking Russell straight in the eye. "If I thought my professional competence was being questioned, I'd resent it like hell. As it is, I know what's involved and I can do with all the help that's on offer. If the worse does come to the worst, there'll be somebody else to help me carry the can."

"Is it safe to assume that things aren't going too well at the moment?" Bewick asked.

"That's something of an understatement, I'm afraid." Lopes's smile was bitter. "So far we don't seem to be making any headway at all. Incidentally, this arrived today. The originals were hand-delivered to headquarters early this afternoon. Needless to say, nobody managed to notice who the hand belonged to."

Lopes passed Russell a copy of the second ransom demand together with the photograph which had accompanied it. The note, handwritten in block capitals, was brief and to the point: AS YOU CAN SEE, THE HOSTAGES ARE ALIVE AND WELL. HOW LONG THEY REMAIN SO IS IN YOUR HANDS. WE EXPECT TO HEAR ABOUT THE WAGE INCREASES AT THE WHITE FACTORIES BY MONDAY. NEGOTIATIONS FOR PAYMENT OF THE RANSOM CAN FOLLOW. It was signed: A MEMBER OF THE MADURAN LIBERATION ARMY. The photograph showed the Whites and Janine Haywood standing bunched together. Mrs. White was holding a newspaper in front of her, the date and headline clearly visible. Behind the figures there were a lot of trees. Once he had finished his examination, Russell handed the note and photograph on to Bewick.

"Do you want me to translate for you?" he asked.

"No, thanks. There's no need."

For an instant, a glimmer of surprise registered on Russell's face. This gave Bewick quite a lift. He was fed up with being treated as part of Russell's baggage.

"Fluent Portuguese is just one of my many accomplishments," he explained modestly. "It's one of the reasons Dietrich sent me with you."

Russell dipped his head in acknowledgement before turning back to Lopes.

"Does the photograph tell you anything?"

"It's a Polaroid and that's about all."

"Have you tried enhancing it?"

"I have and it still tells me sod all. However much we magnify the image, we're not going to be able to identify individual trees. The only thing the photograph does is confirm something we'd guessed already. The kidnappers are somewhere in the mountains and they're fairly close to Viana. As Mrs. White is holding yesterday's paper, they can't be very far away."

"How about their demands?" Bewick asked. "Are you taking them seriously? The threat comes across loud and clear. Unless you do something, come Monday they're likely to start killing hostages."

"I know. That's why the headlines in Monday's newspaper will say that Mr. White is selling his interests on the island to the Maduran government for a nominal price. Hopefully, that should be enough to satisfy the kidnappers. With any luck, it might even encourage them to establish telephone contact about the money. These notes are no bloody use to us at all."

The superintendent tried to cheer himself up by refilling his glass. Then he passed the whisky bottle on.

"Exactly what do you have so far?" Russell enquired.

"Next to nothing, I'm ashamed to say. A few people did see the post office van on the way up to the Whites' villa but none of them really noticed the men inside. A couple of witnesses were certain they were wearing uniforms, but that's as far as they'd commit themselves. We have no idea at all about the vehicle they changed to after they'd ditched the post office van. For all we know, they could have walked."

"How about forensics?"

"They've turned up bugger all. None of the fingerprints we lifted from the van, the Whites' villa or the post office match anything we have on file. We know a hell of a lot about how the maid was killed and virtually nothing about who killed her. Here, you can take a look at these if you have strong stomachs."

The official police photographs of Maria Ribeiro's corpse were in Lopes's briefcase and he shared them out between Russell and Bewick. As the superintendent had promised, they didn't make for pretty viewing.

"There were forty-seven separate stab wounds," he said. "Most of them were in the breasts and around the vagina. Both nipples were sliced off and there seems to have been some attempt to cut out the clitoris as well. The killer had sex with the Robeiro girl shortly before he murdered her."

"Did you get a blood type from the semen?"

"Naturally—it was group O. Even if we made every male on the island jack off and give us a specimen, we wouldn't be much further forward."

"What about hair?"

"We found pubic and cranial. All that tells us is that the murderer was in his mid-twenties, Caucasian and had dark hair. He was probably about average height, which is really helpful. We don't have to bother about any blond Negro dwarves we run into."

While Lopes and Russell were talking, Bewick flicked through the photographs again. He had seen plenty of dead bodies before and didn't consider himself to be particularly squeamish. Even so, what he had in front of him sickened him.

"It must have been a madman," he said half to himself. "Have there been any similar sex killings on Madura recently?"

"No, thank God. There was one murder about three years ago but it wasn't in the same league. A local girl was beaten up, then raped and strangled. It might even have happened while you were over here before, Alan."

"I wouldn't know," Russell answered. "There were too many other things on my mind for me to pay much attention to the local news."

"Did you catch the murderer?"

"Oh yes." Lopes was smiling, amused to see how closely Bewick's thoughts mirrored his own. "To be more precise, the killer did himself in. He signed a confession and then jumped off a high cliff. In any case, they were completely different types of killings. The one three years ago was a rape which went too far. As you pointed out yourself, the murder of the maid was committed by a madman. That's one of the things which is worrying me most. Your Miss Haywood is about the same age as Maria Ribeiro."

This should have been a sobering thought. However, it didn't stop the whisky bottle being passed round again.

"If the killer was the maid's boyfriend, there must be somebody who saw the two of them together."

"You'd think so, wouldn't you?" Lopes pulled a face as he spoke. "Lover boy was either very, very lucky or very, very careful. Several of the maid's friends knew she had a new boyfriend. None of them actually saw him or even knew his name."

"How about the family?"

"It's the same old story, I'm afraid. When I said I had next to nothing, I was boasting. The bottom line is that we don't have anything at all. That's why you two are welcome. I think I've covered all the bases, but you might come up with an angle I've overlooked."

For a moment or two the room was silent. It was left to Bewick to get them back on track.

"Presumably you've been leaning on the local criminal fraternity."

"I've applied more pressure than they'd ever have thought possible. Believe me, if anybody knew anything, they'd be queuing up to tell me. But they haven't. The MLA is as new to them as it is to me and there have been no whispers at all about the kidnapping. I'd hazard a guess that this is the kidnappers' first criminal venture. It's a one-off job which will make them all rich. If I'm right, that should make catching them about ten times more difficult than if they were villains we already had on file."

"It sounded like amateur night when I read the preliminary report," Russell commented. "Looking on the bright side, it's reasonable to expect amateurs to make mistakes."

"Is this your suggested strategy, Alan?" Lopes was grinning. "We sit around and wait for the perpetrators to toss a few clues in our laps."

"I did intend to be a tiny bit more positive than that." Russell responded with a grin of his own. "For a start, I'd like copies of everything you have on file to date."

"Paperwork is about all I do have at the moment and you're welcome to it. I'll have duplicates of all the report sheets sent over."

"Fine. The second thing I want is a list of any activities on the island which can be remotely described as terrorist-inspired. The last five years should be enough to begin with."

"You could go back twenty years and the results would be the same. There's never been a terrorist on Madura."

"How about kidnappings?"

"Exactly the same. There's never been one unless you count the odd elopement."

"In that case I'll settle for the names and membership lists of any local extremist organizations. Everything from animal rights protesters to any religious splinter groups. Presumably you keep some form of shit list."

"We do. I'll have it photocopied."

"When you've done that, have a word with the personnel managers at White's factories. I'm after the details of any disputes in the past five years, no matter how trivial. More important, I want the names and addresses of any workers who have been sacked during the same period of time."

"You think there may be a personal angle?"

The question came from Bewick.

"If I were Derek White, I'd be thinking it was very personal," Russell told him. "It's his wife and son that have been snatched and his money the kidnappers are after. Come to that, it's his factories which are the other target."

"The same thought had occurred to me," Lopes said. "I already have somebody working on it. I'll pass the results on to you as soon as I have them."

"Do that. There's only one other point I can think of at the moment. The kidnappers will probably plan to leave Madura once the ransom has been paid. Can you prepare a breakdown of the options open to them? It would be handy to know the names of any plane or boat owners who aren't too fussy about the cargoes they carry."

"You can forget about planes—there aren't any. As far as boats are concerned, you'll end up with the name of just about every fisherman on the island. Smuggling is our national pastime. Is there anything else?"

"Not for the time being. I would like a daily update of what you're doing, though."

"Sure. I assume you'll be keeping me informed of any progress you're making."

"Of course."

This was a lie and Russell suspected that Lopes knew it.

"There is one last thing, Superintendent." Bewick had decided it was time to remind everybody that he was still there. "I know you've been over it yourself, but I'd still like a look at the file on that other murder. And can you give me the names of any other women who have gone missing on the island recently?"

"I'll send it over with the rest of the stuff in the morning. Another drink anybody?"

Weapons, Russell thought to himself, looking out of the window at the street below. The kidnappers must have had weapons of some description. If they had, they couldn't do what he had done—fly them in on an RAF transport and bypass customs. Shotguns were a possibility, of course, but not very likely. Even with the barrels sawn off, they remained cumbersome and weren't really suited to the kidnappers' needs. Logic dictated that they should have equipped themselves with handguns. Although Russell wasn't familiar with the Maduran gun laws, he was positive that they would be strict.

He turned from the window and looked across at Bewick. The younger man was seated at the table, wading through some of the paperwork Lopes had dumped on them.

"Have you found anything there about guns?" Russell asked.

"Not so far."

"The kidnappers must have been armed."

"That seems a reasonable enough assumption." Bewick was beginning to look interested. "There can't be too many arms dealers on an island this size."

"The question is, how do we find out who they are?"

"That's easy. We ask your friend Lopes."

"No." Russell was shaking his head. "It's too much like an admission of failure. We save him for our last resort."

"In that case, we get back to Dietrich. I'm sure he could find out for us."

"Too clumsy and time-consuming. Where's your sense of style?"

Although Russell's face was deadpan, Bewick could sense the smile inside. It was a test and for a moment Bewick was sure he would fail. Then the answer came to him.

"Hang on a second," he said, hunting through the papers in front of him. "I may have something here."

It took him a minute or so to locate what he was looking for. When he had finally found the correct sheet of paper, he held it out to Russell with a flourish.

"Patricio Spinoza," he said. "He's one of the local criminals Lopes leaned on for information. Reading between the lines, I'd say he was Viana's version of Mr. Big. He'd know who the local arms dealers were."

"You may be right." Russell was skimming rapidly through the report. "He's certainly worth a visit. Do you want to come with me?"

"Why not."

Dietrich had told him to watch the maestro at work. Besides, anything was better than the stodgy, ungrammatical prose of the police reports.

Dougal Allenby was twenty-four years old. Back in Ulster, he already had seven killings to his credit, although he himself didn't count three of them. However satisfying the experience might have been, blowing the Army border patrol to kingdom come had been Mickey Mouse stuff. A little kid could as easily have pushed the remote-control switch. In his own personal tally, Allenby only counted the men who had died at the end of his gun. These were the killings which had made his rep and now he was after the biggest scalp of them all. It didn't even occur to him that he might fail.

He had identified Russell while he was crossing the hotel lobby. By the time he and his companion hit the street, Allenby's back was already turned. The window of the souvenir shop acted as a mirror as he watched the two Englishmen walk away, and he didn't set off after them until they were almost fifty yards down the road. For all his natural arrogance, Allenby knew Russell wasn't a man to trifle with. After all, Russell was the bastard who had murdered his father.

In the area around the Gorgulho, trouble came in many forms. Usually the common denominator was either alcohol or women, and quite frequently the cause was a combination of the two. Very occasionally two of the women went for each other, and this was the nastiest of all. Knives, razors and the odd hatpin became the order of the day and this was when Patricio was seen to move the fastest. But he could cope, the same way he could cope with any other trouble which came in his direction. The Gorgulho and the streets around it were his territory. This might not be much of an empire but it was his and Patricio ruled it with a rod of iron.

Not that he suffered from any delusions of grandeur. Patricio knew his place in the order of things and he was well aware of his limitations. The Englishman was one of them. This was something Patricio had realized within the first few seconds after the two men had come through the swing doors. He had met men like them before—not many, but enough to know they were a breed you took care to walk around. Even before he opened his mouth, the older of the two reminded Patricio of Didier, the Frenchman he had seen in his Lisbon days. Lobo had been big then, very big indeed, but Didier had taken him and his two top lieutenants without even breaking into a sweat. Didier had displayed the same total confidence in himself, the same ease in what should have been an alien environment. The simple act of walking through the door had made it the Englishman's bar, his to do with as he liked. Although he had half a dozen of his own men within call, Patricio wasn't about to contest this assumption. He had seen what Didier could do and this was warning enough.

None of what he was thinking showed on Patricio's face as he watched the two strangers making their way to the bar. He was certain that it must be him they had come to see. He hoped they would make no demands of him that he couldn't meet.

"Senhor Spinoza?"

"That's me. All my friends call me Patricio."

"It's nice to meet you, Senhor Spinoza. My name is Russell. I was told you might be able to help me."

The Englishman's Portuguese was very good, both fluent and colloquial. This was no more than Patricio would have expected.

"I always do my best to be helpful," he said. "Would you like a drink?"

"Not now, thank you. Is there somewhere we can talk privately?"

"You can come through to my office."

Patricio led the way, his bulk dwarfing the two men behind him.

Although he was definitely apprehensive, he didn't feel immediately threatened. Nobody who wished him harm could afford the prices these men would command. Patricio doubted whether he could have afforded them himself. Any danger would arise from what they wanted of him.

"It's about guns." Now they were seated in the office, it was the younger of the two who had taken over. "We'd like to know where we can buy them."

"Guns are something we can do without on Madura."

There was genuine distaste in Patricio's voice.

"We're not overfond of them ourselves. All the same, the information is of some importance to us."

"In that case it's doubly unfortunate I can't help you."

The two Englishmen exchanged glances. Then Russell took over again.

"Senhor Spinoza," he said. "We bear you no ill will. At the moment we're asking you for your assistance as politely as we know how. There is a bottom line, though. It's information we have to have."

"Is that a threat?"

"Not at all." Russell's smile was warm and friendly and Patricio didn't trust it at all. "If I do ever threaten you, you'll know without having to ask. I was simply explaining the situation."

Like hell you were, Patricio thought without any real rancour. At least the squeeze was being applied with a degree of style. Nevertheless, nothing had happened which gave him any reason to modify his original impression. What you got was what you saw. It still looked like a lot of trouble to Spinoza if he should cross the two Englishmen.

"There seems to have been misunderstandings on both sides," he said. "When I told you I couldn't help, I wasn't refusing you my assistance. I meant there were no arms dealers on Madura."

"Not one?"

"None at all."

"So where would you go if you needed weapons?"

"That all depends. What kind of weapons are we talking about?"

"Let's say Armalite rifles, Smith & Wesson handguns, that kind of thing."

"I'd have them smuggled in from the African mainland. Guns are easy to come by over there."

Russell was sure that Spinoza was telling him the truth. He was equally certain that something had been left unsaid.

"Are you saying there's no source for guns of any kind on the island?"

"Not quite."

The handgun Patricio produced from the desk drawer was bulky and clumsy. After Patricio had passed it across to him, Russell could see it was one of the old Savage automatics.

"There is a source for antiques like this," Patricio explained.

"Who sells them?"

"Strictly speaking, they're not for sale. The gun you're holding came from the old police armoury. There were a lot of weapons left behind when the Portuguese pulled out after independence."

"If it's not a rude question, how did you lay your hands on it?"

"Through a policeman, of course. And, before you ask, this was over six years ago. The man who obtained it for me has left the police force and the island. The last I heard of him, he was living in Portimão in the Algarve. All the same, the old armoury is the sole source of weapons on Madura. If you have the right contacts, it's probably as easy to get a piece there now as it was a few years back."

Bewick was about to enquire who these contacts might be when he caught Russell's slight shake of the head. Although he stifled the question, Bewick could do nothing about the sudden flare of resentment.

"You talked about smuggling in weapons from the African mainland," Russell said. "Who would we see about that?"

This made Patricio laugh.

"Just about anybody who has a boat," he answered. "You must have heard that smuggling and Madura are virtually synonymous."

"We're talking about a special kind of boat. There are patrol boats out there. There's one hell of a difference between being caught with a few cartons of American cigarettes and a boatload of AK-47s. The sort of person I'm thinking of wouldn't be a moonlighting fisherman. He'd have to be a specialist."

"That takes us into dangerous territory." Patricio was beginning to wish he hadn't been quite so trusting when he handed over the Savage. The gun still hadn't been returned to him. "Once I start naming names, I'll be betraying friends."

"Betrayal doesn't come into it. Everything you tell us is in the strictest confidence."

"So you say."

"It happens to be the truth." When he put his mind to it, Russell could sound awfully convincing. "We're no more interested in smugglers as such than we are in arms dealers. Our interest is in a group of people who might be using their services."

It's that damn kidnapping, Patricio suddenly realized. It couldn't be anything else and this meant he had to modify his assessment of the two men in his office. They weren't contract killers, but they weren't policemen either. They were something far more dangerous. If Patricio was right, they had an official government licence to kill. They came from the shadowy half-world he knew of only by rumour. He had no great desire to learn any more at first hand.

"O.K.," he said, pulling a piece of paper towards him and picking up a pen. "I'll give you a couple of names. Make sure you leave me out of it when you see them."

When Patricio had finished writing, Russell took the paper from him. He put it into his shirt pocket without even glancing at it.

"There's one final matter before we go," he said. "It's more a business proposition than a favour."

"Yes?"

All Patricio wanted was for them to leave. Although neither of them had so much as raised his voice, they frightened him more with every second.

"We were followed here," Russell explained. "It's a man in his mid-twenties. Sandy hair, very pale face, lemon shirt and jeans. He might be in the bar by now, but he's more likely to be outside in the street."

Patricio nodded.

"He shouldn't be hard to spot."

"He'll probably be coming after us again when we leave. I'd like you to have a couple of your men follow him. Unobtrusively. Find out who he is, where he goes, whom he meets. Do you think you can handle it?"

"That's no problem. I'll just need a couple of minutes to set it up."

"Fine. Drop in anything you learn at the Méridien. I'm in room 1046. The name is Russell in case you've forgotten."

"I haven't."

"Do you want me to pay something on account?"

Russell was already reaching for the wallet in his back pocket.

"This is on the house." Russell was the kind of man Patricio would always be prepared to do favours for. "Like I said, just give me a minute or two to make the arrangements."

It wasn't until Patricio had left the office that Bewick turned to Russell.

"I didn't notice anybody tagging us," he said.

"I know."

The condemnation was there in Russell's voice.

SEVEN

The two of them had never been close and Raul certainly didn't trust the older man. Nevertheless, Cesar was an essential element in his planning. He had the steel which both Paolo and Fernando lacked. Cesar was the only one of the three who shared Raul's own lack of moral scruple. This was why Raul treated him with a patience he would never have displayed with either of the others. Later on, when it was all over, Cesar would have to be dealt with. For the time being Raul couldn't afford to upset him.

"I still say it's taking far too long," Cesar persisted.

"And I still say you're not thinking straight." Raul deliberately kept his tone mild. "My way gives us the best chance of walking off with the money."

"We could have it already."

"We could already be behind bars."

Raul rose to his feet. The two of them were inside the small, rough stone cottage which was their base. From the door there were only the mountains and the sky to be seen. Raul found this restful. Ever since he had been a child, the cottage had been one of his favourite places.

"The longer we spin it out, the more likely we are to be caught." Cesar was sticking to his guns and Raul had to fight down a momentary flash of annoyance. "Why keep messing around with those demands about White Industries? They're simply an irrelevance. It's the money we're after."

"They're a necessary irrelevance. Our demands help to confuse the issue."

"They confuse the hell out of me."

So far Cesar hadn't yielded an inch. Raul turned to face him again, framed in the bright sunlight which was streaming through the doorway.

"Tell me something, Cesar. How badly do you want your share of the ransom?"

"As badly as I ever wanted anything in my life."

There was no hesitation at all.

"So do I." This was a lie, for Raul knew the money was only a small part of it for him. "That's why I spent so long planning this. It's why I read everything I could find about previous kidnappings. Do you know what I discovered?"

"Tell me."

The scepticism was there in Cesar's voice.

"Nearly all the kidnappers were caught, Cesar. Either they left too many clues behind for the police to find or they fouled up on the ransom demand. We didn't leave anything—I made sure of that—and we have Fernando inside police headquarters. Nobody can take us by surprise and I don't intend to make any mistakes over the ransom. We're not going to rush, because there's no need. We're perfectly safe up here."

There was another factor as well, the best guarantee of all, but this was Raul's secret.

"That doesn't explain the stipulations about the factories."

"It's simple, Cesar—they can't possibly be met. A fifty percent wage increase would be economic suicide."

"Now I'm more confused than ever."

"Think about it. If the demands can't be met, we get the chance to demonstrate two things. We're not prepared to compromise and we don't make idle threats. After Monday, White will be only too happy to pay the ransom. A million dollars will seem cheap."

For a moment Cesar didn't speak. With the sunlight directly behind Raul, it was impossible to see his face but there was no mistaking the conviction in his voice. The crazy bastard really is crazy, Cesar thought.

"You're going to kill one of the hostages?"

"That's what I've promised the police."

"Which one will it be?"

"The son, I think. Then White will know we really mean business."

"He might be intending to pay the ransom anyway."

"And he might not. My way there won't be any doubt. Do you have any objections?"

After a few seconds, Cesar slowly shook his head.

"You're the boss," he said. "What do Paolo and Fernando think?"

"By the time they know, it will already be done. They'll go along with it."

They would too, Cesar thought. He was beginning to be convinced that disposing of Raul would be doing society a favour.

"Can we go as far as the river?" Janine asked.

"I don't know."

Although he was the one with the gun, Paolo felt awkward and nervous. Attractive women always made him feel inadequate. In his own mind, he knew he was.

"Come on. It won't take us a moment."

She was already moving on ahead and Paolo's only choice was to follow her. It's as though I'm the prisoner, he thought. Not that he would have minded being in Janine's power one little bit. She could have done any evil thing to him she liked. Simply watching the movement of her buttocks inside the stretch jeans was sufficient to get him aroused. It was as though each one was independently sprung and Paolo carefully filed the memory away. For the past two nights it had been the image of Janine which had filled his mind as he masturbated. He was sure it would be the same for some time to come.

"Will the water be cold?"

Janine had come to a halt on the bank where the river widened to form a small pool and she was looking back at Paolo over her shoulder. Not for the first time he registered that her eyes were an incredibly clear blue, her hair so blond it was almost white. She reminded Paolo of a photograph he had once seen of the young Brigitte Bardot.

"I should think it's freezing," he told her. "We're pretty high up."

"Well, I don't care if it is. I'm going in anyway."

"No."

The command came out much sharper than Paolo had intended but he was too late. Janine had started pulling the sweater over her head.

"Don't be so stuffy, Paolo," she said once her head was free. "I won't be a minute."

"I said no."

Although there was a T-shirt beneath her sweater, there was no bra and Janine knew her nipples were jutting out prettily. Her little act was beginning to turn her on, so God alone knew what it was doing to Paolo. The way he was staring at her, she'd probably have to scrape his eyeballs off her tits.

"Please, Paolo," she pleaded, giving him the helpless-female bit. "I feel absolutely filthy after all that time in the cellar. I really won't be long."

Paolo hesitated. He knew that if Janine had been with Raul or Cesar, she would have stopped at the first command. He also knew that he very much wanted her to remove some more of her clothing.

"All right." Even to Paolo's own ears, his voice sounded strange. "You can have five minutes, no more. Then we have to be getting back."

"Thank you, Paolo."

She flashed him her best Grade A grateful smile before turning her back on him while she stepped out of her jeans. Paolo seemed to like her bum well enough and she had her strategy carefully planned. Janine would have happily stripped off naked and let him count her pubic hairs if she had thought it would do any good. This wasn't the way, though. Too much of the wanton and she might scare him off. All that was on the agenda for today was the wet-T-shirt-and-knickers routine, a hint of the goodies on offer. This should keep Paolo well and truly hooked until she had an opportunity of playing the poor frightened little girl looking for comfort. After this, it should be a matter of helping Paolo prove he was a man, not a mouse.

Jumping into the pool without testing the water first was a mistake. Although Janine had been prepared for the water to be chilly, she hadn't expected it to be so cold that it took her breath away. She could almost feel herself turning blue. The stony bottom and the strength of the current came as something of a shock as well. Her entire body was becoming a block of ice, her feet felt as though they were being cut to ribbons and she was in danger of being swept all the way down to the Atlantic. Somehow Janine forced herself to duck the top half of her body beneath the water. It was the only way to get the T-shirt soaked. Besides, she hadn't been completely untruthful with Paolo. She really did feel filthy after the days cooped up in the cellar.

Scrubbing away at her skin and hair only lasted for a minute. By then her teeth were chattering and goose pimples were growing on her goose pimples. Cleanliness might be next to godliness, but it was also bloody close to hypothermia.

"I'm coming out," she announced. "I'm freezing."

"I did warn you."

"Say you told me so later. Right now I need a hand up the bank."

This wasn't strictly necessary but every little thing helped. While she waited with her hand outstretched, Janine debated whether or not to allow Paolo to pull her right into his arms. In the end she decided against. It might simply dampen Paolo's ardour. However good she looked, she would feel distinctly wet and clammy to the touch. It served her purposes better to take a step back after Paolo had helped her from the river and give him the full frontal.

If Janine was feeling cold, Paolo certainly wasn't. His cheeks seemed to be on fire and he knew he ought to turn his head away. Unfortunately, all he could do was stare. With the thin material of the T-shirt plastered to her body, Janine was effectively nude from the waist upwards. He could see every detail of her full breasts, right down to the small mole by one areola. Her knickers were transparent as well. The soft tendrils of blond hair were clearly visible, as were the outer lips of her vagina. It was just about the most erotic moment in Paolo's limited experience. When Janine shivered, she only added to the effect, her breasts moving deliciously.

"I'm cold," she said. "Hand me my clothes, will you?"

Paolo was temporarily incapable of movement. In any case, he wanted the moment to last forever. Knowing his luck, it might never be repeated.

"Come on, Paolo. I'm catching my death."

"It's all right," Cesar said, stepping into view. "I'll do it."

He had been standing in the trees for some time, appreciating the performance as much as Paolo. Now he had decided enough was enough. With Paolo as the target it was a case of casting pearls before swine. Besides, there was the poor kid's health to consider. If he didn't keel over first from high blood pressure, he was likely to have a permanent kink where his jeans were restricting him.

The unexpected interruption had completely shattered the spell. Paolo spun round guiltily and, now she didn't have his lust to feed off, Janine realized just how cold she was. When she shivered again, it was perfectly genuine.

"Go on, Paolo," Cesar told him. "Raul wants a word with you. He asked me to take over guard duty."

After one last look at Janine, Paolo set off along the path, too embarrassed to speak. Cesar watched him until he was out of sight among the trees. When he turned back to face Janine, he was grinning.

"I wonder why Paolo is walking all hunched over."

"Very funny," Janine said tartly. "May I have my clothes, please?"

"Sure."

Although Cesar bent down to pick up the sweater and jeans, he made no immediate move to hand them over. Unlike Paolo, there was no embarrassment at all as he paused to scrutinize her body. To her surprise, it was Janine who was embarrassed. In fact, she had to fight the temptation to cover herself. The time to play the coy virgin had passed many years before.

"It's a great body," Cesar told her, "but you were wasting it on young Paolo."

"I don't know what you mean."

"Of course you do. The poor little sod will be having wet dreams about you for months. I may have the odd one or two myself."

"Let me get dressed then. That should solve your problem for you."

Janine could feel the situation slipping out of her control. She wasn't entirely sure whether this was something she regretted or not. At first it had been the thought of how she was manipulating Paolo which had turned her on. Now it was Cesar's open admiration which was making her horny. There had always been a strong streak of the exhibitionist in her.

"You only made one mistake," Cesar went on, ignoring her request. "O.K., you could probably twist Paolo round your little finger, or any other part of your anatomy, come to that. The trouble is, he'd only twist so far. Paolo is scared shitless of Raul. You could screw Paolo's brains out and he still wouldn't dare to stand up to Raul. When it came right down to it, Paolo would be no real protection at all. I assume that's what you're after."

To give him his due, Cesar had summed up the situation pretty accurately. Janine suspected he was equally correct about Paolo's relationship with Raul. Paolo didn't strike her as somebody with a great deal of backbone.

"It was something like that," she admitted slowly, nodding her head.

"I thought as much. Now me, I'm different. I don't give a shit about Raul. I watch my back when he's around because he's a certified maniac but I can handle him if I have to. All things considered, I'd say I'm a much better bet than Paolo."

As he finished speaking, Cesar reached out to touch Janine between her legs. Although he was only cupping her in the palm of his hand, it felt good. So good that Janine found herself pushing down against his hand, inviting even more intimate contact. Cesar might be as trustworthy as a rattlesnake, but she definitely hadn't been designed for the monastic life and she seemed to have been up in the mountains forever. It would be nice to have her ashes well and truly hauled.

"Perhaps we can work something out," she said, her voice slightly husky.

"Later," Cesar told her. "I believe in talking afterwards."

You won't have the breath left, Janine promised herself as she allowed Cesar to guide her into the trees. She was no longer feeling at all cold.

The sex had been pretty damn good and he lay back luxuriously, the cigarette sticking up jauntily from his lips. It was about the only thing he could get to stick up after the last couple of hours. Alicia might not be the best-looking woman James Anderson had ever known, but she certainly knew her business. This was all Anderson asked of his women. As far as he was concerned, romance was for the birds. Just give him somebody who screwed like a rattlesnake and he was happy. Paying afterwards didn't worry him either. It never had, not even when he was young. He had always preferred his sex straight, without any entanglements or hassle.

Anderson supposed he ought to be getting up, but he couldn't think what the hell for. Alicia had mixed him a drink before she left, his cigarettes and lighter were right beside him and he was comfortable on the bunk. The aroma of cheap perfume and energetic sex might not be subtle but it added to his sense of well-being.

Coming to Madura had been one of the really smart moves in his life. Back in the U.S. of A. he had sampled jails in three of the seaboard states without enjoying any of them. Over here the money might not be so good but he lived well enough. More important, the police left him alone provided he stuck to the local ground rules. Christ, they probably thought of him as a national asset. It was smuggling which kept the island afloat economically and he had certainly done his share to keep the wheels turning. Best of all, though, he was safe on Madura. He didn't have to worry about some hopped-up Colombian hacking off his balls with a blunt knife.

The cigarette finished, Anderson was drifting off to sleep when he felt rather than heard the visitor come aboard. He and the *Amico* had been together so long that even the slight shift of balance as somebody stepped on the deck was enough to alert him. He rolled off the bunk immediately. As soon as he had his jeans and shirt on, he pulled the Police Special out of its drawer. Tucked into his waistband, it fit snug against the small of his back. Madura might be safe, but old habits died hard.

"Is anybody home?"

The voice was unmistakably English, which did absolutely nothing to endear the visitor to Anderson. It was an Englishman who had sliced off the lobe of his right ear in Fort Lauderdale. This was before Anderson had managed to get the bastard down and kick his teeth out through the back of his neck.

Anderson went up the aft companionway, hitting the deck behind his visitor. On first impressions, he didn't look like too much trouble. He was slightly over medium height with a good pair of shoulders but nothing Anderson himself couldn't match. Then the Englishman swung round and Anderson had to start revising his opinion. There was no way the visitor could have heard Anderson's bare feet, yet he had known he was there. He had actually sensed his arrival.

"Ah, there you are," Russell said. "I was beginning to think you weren't aboard. It is James Anderson, isn't it?"

"That's right. Who the hell are you?"

"Russell, Alan Russell. I wanted to ask you a few questions."

"Why? Are you the rep for a quiz show or something?"

Like Patricio Spinoza, Anderson had seen enough trouble in its various forms to recognize it when it came his way. Russell made Anderson uneasy. He tried to mask his nervousness with a show of belligerence.

"No, I'm not."

"In that case, I suggest you take your questions someplace else. I'm not interested."

"Perhaps I should take them to Ramón Lorca."

It was as though somebody had kicked Anderson hard in the crotch. Lorca was the man who had paid for the *Amico*. He was also the hopped-up Colombian with the blunt knife that Anderson used to have nightmares about.

"Maybe I was a mite hasty," he conceded. "If you'd like to come belowdecks, I'll mix us both a drink."

Anderson allowed Russell to go ahead of him down the companionway, a gesture which had nothing at all to do with good manners. His plan, such as it was, was pretty basic and had been improvised on the spur of the moment. All the same, Anderson couldn't think of any modifications he wanted to make to it on the way down the steep steps. Once they were at the bottom, he was going to pull the Police Special out of the back of his jeans. Then he'd hold it to the Englishman's head while he asked a few pertinent questions of his own.

What happened next depended entirely on the answers. In all probability it would involve steering the *Amico* to a deep part of the Atlantic and dropping Russell overboard with an anchor tied to his legs. This wasn't a prospect which worried Anderson nearly as much as the possibility of having to leave Madura. He had killed before when it was necessary and he still slept easy at nights.

The first part of the plan went perfectly. It was only when Anderson had the gun in his hands that things started to go wrong. As far as he could tell, Russell ducked and sidestepped and turned, though not necessarily in that order. Anderson couldn't even remember whether Russell used one hand or two to grab hold of his wrist. All he could be absolutely positive about was that he was suddenly airborne. And that his body was twisting with the momentum of the throw so that he didn't have a hope in hell of landing properly.

He was right. His back caught the edge of the table as he came down and his forehead connected solidly with a chair. Anderson was hurt and he was dazed but he had been hurt and dazed before. And he had come up off the floor to win. This time there was the Police Special lying temptingly on the carpet, only a few feet away. Even in his slightly battered condition, he could reach it well before Russell. At least, Anderson thought he could. The only trouble was, the Englishman could see the gun as well and he didn't appear to give a damn. It was this which sowed the seeds of doubt in Anderson's mind.

"That was a freebie," Russell explained. "Try anything else and I'm going to break one of your arms."

There was an awful lot of conviction in the bastard's voice. Anderson took another long, hard look at the revolver before he pushed himself stiffly to his feet, turning his back on temptation.

"How about if I mixed us those drinks I promised?"

"That sounds like a great idea," Russell told him.

It pleased him to know he wouldn't have to damage the American any more. He really hadn't come on board to pick a fight.

"Tell me something," Anderson said, still looking at the Police Special out of the corner of one eye. "Who was it who sicked you onto me?"

"Superintendent Lopes," Russell answered.

This wasn't strictly accurate. Both Lopes and Spinoza had provided him with lists of the major smugglers on the island. Anderson's was the only name which had figured on one list and not the other.

"That's all right then. Just so long as it wasn't one of my so-called friends." Anderson took a long pull at his drink. "Are you a policeman too?"

"No. And in case you're wondering, I don't have any connection with Lorca either."

"So who are you then?"

"The man who's come to ask you some questions."

Russell couldn't see any need for a fuller explanation.

"What if I don't want to answer them?"

"You'd suddenly find yourself with a lot of problems."

Anderson nodded his head in acknowledgement. Since Russell had mentioned Lopes, the gun no longer played any part in his plans. And Russell knew about Lorca too. That gave him two powerful strings to his bow. Whichever one Russell chose to use, Anderson was likely to end up in deep shit. He guessed he was going to answer the questions.

"What do you want to know?"

"For a start, what bookings do you have for next week?"

"That's easy enough. I'm taking a bunch of German tourists out fishing on Tuesday. Apart from that I'm open to offers."

"Let's not play games, Anderson." Russell sounded very patient.

"We're talking about your extralegal activities, the night work that earns you your living."

"You're interested in smuggling then?"

Anderson wasn't attempting to be difficult. It worried him not being able to put a handle to Russell.

"Maybe," Russell told him. "I don't know yet. It all depends whether anybody has contacted you recently about a one-way trip out of Madura."

"I see."

And he did too. Like Patricio, Anderson had heard a lot of rumours about the kidnapping up at the Whites' villa. Until now he hadn't made the connection with Cesar. When he thought about it, though, all the pieces fit. In the first place, Cesar had completely dropped out of sight for the past few days. Then again, it was the first time he had ever made contact through that gorgeous sister of his and a trip to the African mainland with no specified return date was unusual too. Normally Anderson would have been looking for an angle he could use to his own advantage. Unfortunately, he stood to lose too much. This was a game he would have to play by the Englishman's rules.

"Well?" Russell prompted.

"Next Wednesday night," Anderson said. "A man called Cesar Freitas."

"It's a one-way trip?"

"Sort of. The story I heard, he was going to do some shopping around in Morocco. When he was ready to come back, he'd let me know."

"How many others will be travelling with him?"

"None. Cesar will be travelling alone."

"You're sure of that?"

"I'm positive."

Russell was surprised, but not unduly so. He was more convinced than ever that the terrorist angle was nothing more than a blind. It was the money the kidnappers were after. Once they had it, there were any number of options open to them.

"Did you speak to Freitas yourself?"

"No. He sent his sister Pilar to make the arrangements for him. She's the resident singer at the Ipanema."

"How about payment?"

"That's made on the night. If it was a new customer, I'd want something up front, but Cesar and I go back a while. We've done a lot of business together."

"He's a friend of yours?"

"In my business I don't have friends. Just people I can trust more than others."

"But you do know him fairly well."

"As well as anybody, I guess. Cesar is pretty much of a loner."

"Tell me about him."

With Russell's prompting, Anderson managed to provide a fairly full profile. After the American had finished, Russell was silent for a minute or two while he thought everything through. When he was ready, he told Anderson precisely what he wanted him to do. It wasn't difficult and there wasn't anything he could seriously object to. However, Russell left Anderson with a final word of warning.

"Remember, Freitas isn't to know about my visit," he said. "I don't want him scared off."

"Yeah, I understand."

"I don't think you do." Russell's voice had gone very soft. "If you foul this up, it won't be the Colombian or the police you have to worry about. I'll be the one coming after you. You'd better believe that what I'd do to you would make Lorca seem like a Boy Scout."

Looking into Russell's eyes, Anderson did believe him. Implicitly.

EIGHT

Bewick pushed the file away from him and leaned back wearily in his chair. He had been through the damn thing three times already without being able to make head or tail of it. It was rather like an Agatha Christie novel. For most of the report, all the evidence pointed clearly in one direction. Then, right at the very end, the case was wrapped up with a totally unexpected conclusion. There was no sense to it at all.

Come to that, he wasn't doing much better with Russell. Logically, there was only the one way to handle the investigation. You did what Bewick himself was doing, sift through the mountains of paperwork until you found something which had been overlooked. Not Russell, though. To the best of Bewick's knowledge, Russell had done no more than glance at the stuff the superintendent had dumped on them. He obviously preferred to ignore the main investigation and shoot off along whatever tangent took his fancy. The worst of it was, the bastard seemed to be getting results. This was something which really pissed Bewick off.

There were some compensations, mind you. Travel with Russell and you evidently went first class because the Méridien was definitely a few cuts above the back-street hotels Bewick was normally shoved into. For a start, there was more furniture in the room than Bewick had in his London flat. It was better quality too, especially the leather-topped desk he was sitting at. Everything else was slightly over the top as well. Nonswimmers would need water wings in the bath, the service booklet was thicker than most novels and the mini-bar would keep an alcoholic happy for weeks. It was a lifestyle Bewick could become accustomed to without any great pain.

The knock at the door snapped him out of his reverie. He picked up the Smith & Wesson from the desktop and walked to the door. If it had been much farther, he would have had to stop for a rest.

"Who is it?"

"Me," Russell answered.

Once he was inside, Russell helped himself to a cold Budweiser from the fridge. Bewick followed his example before dropping into one of the armchairs.

"Any luck?" Bewick asked.

"Some." Russell was being his normal communicative self. "What's the score on our friend from the Hotel Afonso?"

"Friends," Bewick corrected him. "There are three of them, all travelling on British passports, all of them with Irish accents."

"Perhaps there's a potato convention. Are there any names to go with the passports?"

"Sure." Bewick handed the slip of paper across. "Mind you, they're about as genuine as Mary Poppins. The one calling himself Bertram is Frank Dowd. I can't swear to it but I think Henderson is really Pat Behan. He fits the description as I remember it."

"That figures." Dowd and Behan had been a team since before Russell had gone to Northern Ireland, in bed and out of it. Neither of them were to be taken lightly. "How about the young one?"

"Robert Anthony Atkinson is what his passport says. That's all I know. Shall I phone a description through to Dietrich and see what he can dig up for us?"

"It's not worth the bother. He'll be some youngster with an inflated reputation. Fancy another beer?"

"Why not."

Russell fetched a couple of frosted cans, tossing one to Bewick before going to stand at the window. The room was on the tenth floor and there was a magnificent view over Viana and the harbour. In the bright sunlight, the mountains beyond looked almost close enough to touch.

"They ought to be taken out," Bewick said, wiping froth from his top lip.

"I agree."

"Sooner rather than later might be an idea."

"Immediately would be best of all. We can do without them breathing down our necks."

"Do we handle it ourselves?"

"No." Russell had turned from the window and Bewick could see the half-smile on his lips. "I'm not being paid to sort out the IRA."

"Will Lopes be able to cope?"

"He'll have to once they've been dropped in his lap."

"We could do with one of them alive."

"Two would be even better. Come on. Finish your beer so we can go and ruin the superintendent's day."

As he drained the last of the liquid from the can, Bewick decided he still wasn't liking Russell any more.

There were no boats at the Viana Yacht Club. In fact, the only water in sight was in the swimming pool. When it had been founded in 1904, the club had occupied a prime site on the seafront and the sailing connection had been strong. There had been a solid core of English expatriates and a few Germans mixed in with what had passed as the cream of Maduran society. However, time changed all things. Long before the big harbour expansion in the 1960s had occasioned a change of premises, the character of the club had been transformed. The people who could afford the yachts had transferred their allegiance to the newer Leopoldville Tennis Club while the Yacht Club had been passed on to the middle classes.

For all this, Lopes liked it well enough. It served the basic function of any good club anywhere, a protective bubble against the real world outside. Today, with the two Englishmen as his guests, he felt less protected than usual. Russell in particular made him uneasy.

"Why have you handed them to me?" he asked.

"Common courtesy," Russell told him. "After all, it's your island."

"I appreciate the gesture."

Like hell I do, Lopes thought. He had a pretty shrewd idea of how far Russell's ideas of courtesy went.

"We thought it might be useful if at least one of them was captured alive," Bewick said.

"I'll do my best but I can't give any guarantees. I prefer dead Irishmen to losing any of my own men."

"That's understood. When will you move against them?"

"That depends. Are you still being followed, Alan?"

"On and off. It could be I'm simply an optional extra and it's the Haywood woman they're really after."

"You think they're here to negotiate for her?"

"No." Russell made this very definite. "I'm not even convinced they know she's been kidnapped."

This was Lopes's opinion as well. Just the same, he hoped he and Russell hadn't reached their judgement from the same starting point.

"We don't want them splitting up, do we?" he said thoughtfully. "Tonight might be a good time to hit them, after they're safely tucked up in their beds."

"That seems reasonable."

"Are you coming along to watch Madura's finest in action?"

"I think not," Russell answered. "I'll be in bed too. I need my eight hours sleep a night."

Sure, Lopes thought cynically. What you mean is that Dietrich won't be paying you overtime. It was an attitude he could sympathize with. Only a fool risked getting his arse shot off when it wasn't necessary.

"I'll come along if you don't have any objections," Bewick said. "One of us ought to show the flag."

"Suit yourself. Assuming our birds do come home to roost, I'll send a car to collect you just before midnight."

A group of four young women walked through the bar towards the pool and all three men watched them. Modesty was the keynote for swimming costumes at the Yacht Club but the girls were still very easy on the eye. Lopes was pleased that neither of the Englishmen made any comment. Salacity wasn't something he enjoyed or participated in. Mind you, he didn't suppose he was participating in much at the moment. It was almost two years since Alfreda had died and he hadn't touched another woman since. Retirement threatened to be a long, lonely haul. It was still preferable to putting up with Targa for any longer.

"What progress are you making, Alan?" he asked once the women were out of sight.

"About what you'd expect. One thing has occurred to me, though."

"What's that?"

"Have you considered the possibility that a police officer might be involved in the kidnapping?"

Although he did his best, Lopes knew he had been unable to prevent the shock from registering on his face. It was the last question he would have wanted Russell to ask. He had enough on his plate as it was.

"Why do you ask?"

Even to his own ears, Lopes sounded defensive.

"There's nothing tangible. It's just a feeling."

"One of your famous hunches?"

"Something like that. I'm told the only source of firearms on the island is the police armoury."

"We can't be sure the kidnappers were armed."

"I'd bet on it, wouldn't you?"

This wasn't something Lopes cared to dispute.

The street was full of policemen and so was the hotel lobby. Almost every doorway boasted at least one armed man and there were sharp-shooters on the rooftops opposite the Afonso. Inside the hotel itself there were another dozen men. This was the strike force, divided into three groups of four. One group would take the room Dowd and Behan were sharing while another had responsibility for the man who called himself Atkinson. The third group was a mobile reserve within the hotel in case anything went wrong.

This seemed unlikely. All three Irishmen were known to be in their rooms and the lights had been out for over an hour. They should be taken in their beds, seized before they had an opportunity to realize they were in danger. This was the theory and Bewick couldn't fault it. He wouldn't have organized things much differently if he had been in charge.

It was the Irishmen he couldn't understand. Bewick had booked into hotels in hostile territory himself. Under such circumstances, it was axiomatic to have an emergency escape route planned. You visualized the very worst that could happen and made your plans accordingly. From where he stood, in a doorway opposite the Afonso, Bewick could allow Atkinson an outside chance. His room was situated at the side of the hotel. A twelve-foot drop from his window, a quick scramble across the flat roof of the car showroom next to the hotel and a slightly longer drop would see him into an alley away from the main centre of operations. Of course, Lopes would have the roof and the alley covered, but at least Atkinson had some kind of a bolt-hole.

Dowd and Behan most certainly didn't. Their room was at the very front of the hotel, overlooking the street. Where they were, up on the fifth floor, their only line of retreat would be through the hotel itself. This was downright sloppy and Bewick couldn't understand the oversight. Perhaps they had been influenced by the holiday atmosphere on Madura.

Leaving his doorway, Bewick walked across the road to the hotel. Before he went inside, he turned to take a final look at the police dispositions and, once again, he couldn't find any fault. Although he could see the hidden men, he knew where to look. To a casual observer the street was as quiet as it should have been at one in the morning.

The superintendent had just finished his final briefing to the strike force when Bewick strolled across the lobby to join him. A couple of the hotel staff were hovering nervously in the background. Nobody was paying them any attention and Bewick didn't either.

"All set?" he enquired.

"The men are about to go upstairs now," Lopes told him. "They go through the doors in fifteen minutes."

Although there was no real need, both men were keeping their voices low. The last few minutes were always very tense.

"They'll get one hell of a shock if the Irishmen have done a midnight flit."

"No chance." Lopes managed a thin smile. "There's a couple of my men upstairs already. Everybody is where they ought to be."

"So you might take all three of them alive."

"We might."

Lopes was very sensibly refusing to commit himself.

"Anything you want me to do?"

"Just keep out of my hair until it's over. There's a lot to do."

"Sure."

Rather than hang around in the lobby, Bewick went outside again. Standing at the top of the steps, he lit himself a cigarette. He didn't have to wonder what the men in the strike groups would be feeling, because he knew. Each and every one of them would be aware that in a few minutes they would be bursting into rooms which contained men who were armed and dangerous. It was a time when sphincter control became very important.

As he stood there, Bewick found his thoughts returning to Russell. It was difficult for him to assess how much personal dislike and resentment was affecting his judgement. In the end, he decided he was being as objective as possible under the circumstances. Russell was definitely up to something and this wasn't necessarily what Dietrich had had in mind. Unfortunately, Bewick still wasn't sure what he could do about it.

Almost without thinking, he had started walking along the front of the hotel. When he reached the lighted window of the showroom, he stopped for a moment, examining the selection of cars on offer. There wasn't an English one among them, which was no more than Bewick would have expected.

Checking his watch, he saw there were still a few minutes to go and he walked on to the corner of the alley before he turned. He had already taken a couple of steps back towards the hotel when the voice from the alley stopped him in his tracks. It seemed sufficient reason to pull the Smith & Wesson from its holster.

Allenby came awake instantly. For a second he simply lay there, staring into the darkness as he listened to the shrill of the telephone. Then he rolled over and scooped the receiver from its hook.

"Yes."

"Is that Atkinson?"

Although the caller was speaking in English, Allenby couldn't identify the voice. The accent was equally difficult to place.

"It is."

"Excellent. I just rang to warn you that the police have surrounded the hotel. They should be coming in through your door in approximately ten minutes. Good night."

"What . . . ?"

There was no point in completing the question because the phone was dead. So was Allenby likely to be if the information was correct. The only window which overlooked the street was in the bathroom. Padding through to it in the dark, Allenby pushed the window open a crack. Although it wasn't the best of angles, the street seemed peaceful enough at first glance. This was no more than he would have expected, police raid or not. It was the doorways and rooftops Allenby was interested in.

"Shit."

The policeman on the roof opposite had only moved slightly but it was enough. This was for real, not some April Fool. Still in the darkness, Allenby returned to the bedroom and started pulling on his clothes. The whys and wherefores would have to wait. For the moment, his only interest was to get the hell out of the hotel.

While he was zipping up his jeans, Allenby briefly considered trying to warn Dowd and Behan. However, he rejected the idea almost as soon as it occurred to him. A phone call would have to go through the hotel switchboard and the police would surely be monitoring it. The only alternative involved stepping into the lighted corridor outside his room. If the police were in the street, they'd be in the corridor too. Unless the mysterious guardian angel had thought to warn them as well, Dowd and Behan would have to look out for themselves. They knew the rules as well as Allenby did.

The most dangerous moment was going to be when he went out through the window. There could well be a policeman posted on the showroom roof. Against this, there was nowhere else for him to go. Allenby did it fast, gun in hand, and his trainers made no sound as he landed on the rough concrete.

For a second, Allenby lay on his belly, body cringing in anticipation of the bullets slapping into his flesh. But there were none, nor any shouts of alarm. The police on the rooftops opposite hadn't seen him and the showroom roof was deserted. Although there were patches of dark shadow which might have concealed a man, Allenby knew he must be alone. If the police had been there, they would have taken him the moment he appeared at the window.

Acutely aware of the seconds ticking away, he began to crawl, using the low parapet as cover. Once he was above the alley, he stopped again, making a conscious effort to control his breathing. He was sweating like a pig and he took the time to wipe the palms of his hands on his jeans. Although the grip of his Beretta was taped, he couldn't afford to leave anything to chance. There would certainly be police posted in the alley.

Strangely enough, Allenby didn't feel at all afraid. A strong streak of fatalism had always been part of his nature. If this was his night to die, so be it, but as sure as hell he didn't intend to die alone. This was a thought which comforted him as he went up and over the parapet in one continuous movement. It wasn't nearly such a good landing this time, but Allenby managed to turn his stumble into a roll, eyes already searching for a target.

"Stay where you are."

The first policeman was no more than five metres away. If he had had any sense, he would have remained by the wall, not stepped into the middle of the alley where he was backlit by the streetlights. Allenby shot him twice, once in the chest and again in the head, holding the Beretta with both hands and firing with great precision. Then he was rolling again, panicking slightly because he couldn't spot any of the dead man's companions. At the street end of the alley, somebody's head popped round the corner. Allenby loosed off a wild snap shot to discourage the owner as he pushed himself to his feet. The bitter taste of defeat was there in his mouth. He still couldn't see where the other policemen were, and he swung round defensively, the Beretta held out in front of him.

It took him a few moments to realize there was nobody else. By then Allenby was already running. It was only a dozen strides to the end of the alley, and once he was around the corner, he ran as he had never run before. Although the entire area behind the hotel was a maze, Allenby had walked the route so many times that he could operate on automatic pilot. Even the dark was no real hindrance. If he really was through the police cordon, something Allenby found it difficult to believe, they weren't going to trap him again. The sound of gunfire from the hotel only added speed to his legs. There was something he still had to do, the work he had been trained for.

Bewick could take a hint as well as the next man. When somebody put a bullet within a foot of his left ear, he knew he wasn't wanted. Besides, there was no need to go into the alley. He had heard the policeman's instructions to halt, followed by the two silenced reports. Atkinson had then fired a third shot at him. Now was the time for the police to strike back. Leaning against the showroom wall, Bewick waited confidently for the police fusillade. When this didn't materialize, he crouched down and poked his head around the corner for a second time. The alley was deserted. Apart from the body sprawled on the ground a third of the way down, there was nobody there.

Pursuit was pointless and Bewick was checking the police officer for a pulse which wasn't there when he heard the shooting from the hotel. Although the gunfire only lasted for a matter of seconds, it sounded like the St. Valentine's Day massacre all over again. Or the bloody finale to another of Madura's amateur nights. The thought did nothing to improve his temper.

He was still in an angry mood when he swept back into the hotel lobby but there was no Lopes to vent his spleen on. A sergeant directed Bewick to the fifth floor, where he found the superintendent at the front of the crowd which was examining his hit squad's handiwork. Behan had never even made it out of bed while Dowd's naked body was in the middle of the floor. Judging by the amount of blood, both men had enough bullets in them for the lead to be mined.

"What happened?" Bewick asked.

"You can see for yourself. My men were a trifle trigger-happy."

Lopes sounded as pissed off as Bewick felt.

"What happened with Atkinson?"

"I'm not quite sure," Lopes admitted. "He went out of the window t his room. Don't worry, though. The men posted in the have him."

n't have any men in the alley." Bewick put heavy emphasis "men." "The only officer who was there is dead. Atkinson got clear away."

"You are joking, aren't you?"

"I only wish I was."

"Holy shit." This came out almost as a groan. "I don't believe it."

For the next few minutes Lopes was busy delivering a series of rapid-fire instructions to the policemen nearest to him. An ambulance was needed for the dead officer in the alley, the search for Atkinson had to be organized and a certain Captain Pereira's testicles were to be delivered to Lopes on a platter. Bewick gathered that it had been the captain's responsibility to arrange for cover in the alley.

"What a cock-up," Lopes said disgustedly once everything was in hand. "I know what you must be thinking but we're not normally this inefficient."

"It could have happened to anybody."

Bewick was simply being polite. He thought it was a complete cock-up too and he couldn't see any excuses.

"There is a silver lining, though." Lopes was desperately trying to sound optimistic. "Atkinson can't have gone very far. We should have him in the bag by morning."

"If you're lucky." Bewick was sceptical. "His type would have been on the run since adolescence."

"This isn't Belfast, though. He doesn't have anywhere to go to ground on the island."

"Perhaps that isn't what he wants." The thought had only just occurred to Bewick and he was cursing himself for being so slow. "I need to make a phone call."

"Be my guest."

Although Lopes was clearly puzzled, Bewick didn't have the time to explain. It only took the switchboard a matter of seconds to put him through to the number he wanted. He let the phone ring for over a minute without receiving any response. Then, cursing under his breath, Bewick slammed down the receiver and swung round to face Lopes.

"Can I have the use of a car?"

"Why?"

"Nobody is answering the phone at the Méridien."

"You think that's where Atkinson has gone?"

The superintendent had understood the implications immediately.

"Like you said, he doesn't have anywhere to run to. And all Irishmen are crazy bastards."

"We'll use my car."

Bewick's sense of urgency had communicated itself to Lopes and he was already shouldering his way to the door. Bewick stayed close behind him. If he was right and Atkinson had decided to go down fighting, Russell was the man he would most like to take with him.

He was as close to death as he had ever been. Russell had known this from the moment the light had clicked on and he had seen Atkinson standing beside the bed. The only good news was that the light had come on at all. It indicated that Atkinson wanted to talk first.

"You're making a mistake," Russell said.

"I think not, Mr. bloody Russell. You see, I know just who and what you are."

"That wasn't what I meant." Russell was keeping his tone conversational. "You're breaking the assassin's golden rule. If you're going to use a gun, use it straightaway. Don't waste time talking."

"Rules are made to be broken."

The Irishman had seated himself in a chair some six feet from the bed. Close to he seemed even younger than Russell had thought when he first saw him in the street. Not that Russell found this a source of comfort. Everybody, from a baby to a geriatric, was capable of pulling a trigger. It was the ability to kill another human being in cold blood which really counted. Russell didn't doubt that Atkinson had this capacity in abundance.

"Stay exactly where you are, Mr. Russell." Russell had been lying on his left side. He had started to ease himself over onto his back when the sharp command stopped him. "If you move a muscle, you're dead."

"I thought I was dead anyway."

"That's as may be, but you know how the saying goes. While there's life there's hope."

Atkinson's confident air suggested he didn't have much faith in the dictum. To Russell's mind he was a cocky little sod.

"Where are your two friends, Dowd and Behan?" he asked.

"Back at the hotel. They're either dead or captured."

"At least that's something. How did you manage to get away?"

"A mysterious well-wisher phoned a warning."

"Lucky you. I didn't realize you had friends on the island."

"Nor did I. It's a shame he didn't leave his name."

"An address would have been handy as well," Russell pointed out. "You're going to need a place to lie low. The entire Maduran police force must be after you by now."

"Maybe they are. That still leaves me in better shape than you."

This was undeniably true. Russell guessed it would be very soon now. They didn't seem to have anything left to say to each other.

"You must be wondering why you're not dead already."

It was as though Atkinson was a mind reader.

"The thought had occurred to me."

"I wanted to make sure you knew who it was who killed you. My name is Dougal Allenby."

"What am I supposed to say? Pleased to meet you?"

"Doesn't the name mean anything to you?"

"Not a thing. You'd only have just been out of nappies when I was in Belfast."

"How about Colin Allenby?"

There was a new intensity about the Irishman now. This made Russell pick his words carefully.

"Him I knew," he said. "The man was a raving psychopath. Setting him up for the SAS was one of the best day's work I ever did."

"So you admit it then?"

Allenby had gone very pale.

"Why shouldn't I? It's something I'm proud of. If I knew where he was buried, I'd probably pay a visit so I could spit on his grave. Was Crazy Colin a relative of yours by any chance?"

"He was my father, you bastard."

The Beretta was already being raised as Allenby spoke.

One bullet in the throat, Bewick noted dispassionately. This was all it had taken. The night porter was lying behind the reception counter, his head resting in a pool of blood. Beyond him, the telephonist was slumped forward in her chair, one hand still stretched out towards the switchboard. She had been shot in the back of the head. The third body was partly concealed behind one of the pillars in the reception area. He was wearing a green jacket and there was a tray on the floor beside him. It looked as though room service at the Méridien was temporarily discontinued.

The lift seemed to be taking an age to descend. Eyes fixed on the floor indicator, Bewick willed it to move faster. The staircase was a temptation which he resisted. Atkinson was probably still in the building. If he was, Bewick didn't want to confront him after running up twenty flights of stairs. Breathlessness and unsteady hands went together.

Lopes was busy issuing terse instructions to his driver. Although his car had come on ahead, swarms of policemen should be converging on the Méridien in a matter of minutes. They would almost certainly be too late to be of any assistance. Bewick had already decided that if Atkinson was going to be stopped, he was the one who would have to do it. It was something of a surprise when Lopes bustled across to join him as the lift finally reached the ground floor.

"I didn't think police superintendents ever put themselves on the firing line," he said.

"Alan Russell is my friend." Lopes spoke with a kind of dignity. "Besides, it's my fault he's in danger."

There was no arguing with this. Bewick had pressed the button for the twelfth floor and he could read the question in Lopes's eyes.

"We walk down a couple of floors," he explained. "I don't want the lift doors to open on the tenth floor and find Atkinson waiting on the other side. He's already shot his quota for the night."

He very much hoped Russell wasn't included in it because Bewick knew he had to share the guilt with Lopes. If he had been thinking straight, he should have phoned Russell the moment he had learned Atkinson was on the loose. The two hotels were less than a mile apart and Bewick knew how important a symbol Russell was in Provo eyes. Somehow, the fact that he didn't like Russell very much made Bewick feel worse. This was a thought he pushed firmly to the back of his mind. The job ahead demanded total concentration.

"You keep behind me when we leave the lift," he told Lopes. "Follow my lead."

"I don't need to be mollycoddled." The superintendent sounded offended. "I've done this sort of thing before."

"Not recently, you haven't. Besides, you're the bigger target."

"Unfortunately, that's true."

Although there was a thin sheen of sweat on Lopes's face, his hands were steady enough as he checked his service revolver. Bewick guessed the superintendent would do a good job of covering his back.

The moment the lift stopped on the twelfth floor, Bewick was jabbing at the button to open the doors. He couldn't rid himself of the conviction that they were too far behind Atkinson to do any good. In Bewick's mind, Russell was already dead.

The corridor outside the lift was deserted. Apart from the subdued sound of snoring from one of the rooms, everything was quiet. With the thick carpeting, Bewick didn't need to worry about noise and he took the stairs at a run. The adrenaline was coursing now and all his senses were at their sharpest. It wasn't until he reached the last flight that he slowed down. Now he took each stair as though he was walking on eggs. The slightly laboured breathing of Lopes behind him was an irritant he ignored.

At the bottom of the stairs Bewick stopped, listening for any indications of a hostile presence. There was nothing and he cautiously peeped round the corner. The corridor was clear all the way to the closed door of Russell's room. Bewick signalled to Lopes to follow him and started down the corridor, keeping close to the wall. Halfway to Russell's room caution became unnecessary. The noise of the two shots from inside the room was muffled but unmistakable.

The damn duvet had caught fire. Russell had rolled it up into a ball and was jumping up and down on it with his bare feet when the door of his room was kicked open. He was still tense and the backward roll over the

ιs instinctive. For a second or two, Russell simply lay on the
peering round the end of the bed. The doorway was empty but at
least one man had ducked into the bathroom.

"Is that you Bewick?"

"Yes."

Bewick sounded equally tense.

"Who else is with you?"

"Superintendent Lopes."

"Well, he can start fixing my door while you bring me a wastepaper
basket full of water. Otherwise the entire hotel is likely to burn down."

Russell went back to stamping on the smouldering duvet. The water
seemed to do the trick but he jumped on it a bit more to make sure.
Bewick was far more interested in the body slumped in the chair than he
was in the damage to hotel property. The same would probably have
been true of Lopes if he hadn't been busy at the door, shepherding away
those hotel guests who had been woken up by the disturbance.

"What happened?" Bewick asked, indicating the dead man.

"He talked far too much."

This had been Allenby's second mistake. The one which had really
killed him had come earlier. He should have switched off the lights in
the corridor before he opened the door. The sudden sliver of illumination as he had slipped inside the door had been as good as an alarm bell
to somebody who slept as lightly as Russell. And he always kept a
weapon near to hand.

"You had the gun under the bedclothes."

Bewick made this a statement. Considering the state of the duvet,
this hardly qualified him as a master of deduction.

"That's right."

"But you let him talk a little before you shot him."

"Try stopping an Irishman. They're all in love with the sound of
their own voices."

"Did he say anything interesting?"

"Not really. What I want to know is how he managed to slip through
the police net."

"So do I," Lopes agreed. Now more policemen had arrived, he had
come into the room to join them and he was doing his best to look
contrite. "I shan't ever forgive myself."

"Nor will the hotel management. You made a hell of a mess of their
door."

"While I'm sorting that out, it might not be a bad idea if you two
retired to Mike's room. Pretty soon it's going to be like a three-ring
circus in here."

"You won't need us then?"

"Not officially, no. The less you figure in this, the better."

This wasn't a point either Russell or Bewick chose to dispute.

NINE

An hour ago Cesar had been enjoying himself. Now he was on the verge of panic and this had nothing to do with a change of environment. He still sat on the same bench overlooking the same beach. The sun continued to shine and there were just as many well-filled bikinis for him to admire. Sixty minutes previously the sight of all the nubile, scantily clad bodies had filled him with lust but right now sex was the last thing on his mind. The big difference was that an hour ago he had been waiting for Fernando to keep their rendezvous. As of this minute, he was still waiting, but Fernando was forty minutes overdue.

It was no good trying to kid himself that Fernando had forgotten the appointment, because he was one of the most organized people Cesar had ever met. Besides, the meeting was far too important to slip anybody's mind. No, if Fernando wasn't coming, it was because he couldn't and this was bad news for everybody.

For the moment, Cesar's concern was entirely selfish. The local police didn't give a toss for Amnesty International. When they wanted a suspect to talk, he talked. The only element of doubt was whether the suspect saw the light while he was still capable of doing things like walking or holding a knife and fork. Assuming Fernando had been pulled in, he would have spilled everything he knew. This wouldn't include the location of the hideout, because he didn't know it, but it would sure as hell include his rendezvous with Cesar. Half the Maduran police force could be watching him at this very moment. This was one of the reasons Cesar had remained on the bench. If it was a stakeout, he needed to know exactly what he intended to do before he stood up.

Cesar lit himself a cigarette and gazed sightlessly down at the beach. It wasn't easy to stay calm when he knew his entire future might be riding on what he did in the next few seconds. And he had to bear in mind the possibility that he could be wrong. It would be as stupid to blow the whole deal for nothing as it would be to lead the police back to the hideout.

Fortunately, the first step was relatively straightforward. If he couldn't see Fernando, he had to see Pilar and there was no point in trying anything tricky before then. It didn't make sense to try to lose anybody watching him when he was heading directly to the one address in Viana where he could be expected to go. The fun was likely to begin after he had left his sister and Cesar was very glad she had no idea what he was doing.

Let's do it, then, Cesar thought to himself, grinding out his cigarette and rising to his feet. Almost immediately he discovered that walking naturally had become something he had to think about. His legs and back suddenly felt unnaturally stiff. It was as though he was centre stage, in the full glare of the floodlights. Although nobody he could see seemed to be taking particular notice of him, this didn't mean a damn. The ones who counted would be behind him and Cesar didn't have eyes in the back of his head.

It was so glaringly obvious, Russell was sure he must have overlooked something. After he had read the report through a second time, it was still there, staring him in the face. Although he was no policeman, he was no stranger to the investigative process. He knew he would never have allowed the matter to rest there.

"Why didn't you show me this before?" he asked.

"I didn't think you'd be particularly interested." Bewick had looked up from the papers he was going through at the desk. "You were too busy doing your own thing. Besides, the report didn't seem relevant. It's all ancient history. The police got their man, even if it was more by luck than judgement."

"Is that what you really think?"

Bewick didn't answer immediately.

"No," he admitted finally, "but it doesn't appear to tie in with anything we're interested in. There are no similarities with the killing up at the Whites' villa."

"Maybe not." Russell was pretty sure Bewick was holding something back. He did this often enough himself to recognize the signs. "Indulge me, though. Who do you think killed the Cavalcanti girl?"

"It's there in black and white. The murderer wrote a full confession and then committed suicide."

"That's the officially approved version. I asked what you thought."

"O.K." Bewick shrugged. "I'd say all the evidence pointed at the brother. Without the confession, I wouldn't have any hesitation in saying he was the murderer. Reading between the lines, the police thought that way too."

"Exactly. And if it was the brother, he's pretty sick. Incestuous rape murderers aren't your ordinary, run-of-the-mill citizens."

"It isn't the typical psychological profile for a terrorist or kidnapper either."

Russell conceded the point with a dip of his head. However, it did nothing to change his mind, especially as he possessed information that Bewick didn't.

"Take a look at this," he suggested, pushing two typed sheets of paper towards Bewick. "It's the list of men who have been sacked or laid off by White Industries. The name you're looking for is halfway down the second page."

It only took Bewick a couple of seconds to find it.

"Raul Cavalcanti," he said, raising his head to look at Russell. "He was sacked just over a year ago."

"Quite a coincidence, isn't it?"

"You could put it that way. Do we know why he was given the push?"

"Not yet. That's something you're going to find out for us. In fact, I want everything you can dig up on friend Raul."

"Do I work through Lopes?"

"I think not. Let's see how you manage on your own."

"It would be quicker through the police."

"Sure, and half of Madura would probably know what we were doing before the day was out. Let's keep this between ourselves for the time being."

"O.K. What will you be doing?"

"Interviewing a lady."

"Anybody I know?"

"Pilar Freitas," Russell said. "You probably recognize the name."

Bewick did, but he checked the report again after Russell had left. Then he had the hotel switchboard place a call for him to London.

"How's it going, dear boy?" Dietrich enquired.

"Slowly, sir."

"That doesn't sound very promising."

"It isn't. Has anything come through from Belfast yet?"

"Not so far, I'm afraid, but I'm pushing every button I can."

Bewick was disappointed. Somebody must have tipped off the Provos about the situation on Madura and this could be the key to everything.

"You will let me know as soon as you hear anything, won't you, sir?"

"Of course, dear boy. How's Russell bearing up?"

"Remarkably well. He probably knows a hell of a lot more than he's admitting to."

"He always does. You could say it's his trademark."

Although Dietrich had interpreted the remark as a compliment, this wasn't how Bewick had intended it. Not that he did anything to correct the misunderstanding. Bewick knew he would need incontrovertible proof before he dared voice his suspicions.

Built of stone which had been hewn from the surrounding mountains and thatched with reeds brought up from the lowlands, the cottage had an ageless quality about it. Raul found it difficult to visualize a time when it hadn't stood on the small plateau. However, the cellars were a recent addition. He could even put a date to their excavation. It had been 1932, the first year of what the Madurans still referred to as the Contraband War, a reflection of the islanders' taste for melodrama. There had only been four deaths in the five years the dispute had lasted.

A couple of years previously, twice as many people were killed in a single morning when Guihermo Alves's coach had gone off the road near Barcelos.

Nevertheless, the Contraband War was firmly established in local folklore, a distinct wave in the peaceful sea of Maduran history. Prior to 1932 all smuggling on the island had been in the hands of the Cavalcanti and Pires families. Although they had never been particularly friendly, they had coexisted well enough. Both families knew their territory and, by and large, they had stuck to it. It was in the best interests of both families not to upset the applecart.

This was a fact of life which Mauro Pires hadn't appreciated. When his father had died, leaving him as head of the Pires clan, Mauro had still been young enough to think he could change the world. He had wanted the entire cake for himself and he had set out to destroy the Cavalcantis. For a time it seemed as though he might succeed. With the active connivance of the governor at the time, the Cavalcantis were virtually driven out of Viana. Boats were burned, safe harbours were no longer safe and retailers were forcibly discouraged from dealing with anybody but Mauro.

For a while the Cavalcantis were forced up into the mountains, where they established a new smuggling route across the interior from the north coast. This was why the cellars had been dug. The tiny settlement became the Cavalcantis' fortress while they struggled to survive and plotted their revenge. On Easter Sunday 1937, Mauro Pires died in a hail of bullets outside the cathedral after attending mass. Three months later João Cavalcanti and his two sons faced a firing squad. This marked the end of the war. It also helped to turn the smuggling industry into the free market it had remained ever since.

The feud might be ancient history, but Monte Cavalcanti was still a fact. It was a miniature fortress, virtually impregnable against anything short of an air strike. From where he sat among the rocks, Raul had a clear view of the only path, and for the past twenty minutes he had been watching the solitary figure climb towards him. It was only now, as Cesar struggled up the last incline, that Raul stepped down onto the track. He could see the sweat on Cesar's face and arms and hear his ragged breathing.

"You're out of condition," he said.

"You would be too if you spent half your life climbing up and down this bloody mountain."

"I doubt whether all that extra exercise with the English girl does anything to help."

Cesar had seated himself on a rock while he mopped his brow but now he looked up sharply. The reaction pleased Raul. Although embarrassment would have been too much to hope for, Cesar was definitely startled.

"You know about that, do you?"

"Obviously."

"Do you mind?"

"Not so long as it's simply a diversion. If I had objected, I would have stopped it."

I bet you would, you bastard, Cesar thought to himself. And then it would all have been in the open.

"Here's something you will mind," he said. "Fernando didn't show."

"What do you mean?"

"Exactly what I said. Your friend Fernando didn't turn up at the rendezvous."

"You were at the right place?"

"Of course I was." Cesar sounded insulted. "And I was there in plenty of time."

"What happened to him, then?"

"How the hell would I know? I'm no clairvoyant and, short of strolling into police headquarters, there was no way I could find out. When I spoke to Pilar, she didn't have any idea what might have happened to him either."

"I see." Although he was doing his best to sound concerned, Raul felt nothing except satisfaction. Everything was going like clockwork. "Do you think the police have him?"

"It's a possibility but they can't have had him very long. Otherwise they would have been waiting for me at the rendezvous. I reckon he must have chickened out."

"That's not Fernando's style."

"Maybe not, but he was very upset about what you did to the maid."

"Not enough to make him change his mind." Raul sounded very confident. "Without his share of the ransom he'll never get to Brazil. What's the news about White Industries?"

"You might as well read it for yourself."

The newspaper was in Cesar's back pocket. Once Raul had unfolded it, the headlines leapt out at him. In fact, the entire front and back pages dealt with the story of how White Industries (Madura) were to be transferred to local ownership. Raul only skimmed through the report, but the editor was evidently all in favour of the transfer. He saw it as "a giant step towards Maduran self-sufficiency." Raul was pleased too. It hadn't been part of the plan for his demands to be met in full.

"It seems we have to show the authorities that we mean business."

"Why?" Cesar thought he knew the answer, but he was still curious. "White has gone much further than we could have expected."

"That just isn't good enough, Cesar. We'll be collecting the ransom in forty-eight hours. By then the authorities have to be trained to follow every instruction to the letter."

For a moment Cesar was about to argue. Then he changed his mind.

"You're the boss," he said, rising to his feet.

"That's right," Raul agreed. "I am."

He had known all along what he would have to do. It was something he looked forward to with pleasure.

Pilar Freitas was very nearly beautiful and, on the whole, Russell was glad she fell just short. The few truly beautiful women he had encountered had all seemed strangely sexless. Most of them had looked as though they should be hung on museum walls where they couldn't be touched. Besides, a beautiful face and body didn't necessarily indicate a personality to match.

So far there had been no opportunity for Russell to assess Pilar's personality, but there was no denying her looks. She had a good voice as well and, even in rehearsal, she was putting everything into the song. When she had finished, there was a hollow sound to his clapping in the emptiness of the large room. Pilar dropped him a little curtsey before she walked across to talk to the pianist. It was another couple of minutes before she came to join Russell. He couldn't help noticing how well she moved. Or how good her legs were. It made him wonder whether a dance routine was included in the act.

"I'm sorry to have kept you waiting, Senhor Russell."

She had a pleasant speaking voice too. So far it was full marks all the way.

"That's all right," he told her. "I was enjoying the performance. I may come back for the real thing tonight."

"Do that. You shouldn't have any trouble finding a table on a Monday. In fact, bring all your friends along as well. Paying customers are always welcome."

Her smile was even better than her voice.

"I wouldn't have thought there was any shortage of custom. From what I've heard, the Ipanema is the busiest night spot on the island."

"That isn't the owner's story," Pilar said with a laugh. "If you listened to Pablo, you'd think he was on the verge of bankruptcy."

"My heart bleeds for him. I assume it is his Jaguar I saw parked on the pavement outside."

"It is." Pilar laughed again. "He only uses it on weekdays, though. On Saturdays and Sundays he drives his Cadillac. Incidentally, Pablo didn't mention what it was you wanted to talk to me about."

"Perhaps I can explain over a drink somewhere."

"That's fine provided mine is a coffee. Too much alcohol doesn't do a thing for my voice."

The bar Pilar guided him to was only a few yards down the street, and as soon as they had been served, she repeated her query. As she told Russell, she was intrigued to know what had brought him all the way from England to interview her.

"It's not just you," he explained. "There are others as well. I'm a journalist. I work for a monthly magazine called *True Crime.*"

Suddenly Pilar was no longer smiling. A lot of her vivacity had died away as well.

"It's the Cavalcanti killing, isn't it?"

"I'm afraid so," Russell admitted. "My magazine is doing a major series on rape murders. The editor would like to include an article about Teresa Cavalcanti."

"I thought it was all over and done with." There was no mistaking the distaste in Pilar's voice. "Isn't it about time poor Teresa was left in peace?"

"We're not a sensational magazine," Russell pointed out. "It's a serious study we're doing. I think there's a lot to be learned from the Cavalcanti case."

"Well, all the facts are on file at the local newspaper. If you can read Portuguese as well as you can speak it, you shouldn't have any problems."

"The facts are easy to come by." For the first time Russell was being honest. "It's the background I'm after. After all, you were Teresa's best friend."

"And the man who was supposed to have murdered her was my fiancé." There was a bitter note in her voice now. "You don't have to be afraid to say it."

"There is that too."

"Do you know, there was a time three years ago when I would have walked out of here the moment I learned you were a journalist."

"But now you have it under control."

Russell was doing his best to be soothing. He still thought she was going to walk out on him.

"Not really. It's simply that you took me by surprise. Like I told you, I really thought it was all over and done with. I should have known better."

"Perhaps now is the right time for you to talk about it. You've had an opportunity to put it into perspective."

"No." Pilar's head had started shaking before Russell had finished speaking. "I don't think about what happened and I certainly don't want to discuss it. I'm sorry, but there it is."

"I'm not so sure you can keep it locked away forever." Russell was making another brief foray into honesty. "Facing up to what happened might do you good."

"And it might not. Poking at old wounds only reopens them."

"Bang goes my article then."

"I don't see why. You said there were other people you wanted to talk to. Some of them are probably less sensitive than I am."

"Unfortunately, none of them knew the principals in the case as well as you did."

"Raul did."

"You mean Raul Cavalcanti?"

"That's right. Teresa was his sister and Raimundo was one of his best friends."

"He was number two on the list of people I wanted to interview. I suppose I'll have to promote him. Do you happen to know where I can find him at this time of day?"

"I've no idea," Pilar told him."I haven't seen him to speak to for over two years. I can give you the address where he used to live, if that's any help."

"Thanks a lot. It should save me a little legwork."

It only took Pilar a few seconds to scribble the address on a napkin. Then she rose to her feet and held out her hand. For a woman, her grip was surprisingly firm.

"I really am sorry, Mr. Russell," she said.

"That's all right," he told her. "It was worth coming just for the song."

"If your writing matches your flattery, you must be a very good journalist. Are you really planning to catch the show tonight?"

"I thought I would, provided you don't mind."

"Of course not. I'll arrange for a ticket to be held for you at the door. Goodbye."

"Goodbye, Miss Freitas."

"Au revoir" would have been far more appropriate. Although the direct approach had been a total failure, Russell had never given in easily. There was always more than one way to skin a cat.

"You're letting me go."

"That's what I said."

Raul's smile remained warm and friendly. Even so, Rodney White found it difficult to believe him.

"But why? Has Dad paid the ransom?"

"Not yet. If he had, all three of you would be leaving together."

"You mean Mother and Janine aren't coming with me?"

"Not for the time being."

"In that case, I'm not leaving either."

No matter how firm he tried to sound, Rodney failed to put much conviction into the words. The true, cowardly Rodney wanted to leave at any price. Over the past few days he had discovered just how selfish he was. All the prayers he had offered to the deity he didn't really believe in had been for himself alone. When they had figured at all, Mum and Janine had come a very poor second and third.

"You're being too hasty," Raul said gently. "I want you to make the arrangements for payment of the ransom. The sooner you do that, the sooner your mother and girlfriend will be freed."

"I see."

Although Rodney didn't, the pill Raul was offering him was becoming more palatable by the moment. It offered not only safety but a way to salve his conscience.

"The instructions are in here." Raul tapped the envelope he was holding. "All you have to do is deliver it to police headquarters."

"But I don't know the way through the mountains."

"Of course you don't." Raul's voice was so soothing, it was almost mesmeric. "I'll guide you to the outskirts of Viana. Then I'll give you the instructions and enough money to pay for a taxi."

"It sounds easy enough."

"It is. There is one thing I ought to mention, though. As soon as we leave here, your mother and girlfriend will be moved to another location. Even if you do remember the way back here, the information won't be of any use to the police. We don't want to put temptation in your way, do we?"

Raul was smiling again, and Rodney responded a trifle uncertainly.

"How long will it be before the other are released?" he asked.

"It should all be over within forty-eight hours provided my instructions are followed to the letter. That's not too long to wait, is it?"

"I suppose not."

Self-delusion was a wonderful thing, Raul decided as he guided the Englishman out of the cottage. He was already looking forward to the moment when it would be replaced by disillusion.

TEN

There was no stage door at the Ipanema, so performers, staff and customers all used the main entrance. Except for Pilar, that is. Unless she was going to a party or back to a friend's house, she preferred to use the service entrance. The narrow alley it opened onto ran for some two hundred metres between the Inglesa and the Pátria, offering a useful shortcut back to her apartment. Although the alley itself was unlit, it had never occurred to Pilar to be at all nervous. Violent crime was virtually unheard of on Madura and, in any case, the lights along the Pátria were always in sight. On the odd occasion she had disturbed one of the local youths seeking privacy with a female tourist. Once or twice she had interrupted men urinating behind the trash cans outside the club. Otherwise the alley was hers after the last show had finished at two in the morning. It afforded her a minute or two to unwind after the performance.

Tonight, though, she had company. The young American had evidently just finished relieving himself, because he was zipping up his fly when she stepped out of the door. Pilar's initial reaction was one of amusement. His embarrassment as the light caught him was almost comical.

"I'm sorry, ma'am," he mumbled. "I wasn't expecting company."

"That's all right."

Pilar would have continued past him. Unfortunately, in stepping away from the wall, he had effectively blocked the passage between the rubbish bins. He smelled strongly of whisky.

"Hey, I know you, don't I?" He was leaning forward to examine her in the dim light and the smell of whisky was even stronger. "You're the lady singer from the Ipanema."

"That's right."

"I caught your act the other night. You were great."

"Thank you."

It wasn't a conversation Pilar particularly wanted to prolong. Amiable as the American seemed, she encountered more than enough drunks inside the Ipanema. Besides, she was tired. She made to go past him but where he was standing, there wasn't room without brushing against him.

"You go down there?"

Now there was a note of disbelief in his voice. He was indicating the stretch of alley ahead.

"Yes."

"That's not safe, ma'am, not for a good-looking lady like you."

"It's safe enough." Pilar was becoming irritated. "Madura isn't at all like America. Can you move out of the way, please? It's very late and I'm tired."

"Sure." The American squeezed back against one of the large trash cans to allow her through. "I'll just tag along behind to make sure you're all right."

"There's no need, thank you."

"It's no trouble. I'd hate for anything to happen to you."

It was only now, listening to the uneven footsteps behind her, that Pilar realized how drunk the man was. A couple of times he stumbled. Once he banged his leg against a can and swore out loud. Pilar was becoming increasingly annoyed. If it hadn't meant squeezing past him again, she would have turned back and taken the long way home along the Inglesa.

As soon as they were clear of the trash cans, there was room for the American to move up alongside her. The next time he stumbled, he caught hold of her arm for support. He didn't immediately relinquish it.

"Look," she said angrily, shaking him off. "Can't you leave me alone? I'm quite happy on my own."

"I'm only trying to help. I thought you might appreciate the company."

There was a new note of hurt belligerence in his voice. Pilar was too angry to heed the warning.

"For goodness' sake, just go away. After a performance, I don't want anybody's company."

She started to walk off. Pilar had only managed one step before he grabbed hold of her arm again, swinging her around to face him.

"Let go of me, you animal," she demanded furiously.

Then the world seemed to fall in on her. Although the American only used the flat of his hand, Pilar would have been knocked clear off her feet if he hadn't had hold of her.

"That's not a nice way to talk, Miss High-and-Mighty. Not nice at all." When he rubbed his free hand across his chin, Pilar could hear the rasp of his beard. "It gets me all upset."

As Pilar half hung from his grasp, the whole of one side of her face seemed to be on fire. Anger had given way to fear. The late-night revellers on the Inglesa were no more than fifty metres away. For all the help they were to her, they might as well have been on the moon.

"I'm sorry," she whispered, tasting the blood in her mouth. "I didn't mean to upset you."

"Sorry," the American said disgustedly. "Flighty bitches like you are all the same. You call me names like that and think 'sorry' puts everything all right."

He had started walking, roughly tugging her along with him. Still half dazed, Pilar's first thought was that they were continuing to the end of the alley. Then she realized he was angling towards the recessed doorway of one of the shops and she started to struggle. It was already too late. He had used his weight to bull her into the doorway, trapping her against the glass of a window. Pilar would still have fought, but his hand had gone up to circle her throat. The American was squeezing and squeezing and, through the pain, Pilar could feel herself slipping into unconsciousness. Her legs were buckling beneath her before he thankfully eased the pressure a little.

"Stop it," she mumbled. "Please stop it."

"It's too late for that, lady. First you get to apologize properly."

This is ridiculous, Pilar thought disjointedly. It can't really be this easy. She was a grown woman, yet the American was handling her like a small child. And she daren't even scream. With his hand around her throat, he could kill her before she made a sound. Even though there had been no threats, Pilar knew this was what she risked with any further resistance. There was a casual offhandedness to his violence which was totally chilling.

"Please," she whispered.

"See, I knew you could be nice if you wanted to." The American had been leaning his whole weight against her, but now he eased away slightly. "Back where I come from, women usually do their apologizing on their knees."

With his hand around her neck, forcing her down, Pilar didn't have any choice. As soon as she was kneeling, he shifted his grip, using both hands to hold her where he wanted. The tiles were cold through her stockings, the rough material of his trousers stifling against her face. Pilar had never felt quite so helpless in her life.

"Now, lady." She could hear the excitement in the American's voice and it sickened her. "Here's what . . ."

He never finished. The pressure on her neck was released so suddenly and unexpectedly that Pilar fell forward, banging her chin on the tiles. What was happening in the alley was no more than a blur of impressions. She was vaguely aware that two men were fighting. She knew one of them must have won when she heard the other running unevenly off but none of this seemed to have any real relevance. It didn't even matter who the victor was. Although the physical degradation had been limited, Pilar felt her humiliation was already complete. For a few minutes she had been a nonperson, completely helpless in another's power. She was sure this was an experience which would scar her for life.

"Are you all right?"

Although the grammar was perfect, the slight accent was unmistakable. Raising her head, she recognized the English journalist even through the blur of her tears. The hand on her shoulder was gentle and reassuring.

"No," she answered, her voice trembling.

"Do you need a doctor?"

"It's not that kind of hurt. Get me up from here, will you?"

Her legs weren't functioning properly and Russell virtually had to lift her to her feet. Even when she was upright, Pilar had to lean bodily against him. In contrast to the American, Russell's strength was a source of comfort.

"I can carry you if you'd like."

"There's no need. I think I can still walk."

"Where to?"

"Take me home. Please."

Their start had to be delayed until Pilar had her sobbing back under control.

There were occasions when Russell didn't like himself very much and this was one of them. It was no good trying to salve his conscience by telling himself he was simply doing what was necessary. The same went for any clichés about the good of the many. He knew that innocent bystanders should remain just that. They shouldn't be pressured or exploited or manipulated by people like him. The thing he liked least wasn't so much what he did but how bloody good he was at it.

"One black coffee," he said, putting the cup down on the table in front of Pilar. "Is there anything else you want?"

"No, thank you."

Although she seemed calm enough sitting there on the sofa, Russell knew this apparent composure was only skin deep. He had witnessed shock in enough of its various forms to know just how shaken and vulnerable she was underneath. It was something he was about to exploit.

"Are there any friends or family you'd like me to contact? Ask them to come over?"

"There's no need, thanks."

"What about me? Do you want me to go?"

"No." A hand shot out to grab hold of his wrist. "Please don't leave me just yet."

"O.K. But if I'm staying, I'd better take a look at that cheek of yours."

She was like some trusting little girl as she obediently turned her face up to the light. Once again, Russell was aware of just how attractive he found Pilar Freitas but this was a thought he pushed firmly to the back of his mind. Under different circumstances there might have been possibilities but the present situation precluded any involvement. There were definite limits to how far he was prepared to mess her around.

When he checked her cheekbone, he found some slight puffiness but the swelling seemed to have stopped. Although there would be some minor disfigurement for a day or two, it could probably be concealed with makeup. More or less the same went for her neck. There would be some bruising but nothing serious.

"How are your teeth?" Russell asked. "Are any of them loose?"

Pilar explored with her tongue before she shook her head.

"They seem to be all right."

"Fine." Russell moved away to sit in the armchair beside the sofa. "In that case, I'd say you'll probably live."

"Teresa didn't, did she?" The tremble was back in Pilar's voice. "There was nobody around to help her."

"No, there wasn't."

Pilar appeared to have made the connection by herself. There would be no need for him to do any prodding.

"It was horrible." Pilar shuddered at the memory. "I called him an animal and that's just how he behaved. Like a beast."

"Lust does strange things to people."

On this occasion there was no immediate response. Russell allowed the silence to develop, leaving Pilar to set her own pace. Now she had started talking, she was unlikely to stop.

"Raimundo could never behave like that." There was a defiant note in Pilar's voice as though she was challenging Russell to contradict her. "Not in a million years. He was so gentle and considerate. I never heard him raise his voice, let alone lose his temper."

"All the reports I've read say exactly the same."

There was no need to do more than insert the odd commonplace to keep the flow going.

"They didn't do him justice. Raimundo was a really sweet man." Pilar appeared to be completely unaware of the tears running down her cheeks. "Nothing could turn him into a beast like that man in the alley. Besides, he'd known Teresa for years. He liked her a lot but that was all. I'd have known if there was anything more. I didn't believe Raimundo could have killed her at the time and I still don't believe it now."

This was almost a plea.

"The only evidence against him was his own suicide note."

"That's another thing." Pilar seized on the point eagerly. "Raimundo was religious. I mean really religious, not just somebody who went to church. You know how Catholics feel about suicide, don't you?"

"It's a sin."

"Exactly."

She spoke as though her point was proven. Russell didn't necessarily disagree with her, although his judgement wasn't based on the same foundations.

"You mentioned that Raimundo had known Teresa for years. Did they ever go out together?"

"Oh no." Pilar seemed surprised at the idea. "Teresa sometimes came with the two of us to the cinema or on a picnic, things like that, but they never went out alone. In fact, Teresa didn't even have a proper boyfriend until she and Fernando started going together. That was just before she died. Until then she was always with her brother, Raul."

"Tell me about her," Russell suggested.

By now he had put conscience well behind him. It was much easier for Pilar to talk than to think about her own experiences of the night. All he had to do was make sure she kept headed in the right direction.

Although it was nearly five in the morning when he returned to the Méridien, a light was still shining from under Bewick's door. He answered Russell's knock in his pyjama trousers. This allowed him to display the livid bruising on the right side of his rib cage.

"I think you've cracked one of my ribs," he complained once Russell was inside the room.

"Let's have a look."

Russell wasn't nearly as gentle as he had been with Pilar. His exploratory prodding caused a couple of gasps of pain.

"You're exaggerating," he decided. "There's nothing broken. How did it happen?"

"I went into one of those rubbish bins when you threw me across the alley. Did you have to be quite so rough?"

"It had to be convincing. Besides, you looked as though you might be enjoying yourself too much."

"I was supposed to be convincing too."

"True." Russell conceded the point. "Let's just say it was punishment for your lousy American accent. Do you mind if I have a beer?"

"Help yourself," Bewick told him. "You usually do."

He had a can too, popping the lid before he spoke again.

"Were my injuries suffered in a good cause?" he enquired.

"Oh yes. Once Pilar started talking, there was no stopping her."

"I see you're on first-name terms already."

"It's the intimacy of the confessional. Besides, I'd just saved her from a fate worse than death."

"So what did she have to say?"

Russell's summary included a lot of reading between the lines. It had to because despite Pilar's deep-seated belief in her fiancé's innocence, she had never once pointed an accusing finger at the obvious suspect. Russell doubted whether the idea had ever occurred to her. In his own mind, though, it couldn't have been clearer. The picture Pilar had painted of the relationship between Teresa and Raul Cavalcanti didn't leave any room for doubt. Whether or not there had been any physical expression of their feelings for one another prior to Teresa's death was completely immaterial. The incestuous content was there for anybody with eyes to see.

According to Pilar the siblings had been virtually inseparable. They went everywhere together, they did everything together and they shared their own private jokes. Although both of them had their own friends, these had never been of central importance. As Pilar herself had said, she might have been Teresa's best girlfriend but she had always known she came a poor second to Raul. In fact, Teresa had seemed to worship the very ground her brother walked on. One proof of the strength of the bond between them was that until the very end Teresa had never had a boyfriend. This wasn't because she was at all unattractive. She simply hadn't seemed to need or want anybody else while Raul was around.

"That leaves us with the big question," Bewick commented. "If they were as close as you say, why would the brother rape and kill her?"

"Jealousy." Russell didn't hesitate at all. "In the last few weeks before she was killed, Teresa had finally found herself a boyfriend. She went out on several dates with him."

"You think that was enough to set Raul off?"

Bewick wasn't arguing. He merely wanted to get the facts straight in his own mind.

"Don't you? What picture did you form of Raul Cavalcanti from the people you talked to?"

"Intelligent, quirky, unpredictable, the leader of the pack." There had been remarkable unanimity about this. "He seemed to make a lot of people nervous. One or two hinted that he might be unbalanced."

"That's what I think too. However fond he might have been of his sister, Raul was always the dominant one in the relationship. Teresa always looked up to him. When she found herself a boyfriend, it must have been a blow to his self-esteem. I suspect he saw it as an act of betrayal and that's why he killed her. There may have been lots of other factors we know nothing about but that's the way I read it. Judging by their reports, the Maduran police were thinking along the same lines until they were presented with a full confession."

"O.K.," Bewick agreed. "I'm with you so far. There's one thing I don't understand, though. Why pick on the Freitas girl's fiancé for the fall guy?"

"We'll probably never know." Russell said this with a shrug. "I'd guess it was simply because he happened to be handy. It didn't really matter who Raul used so long as he took the heat off himself. He must have seen the way the police enquiry was going. Whatever else they might say about him, everybody is in agreement about his intelligence."

There was no need for Bewick to ask how the confession had probably been obtained. Like Russell, he had seen the photographs of the dead maid. Raimundo was supposed to have committed suicide by jumping off a cliff into the sea and it had been several days before his body had been recovered. By then the wave and the rocks would have obliterated any marks of torture.

"O.K.," Bewick repeated. "Let's pencil Raul Cavalcanti as a certainty. He appears to have the track record and nobody has seen him around since the kidnapping. Who else do we have?"

"Cesar Freitas—he's Pilar's brother. I'd classify him as a near-certainty. He's active in the smuggling racket and he knows Raul Cavalcanti."

He had also booked a one-way passage off Madura but this wasn't something Russell had divulged to Bewick. It was always useful to have an ace in the hole.

"Did you learn anything useful about him?"

"Not really. Cesar didn't have any direct connection with the Cavalcanti killing, so he didn't come into the conversation a lot. All the same, I have a definite feeling about him. He's just the sort of talent I'd want to recruit if I was Raul Cavalcanti."

"Let's play safe then and say one certainty and a probable."

"And I have a photograph of the probable." Russell tossed the snap-shot onto the table. "I picked it up before I left."

"How about the Freitas girl herself? Do you think she's involved in the kidnapping?"

"Most unlikely." This was a possibility Russell had considered and had rejected almost immediately. "Pilar is the moral member of the family. There's no way she'd get herself involved with kidnapping or murder. On the other hand, if I'm right about Cesar, he might well have been using her. He could have used Pilar for some of the legwork without her knowing what she was doing. I'll do my best to check that the next time I see her."

Russell felt no qualms at all about the information he was deliberately holding back. He and Bewick might be on the same team, but they were playing different games.

"At least we have two names we can fit into the frame," Bewick said. "Do we share the good news with Lopes?"

"No." Russell was very definite about this. "You heard what Dietrich said—he wants us to clear the whole business up ourselves. We're supposed to be several steps ahead of the police and we can't manage that if we pool all our information. Besides, there are three names to put in the frame, not two."

"Three?"

"That's what I said." Russell had finished his beer and he tossed the empty can into the wastepaper basket. "Do you remember my theory about a policeman being involved in the kidnapping?"

"Sure."

"Well, I think I may have found him. How would you feel if I told you that one of Raul Cavalcanti's best friends was a policeman?"

"I'd be very interested."

"You ought to be more than that. It seems this same policeman was the boyfriend Teresa Cavalcanti was going out with just before she was killed."

"O.K., O.K. I'm very, very interested. Why wasn't this included in any of the reports I read?"

"Your guess is as good as mine," Russell said with a shrug. "Anyway, let's assume I'm right for the moment. If you'd set up a kidnapping and you had a policeman on your team, where would you want him to be?"

"I'd have him inside police headquarters. Then he could feed me information about the progress of the investigation."

There was no hesitation at all. Bewick didn't even have to think about his answer.

"Exactly," Russell agreed. "You wouldn't waste him up in the mountains, looking after the hostages. You'd want him going about his normal duties and keeping both ears to the ground. Unless I'm jumping ιυ unwarranted conclusions, we now know precisely where we can find one of the kidnappers."

"And if he's going to be of any use, he has to maintain contact with the rest of the gang." Bewick was finishing Russell's thought processes for him. "Keep him under observation and he should lead us to the hostages. Does this policeman have a name?"

"Naturally. He's Fernando Carreiro."

"Oh shit." Disappointment hit Bewick like a physical blow. "I knew it was too good to be true."

"What do you mean?"

Russell seemed bewildered.

"Fernando Carreiro is an ex-policeman. He was shot dead outside the Hotel Afonso the night of the raid."

"I don't believe it."

Neither did Bewick. It was too much of a coincidence, especially when he already had one coincidence he was trying to swallow. He now knew that Russell had been on Madura at the time Teresa Cavalcanti was killed. Bewick had checked the dates himself.

ELEVEN

"Who is it?" the chief of police asked.

"We can't be sure, sir."

How the hell does Targa manage it? Lopes asked himself. A bloody stupid question for every occasion. The body was almost thirty feet below the point where they were standing, half hidden by bougainvillaea which grew on a trellis above one of the main storm drains. The trellis and flowers had been donated by a worthy citizen of Viana, thinking they would help to improve the appearance of the area. Although his object had undoubtedly been achieved, they weren't doing a thing to make Lopes's job any easier. When the corpse had been thrown over the parapet, it had landed on its stomach. With the head hanging down through the trellis, all Lopes could be sure of was that the victim was a male. And even this wasn't an absolute certainty.

"How are you going to retrieve the body?"

"With great difficulty. We're hoping to haul it up."

"I'll leave you to it, then. Report directly to me the moment you have a positive ID."

"All right, sir."

Although the superintendent was delighted to have Targa out of his hair, he still used a great deal of bad language in the next few hours. So did the officers who went down into the storm drain. The trellis had been designed to support climbing flowers, not fully grown men. While it had managed to withstand the impact of the body landing on it, this had weakened an already fragile structure. Even with safety lines attached, none of the policemen could get near the body.

The easiest means of recovery, of course, would have been to saw through the framework of the trellis and allow the corpse to drop into the drain below. Unfortunately, this was also the easiest way to destroy valuable forensic evidence. Nor would it have done very much to impress the large crowd which had assembled to watch the recovery operation. In the end, Lopes had to requisition a small mobile crane from the harbour and it was almost one o'clock before he was able to take a proper look at the victim. This merely confirmed what Lopes had suspected all morning.

By two o'clock Lopes was in Targa's office. Russell and Bewick were already present, summoned by a hasty phone call, and for the past quarter of an hour Targa had been doing his best to entertain them with what passed as small chat. He was unable to offer them more as the superintendent had yet to inform him of the victim's identity.

"Well?" Targa demanded as soon as Lopes was through the door. "Who is it?"

"I'd have thought it was obvious." Lopes's reply was curt and lacking in respect. "The kidnappers didn't think a change of ownership for White Industries was good enough."

The morning hadn't left Lopes in the best of moods. He also seemed to have been on his feet ever since he climbed out of bed and he dropped into the only available chair without waiting to be asked.

"What's that supposed to mean?"

Targa clearly felt his authority was under threat.

"The maniac who slaughtered the Whites' maid has used the same knife on one of the hostages."

"Which of them was it?" Bewick asked.

"The son, Rodney White."

"Was it a clean kill?"

Like Bewick's, Russell's interest was purely professional.

"Hardly." Lopes accompanied this with a snort of disgust. "If anything, the body was in a worse state than the maid's. I didn't have time to count the stab wounds but young White was definitely emasculated. Old Oliveira won't commit himself until he's done the autopsy but he thinks it may have happened while young White was alive."

"Oh my God." Targa looked as though he was having difficulty believing his ears. "Emasculated?"

"That's right, sir. An important part of Rodney White is still missing. I have a team looking for it in the storm drain."

The superintendent didn't bother to add that the chances of finding it

were remote. During the dry season, the drains were a favourite scaveng-
ing ground for the local dogs.

"Presumably there was a note with the body."

"There was." Lopes awarded Russell a nod of acknowledgement. "I
left the original with forensic but I brought a copy with me."

Like the other messages from the kidnappers, the note was brief and
to the point. It said: I HOPE THIS PROVES HOW SERIOUS I AM. I
SUGGEST YOU HAVE THE RANSOM MONEY READY BY MID-
DAY WEDNESDAY. Russell found the use of the first person particularly significant but this wasn't a thought he shared with the others.

"I didn't bother to copy the signature," Lopes told them. "It was the
same as before."

"What are we going to do?"

Targa's appeal was to the room in general.

"We have the ransom ready by midday tomorrow," Lopes answered.
"Otherwise we're going to find another mutilated hostage."

"And the next one will be Janine Haywood," Bewick added.

"But Senhor White was absolutely adamant." Targa was completely
out of his depth and it showed. "He won't pay the kidnappers a penny."

"Perhaps he'll change his mind now his son has been murdered,"
Lopes said. "If he doesn't, we'll have to dip into the national treasury."

"There's no need for that." Suddenly Russell had become the focus
of attention. "Her Majesty's Government will provide the necessary
cash."

"That's very generous. Very generous indeed."

Relief was making Targa babble.

"There is one proviso, though," Russell continued. "Delivery of the
ransom is to be made by either Bewick or myself."

Although there were several objections Lopes could have raised, he
was too much of a realist to mention them. For his part, the chief of
police was only too glad to grab at the proffered straw. Bewick was
simply amazed. However, he didn't say anything until he and Russell
had left police headquarters some three-quarters of an hour later.

"I wasn't aware that the government had authorized any funds for
the ransom," he said.

"They haven't."

"What?" Bewick had stopped dead on the pavement. "You mean you
were talking off the top of your head back there?"

"I was." Russell was amused by the reaction. "Look, Mike, we have
less than twenty-four hours before the deadline mentioned in the ransom
demand. We don't have a hope in hell of tracking down the kidnappers
before then, even if we do know their names. The only hope we have is
to assume full control. Explain the situation to Dietrich when we get
back to the hotel. He'll understand."

"Let's hope so." If Bewick sounded bitter, this was the way he felt. "If he doesn't, the PM is likely to be losing a stepdaughter."

Russell simply smiled enigmatically and started walking again. At that particular moment in time, Bewick would have liked to nail him to a wall in the Louvre, slap bang in front of the *Mona Lisa*. Then Russell would have had a chance to discover just how irritating that kind of smart-arse smirk could be.

When she opened the door to him, Pilar was wearing a short white terry-cloth bathrobe which barely reached her knees. It immediately made Russell wonder what she might or might not be wearing underneath.

"Hello, Alan." There was no denying the warmth of her welcoming smile. "I wasn't expecting to see you."

"I didn't have any choice. In some parts of the world they'd say I'd assumed responsibility for you by saving your life."

"Do you believe that?"

"No. I'm not even sure I saved your life but I did think I ought to come round to see how you were."

"Come inside and I'll tell you."

Today it was Pilar who made the coffee while Russell sat waiting in the living room. He had to admit she made a better job of it than he had done.

"So how are you?" Russell enquired after Pilar had finally finished fussing around.

"A bit shaky still but not too bad otherwise."

"Is that the truth or are you being incredibly brave?"

Pilar laughed and the robe opened a little across her chest. Russell resolutely kept his eyes on her face.

"Bravery doesn't run in my family," she said. "I really am feeling a lot better."

"You certainly look better than I expected. Your cheek hasn't swollen any more and the bruising hardly shows."

"No." When Pilar raised a hand to her cheek, the robe lost more ground across her bosom. "My throat is painful, though."

"I should imagine it is."

The marks left by Bewick's fingers were still faintly visible. Russell was glad he hadn't been gentle with him.

"Actually, I've had to telephone the Ipanema to say I won't be in for a couple of days. It's the first time I've ever let them down in the season."

"Did you explain why?"

"Oh no." Pilar shifted uncomfortably in her seat. Now the robe was parting at the bottom as well, revealing a smooth expanse of inner thigh. "That's my business."

"You're definitely not going to the police, then?"

Pilar grimaced.

"I don't think I could face it," she said. "All I want to do is forget what happened."

"Perhaps I can do something to help you stop brooding. What will you do tonight if you're not working?"

"I hadn't really thought about it. I suppose I'll sit around and watch television."

"Why not come out and have dinner with me."

Although Pilar didn't answer immediately, she didn't seem hostile to the suggestion.

"You'd be doing me a favour," Russell persisted. "I detest having to eat on my own."

"You're sure you're not just being gallant."

She used the French pronunciation.

"Gallantry doesn't run in my family."

"All right, then." Pilar was suddenly smiling again. Russell was rather surprised to discover how pleased this made him even though every move had been planned in advance. "I'd love to have dinner with you."

"Terrific." Russell rose to his feet. "What time suits you?"

"Eight-ish?"

"In that case I'll have a taxi at the door on the hour. You choose the restaurant and I'll pay the bill."

"That doesn't seem fair," Pilar objected. "You've already done enough for me."

"Nonsense, woman. Besides, you're forgetting that I'm here in Madura on an assignment. That means the meal will go on my expenses. I'll see you at eight."

After Russell had gone, Pilar spent a few moments in front of the mirror, readjusting the robe across her chest. She was also wondering what had prompted her to behave quite so shamelessly. It was a long time since she had last played the coquette.

Deborah White knew she couldn't afford any further delay. She had prevaricated far too long already, hoping against hope that she would have an opportunity to talk with Rodney. But it wasn't going to happen and it was no use deluding herself that the police would rescue them either. If they hadn't arrived by now, they weren't likely to come at all. Deborah had lived on Madura long enough to know exactly what the interior of the island was like. You could hide whole armies there, let alone three hostages.

No, if she and Rodney were to come out of this mess alive, Deborah knew she would have to do something herself. She had realized from the very start that Derek would never pay a ransom. Her husband might spend a large part of his life displaying all the morals of an alley cat, but he still prided himself on being a man of principle. Deborah herself had heard him expound often enough on the follies of submitting to blackmail or extortion. And one thing you could say about Derek, his actions invariably matched his words. Even in the early days, when they had been so madly in love with one another, he would never have paid a penny for her release.

It would have been nice to believe she could leave everything to Rodney, but, much as she loved him, Deborah had very few illusions about her son. For all the surface charm, there was no real backbone underneath. All his life Rodney had tended to shy away from any sort of challenge, preferring to take the line of least resistance. This was the main reason he and his father never got on well together.

If there was going to be an escape, she would have to arrange it and it would have to be done while Paolo was supervising her exercise period. Deborah thought she might just be able to manage him. With either of the others, there would be no chance at all. It was a promise she had made to herself. The next time Paolo was in charge, she would try to escape. And the next time was today. It was Paolo who had unlocked the door of the cellar. It was Paolo who had led her outside and neither of the other kidnappers were anywhere in sight. This was why Deborah's mouth was so dry. Although there were a thousand doubts assailing her, she tried to push them firmly to the back of her mind.

"Can we walk in the woods today?" she asked.

"All right." Paolo didn't seem to have any objections. "Just so long as you don't want to go near the river."

For a while Deborah walked aimlessly, acutely aware of Paolo's presence behind her. Although he no longer constantly carried the gun in his hand, she knew he would be armed. She also knew that she hadn't committed herself yet. It was the next step which would be irrevocable and Deborah wanted to postpone it for as long as possible. I'll count up to a hundred first, she told herself, but after the first century she counted another. Then another and another. She seemed to be wrapped in inertia.

"We'll have to be getting back soon," Paolo said suddenly.

"Already?"

Deborah had lost track of time.

"I'm afraid so."

"Oh." It was now or never. "Can I relieve myself first?"

"Sure. Pick yourself a tree."

Paolo was grinning at her.

"Would you mind turning your back please?"

"Not if it makes things easier for you."

The branch was about a metre long, thicker at one end than the other. Deborah picked it up by the thin end, surprised at the weight. As she stepped quietly towards the unsuspecting Paolo, she forced herself not to think about what she was doing. It was simply an unpleasant necessity.

She didn't hit Paolo hard enough the first time. Although he staggered, he was still on his feet as he started to turn towards her. Grunting out loud with the effort, Deborah hit him again, much harder, and Paolo sank slowly to his knees. There was an almost comical expression on his face as he put one hand to his head and then examined the blood on his fingers.

"What did you . . . ?" he began plaintively.

Deborah didn't allow him an opportunity to finish. This time she swung from side to side, catching Paolo on the side of the jaw and sending him sprawling. Even then he tried to struggle up until Deborah hit him a fourth and final time. The branch might have broken but at least Paolo was lying still, his eyes closed.

Breathing hard, Deborah tossed the broken stump of the branch away. It simply hadn't occurred to her that knocking somebody unconscious could be quite so difficult. She hoped the rest of her escape plan would be easier. With any luck she would have at least half an hour's start and that ought to be plenty, because all she had to do was follow the river down the mountain. Sooner or later it would either reach the coast or join up with one of the bigger river valleys where people lived.

After one last look at the unconscious Paolo, Deborah turned away. However, she only managed a single step before the hand grasped hold of her ankle. Taken completely by surprise, Deborah could only partially stifle her scream. Looking down, she could see that Paolo's eyes were open again and he was hanging on to her like a limpet. When she attempted to pull herself free, Deborah lost her balance and fell to the ground. There was a terrible intensity about Paolo's expression, his face a bloody mask as he used his hold on her ankle to pull himself across the pine needles towards her. Deborah screamed again and kicked him in the face. Apart from opening yet another cut, this had no effect at all. Inch by painful inch, Paolo was pulling himself closer and there was nothing she could do to escape. Deborah was sobbing out loud now and her fingers were scrabbling at the ground in a vain attempt to pull herself free. When her hand closed around the rock, she acted without thinking. Deborah simply turned and smashed it into his face, hitting him again and again until Paolo's fingers finally fell limply from her ankle.

The telephone began ringing while Bewick was still putting the key in the lock. By the time he had the door open and had rushed into the room, it had stopped. He swore nastily under his breath and began pulling off his damp clothes. Although the temperature in Viana was only in the high seventies, there was obviously a major thunderstorm brewing. The humidity was so high, it was like walking around inside a Turkish bath. Bewick was about to step under a cold shower when the telephone rang again. This was the occasion for a second burst of profanity before he padded back to answer it.

"Yes."

"My, my, dear boy. We do sound a trifle terse today."

Dietrich himself sounded as jovial as ever.

"It must be the weather," Bewick explained. "It's so humid here the air has to be chewed and swallowed."

"How you do suffer. If it's any consolation, it hasn't stopped raining in London since you left."

"That makes me feel a bit better," Bewick admitted. "Is there any news from Belfast?"

"That's why I rang you, dear boy. The message about Russell being in Madura was apparently passed on by one James Dennison."

"Dennison? That isn't a name that rings any bells."

"It wouldn't—he's a new one for our files. As far as I can gather, Dennison is some suburban accountant the Provos have retained to do their creative bookkeeping for them. He sets up dummy businesses for them to channel their funds into and the like. As far as we know, he has no links with the organization other than financial. That's almost certainly the reason he was selected as a conduit."

"How did the information reach him?"

"He received an anonymous phone call. We'll probably never know, but the information could have been second- or third-hand by then."

"So we're not much further forward."

"There is one significant point. Dennison phoned Belfast the same day we went to Southwold."

"I see." Bewick felt the first faint stirrings of elation. "How many people were in the know at that stage?"

"You, me and Russell."

"Nobody else?"

"Several others in the department had parts of the picture but we were the only ones aware of the complete setup. I didn't even report to the PM until the following day."

"I know I didn't contact the Provos. Did you, sir?"

"No, I didn't. And Alan wouldn't have had any reason to either."

"I'm not so sure."

It was out now and Bewick felt almost light-headed with relief.

"What exactly are you saying, dear boy?"

"Think about it, sir. The whole situation on Madura could have been tailor-made for one man and one man alone. There was nobody else you could possibly send to the island apart from Russell."

"That's true."

This was a point Dietrich conceded readily enough. It had worried him from the beginning.

"Then there's the kidnapping itself. It all seems to be connected with a killing about three years ago. Russell was on Madura at the time."

"So were thousands of other people."

"None of the others had any reason to set up the kidnapping."

"And Russell had?"

"He needs the money, sir. We both know that."

There was a brief silence while Dietrich considered the implications of what had just been said. Bewick was miserably aware of how thin it must sound. There simply wasn't any adequate means of expressing his suspicions in words.

"You do seem to be leaping to a lot of unwarranted conclusions, Michael."

"If you remember, sir, that's one of the things you pay me for. Besides, there's more. Superintendent Lopes is a good policeman. He's handled everything by the book and he hasn't got anywhere. Russell swans in and manages to find a suspect under every stone."

"I did tell you he was good, dear boy."

"Nobody is that good, sir. Anyway, there's another point to consider. Nothing Russell has come up with takes us any closer to Janine Haywood, however impressive it looks on paper. He finds the name of a policeman who's one of the kidnappers and the policeman is conveniently dead. He provides the names of two other kidnappers and there's no way we can possibly get to them in the time available. Everything is going to come down to what happens when the ransom is handed over. Russell has that arranged, so it's entirely in his hands."

"How does IRA involvement fit in with the scenario you've constructed?"

"It was a smoke screen." Bewick had it clear in his own mind. "Russell stage-managed it to divert suspicion from himself."

"That does sound rather Machiavellian, dear boy."

"You keep telling me how clever Russell is, sir."

"True."

Dietrich remained far from convinced, but he seldom dismissed any theory out of hand. Besides, he could appreciate how the complexities might appeal to Russell. As Bewick had pointed out, it did fit very neatly together, right down to the involvement of Janine Haywood. Russell's feelings about the PM weren't exactly a secret.

"What do you want me to do, sir?"

"What you seem to be doing already. Keep a careful eye on Russell. Try to find out what he knows that he isn't telling you. Meanwhile I'll do a little more poking around here in London. One word of warning, though. Whatever your suspicions, don't lose sight of our main priority."

"I won't, sir."

When Bewick hung up, he was no longer elated. He was absolutely jubilant. It would be a real pleasure to take Mr. High-and-Mighty Russell down a peg or two.

She was going to kill him. Cesar knew it and he didn't give a damn. Until now, he had always prided himself on having spread himself around a bit. If he didn't know it all, he had thought he knew most of it but compared with the English bitch he was an innocent. Being with her was some kind of exquisite torture. She did things which reached every nerve ending in his body and, on occasion, she had him sobbing out loud for release. He knew he would never meet anybody like Janine again. This was probably just as well for his future health.

"That's it," he said. "No more."

Of course she didn't pay any attention at all. Cesar's brain and body were both agreed that he had had enough but she simply wouldn't accept facts. All right, Cesar thought. Let her flog a dead horse if that's what she wants. But the horse wasn't quite dead yet. It was slowly reviving and Cesar groaned out loud, only partly from pleasure.

"Oh Christ," he moaned.

"Just lie still," Janine told him.

Cesar was too exhausted to do anything else. At least, that's what he thought until the sensations began to take over. It was too bloody wonderful for words.

"Not bad, Macho Man." Janine had levered herself up on one elbow so she could look down at him. "How about a cigarette?"

He had just about enough strength left to hunt out the packet and light one for each of them.

"Jesus Christ," he said. "Did you ever think of doing this for a living?"

"What do you think I'm doing now? I'm screwing for my life."

"And I thought it was for love."

"Like hell you did." She blew smoke into his face. "We both know what we're at. How am I doing so far?"

"You're still alive, aren't you?"

"And I'm still stuck up here in the mountains. When are you going to let me go?"

"Why would I want to lose the best piece I've ever had?"

"Because you can't stand the pace much longer."

"That's true."

"Well?"

"Well what?"

"When do you let me go?"

"As soon as the ransom is paid."

"And when is that?"

"Soon."

Although Janine pressed him, this was all Cesar would say. In any case, he was in a hurry to go now, before she started on him again. Once his cigarette was finished, he pulled on his clothes and unlocked the door.

"So you're walking out on me," Janine said from the bed.

"If I stayed any longer, it would be a crawl."

"But you'll be back when you've recovered."

"I'll be back," Cesar promised.

"That's good. There are one or two little tricks I've been saving up as a special treat."

The way she said this almost had Cesar going again and he left hurriedly. God alone knew what she could have left in her repertoire but Cesar knew he would return for a sample before he collected the ransom. Janine was as addictive as heroin.

Suddenly Cesar's mind was cleared of all erotic fantasy, as effectively as if somebody had thrown a bucket of icy water over him. The door of Deborah White's cellar was wide open, which meant Paolo hadn't yet brought her back from the exercise period. Cesar checked his watch. He had been with Janine for over an hour and Paolo had already left before then. For a moment Cesar toyed with the idea that Paolo might be giving her a quick one in the woods, then dismissed it. The White woman wasn't the type to take the lead and this was the only way Paolo was likely to get himself laid. No, there was definitely something wrong. The exercise periods never extended much beyond forty-five minutes.

As he expected, he found Raul in the cottage, busily writing in an exercise book. He closed it as soon as Cesar came in.

"I think we may have trouble," Cesar told him. "Paolo hasn't brought the White woman back yet."

"How long have they been gone?"

"Well over an hour. Do you want me to check?"

"No, I'll do it. By the looks of it, you've had enough exercise already. Do you know which direction they went in?"

"They were heading into the woods when I saw them."

"Fine. You look after things here."

Cesar was interested to note that Raul wasn't in too much of a hurry not to lock the exercise book away in the table drawer before he left.

After ten minutes' searching, there was still no sign of Paolo. The trouble was, Raul had no real idea of what might have happened. All he could do was assume the worst, that the White woman had somehow incapacitated Paolo and tried to escape. In this case, she would have tried for the river. Only an idiot would go higher into the mountains and following the track would have taken her right past the cottage. If he was right, there was no desperate rush. Raul had once experimented with the river route himself and he knew just how rough the going was.

It would take her two hours at the very least to reach the point where the river cut the track. Raul could be there in twenty minutes.

He was actually on the point of turning back when he heard the groan. Not that he was immediately certain it was a groan, or where the sound had come from. Then Paolo groaned again and Raul saw him some twenty metres away, half hidden among the ferns.

Even at that distance, Raul was aware of the blood. The sight fascinated him and he approached on tiptoe, unsure of whether Paolo was aware of his presence or not. By the time he was standing over the dying man, he was positive that Paolo was locked in his own private nightmare. There was nothing at all sentient about the noises he was making and he no longer possessed anything which was recognizable as a face. It amazed him to think that such a slight woman as Deborah White could have inflicted so much damage. It also excited him, and Raul could feel himself hardening inside his trousers. For a few seconds he simply watched Paolo twitching and moaning, still wondering whether any remnants of awareness remained.

"Paolo," he said, his voice almost a whisper. "Can you hear me?"

If he could, there was no indication. Raul prodded him with one foot and still there was no reaction. Paolo just twitched and bled a little more, twitched and bled.

Raul would have liked to stay longer and watch Paolo die, but there was suddenly a new urgency in his desire to find Mrs. White. He already knew how satisfying it was to kill. Now he had the opportunity to observe how the experience affected somebody else. It was an encounter which promised to be even more stimulating than what he was watching now. Before he set off down the mountain, Raul considered it almost a kindness to use the same rock to finish the work Deborah White had begun.

At first, Deborah had fled almost without thinking, her only ambition to be as far away from Paolo as possible. Sheer instinct led her towards the river and then turned her to follow its course downwards. She was totally oblivious to the sharp stones beneath her feet and the branches which were tearing at her face and body. In her mind she was replaying the terrible confrontation with Paolo again and again. And with every repeat, what she had done seemed more and more appalling.

It was the water chute which snapped her back to reality. She had been aware of the swelling volume of noise for some minutes. However, Deborah didn't appreciate the significance until she saw how the river dropped away in front of her in a swirling torrent. The noise made coherent thought difficult but one thing was obvious. She couldn't climb the sheer cliff to her left and crossing the river was out of the question. Unless she was prepared to retrace her footsteps, there was no way around the maelstrom which lay ahead. This was no choice at all because there was no power on earth which could force her to take even a single step back towards where she had left Paolo. Somehow or other, she would have to negotiate the falls.

To Deborah's surprise, the climb down proved to be much easier than she had anticipated. On the other hand, the ravine at the bottom turned out to be far worse than she had visualized. Far, far worse. It seemed to go on forever, twisting and turning back on itself. At times it was so narrow that only a tiny patch of sky was visible overhead. More than once Deborah was tempted to give up but she couldn't. Her course of action had been mapped out for her from the moment she had attacked Paolo. Besides, Rodney's safety depended on her.

Somehow she managed to force herself onwards. A shoe had been lost at the water chute and she daren't look to see what the rocks had done to her unprotected foot. Her nails were broken and bloody from scrabbling her way along the cliff and her entire body seemed to be one huge bruise. Life had boiled down to taking one more step. And then another and another. Deborah was concentrating so hard that when she finally reached the end of the ravine, it took her a few moments to realize that deliverance was at hand. Not only were there no more cliffs but a proper track ran beside the river. Sobbing out loud with relief, Deborah scrambled up the slope towards it.

Raul had been waiting almost half an hour before he saw her working her way along the gorge towards him. Concealed in the shadow of the rocks, he had another ten minutes to observe her before she finally stumbled onto the track. Her dishevelled hair and dirty, scratched face gave her a wild appearance which he found stimulating, but it was the blood on her dress which really excited him. He knew it wasn't her blood and this was why he had been waiting with such eager anticipation. There was a bond between them now, an unbreakable cord which had led her to him.

She was almost level with his hiding place before Raul stepped out of concealment. For a second he thought she was going to faint. Although Deborah didn't actually utter a sound, her mouth fell open and she staggered back as though she had been hit. Raul had to take hold of her shoulders to steady her.

"I've been waiting for you," he said softly.

Deborah felt totally numb. The whole world was disintegrating around her and she didn't care any longer. She had made her effort and it had failed. Now she didn't mind what happened so long as she didn't have to struggle anymore. When Raul pulled her to him, she didn't resist at all. Leaning against him was much easier than standing unaided and the erection pressing against her stomach was simply an irrelevance.

Raul misinterpreted her passivity as willing acceptance. In his mind, they were two of a kind and he kissed her hungrily, thrusting his tongue deep into her mouth while one hand traced the cleft between her buttocks.

"Come on," he whispered after a few moments. "We'll be more comfortable under the trees."

Half supported on his arm, Deborah allowed Raul to lead her into the shade of the trees. Surprisingly tender, he stripped her completely naked before he laid her down on the thick carpet of pine needles. She watched as Raul undressed himself, tearing his clothes off in a fever of anticipation. She felt nothing. Apart from a momentary flicker of surprise to see he was so much bigger than Derek, there was no impact at all. The old Deborah White had passed quietly away at some time during the past few hours. This was all happening to a stranger.

Foreplay was virtually nonexistent. Raul kneaded her breasts for a few seconds, then his hand was down between her legs, fingers exploring her innermost recesses.

"Are you ready?"

Answering would have been too much of an effort. In any case, Deborah's silence was taken for assent. Her thighs were parted, Raul was kneeling over her and still she felt absolutely nothing.

"Hold me," Raul instructed huskily.

Deborah obediently did as she was told, wrapping her arms around Raul as he kissed her again. This time she was aware of the garlic on his breath. She found this vaguely displeasing.

"There's something I have to tell you," Raul was whispering, his lips only a few inches from hers. "Paolo is dead."

"What?"

For the first time Raul had really reached her.

"It's true, darling. Paolo is dead. You killed him."

As he spoke, Raul stabbed deeply into her. Deborah's moan could have meant almost anything. She wasn't sure herself.

TWELVE

In private practice Dr. Oliveira headed a brand-new health centre in the middle of Viana and also acted as a consultant at the general hospital. When he was wearing his public hat at police headquarters, he operated from a dingy little office which was packed with filing cabinets and leftover furniture. Although the fees he was paid by the police were derisory, the doctor didn't mind too much. He was wealthy enough for the money not to be important. In any case, it helped to salve what few qualms of conscience he had about the omissions on his tax returns.

When Lopes rushed in with the postmortem report in his hand, Oliveira was sitting at the battered desk doing nothing in particular.

"You're late," he said, checking his watch. "You must read more slowly than I thought."

"I wasn't in my office when the report was sent up," Lopes explained. "Otherwise I'd have been here sooner. You're sure about this, are you?"

"Do you doubt my professional competence?"

"Why not? I don't see why I should be the odd one out. Everybody knows you can't see, your hands shake and you've been senile for years."

"Thanks for the character reference."

Oliveira was smiling. He was almost seventy and looked much older. More important, he and Lopes had been friends for years.

"Don't mention it. Are you really saying the White boy was sodomized?"

"I obviously underestimated you. I was worried you might not manage a long word like that."

"You're sure about that?" Lopes persisted.

"Unless the victim was a highly trained contortionist, there's no doubt at all."

"Jesus Christ." The superintendent had sunk down into the only other chair in the office. "What kind of a man are we dealing with?"

"Do you want me to baffle you with science or would you prefer terms a child could understand?"

"Why break the habits of a lifetime? Talk to me as though I'm an idiot."

"In that case, I'd say you're dealing with a madman."

"Even I could work that out."

"What more do you want?"

"Can't you give me a psychological profile of the killer?"

"No—it's not my line of country. All I can say is that he appears to be a very sick man. I'd say he's a death freak."

"You mean killing turns him on?"

"All the evidence points in that direction."

"So how do you rate the chances of the remaining hostages?"

"Slim to nonexistent. The man obviously enjoys killing. As I said, he seems to equate it with sexual gratification. I think he's likely to kill the hostages whether the ransom is paid or not. In fact, I'd hazard a guess and say that killing is far more important to him than money or any of the other demands."

"That's what I was beginning to think too."

Lopes sounded gloomy. Everything seemed to be careering out of his control.

"There's another point as well."

"Go on," Lopes said. "Cheer me up some more."

"Well, I wouldn't rate the other kidnappers' chances of survival much higher than those of the hostages. Your killer has the taste for blood now. He's likely to continue killing until somebody stops him."

"And that's your considered professional opinion?"

"On the contrary, it's totally unprofessional guesswork. That doesn't necessarily make it any less valid."

This wasn't a viewpoint Lopes cared to dispute and he left the doctor's office a deeply troubled man. There were very few cards left for him to play.

Russell had expected Pilar to choose one of the glossy establishments in the centre of Viana. Instead, she had directed the taxi driver to a much smaller restaurant on the very outskirts of the capital. As far as Russell could tell, he was the only non-Maduran in the place. However, Pilar had assured him that the food was superb and he had no reason to doubt her. Besides, the meal was merely a secondary concern. The restaurant provided a nice, relaxed ambience for him to mess up her life some more.

"You really do speak Portuguese very well," Pilar said once the waiter had left with their order.

"Does that mean I could pass as an islander?"

"No, your blue eyes would always give you away."

"In that case, I'll have to wear dark glasses."

Pilar laughed.

"Why do you want people to think you're Maduran?"

"I thought that might stop them charging me double everywhere I go."

"You shouldn't complain—most of the tourists are charged at least treble price. Every Maduran knows that all you English are filthy rich."

"This one isn't. Besides, I'm not a tourist. I'm a working man."

"On expenses," Pilar pointed out. "Mind you, I still have difficulty seeing you as a journalist."

"It isn't a very good act, is it?"

He held her gaze while Pilar absorbed the implications of what he had said. As he watched, he could see the defences going up. Until now she had been relaxed and friendly, like a young girl on a date, but that mood was gone now, quite possibly forever.

"What do you mean?" Pilar asked after a moment.

"I've been lying to you." There was no point in mincing words. "I've never worked for a newspaper or magazine in my life."

"Why?" she demanded. "Why lie to me?"

"Because lying to people is a big part of my job."

"Oh." The hurt and sense of betrayal was there in Pilar's eyes. "What do you do, then?"

"We'll talk about it later. Let's eat first."

It was a gamble. Russell knew this, but he had run out of time. If

Pilar had anything left to tell, he had to extract the information tonight and at least he had negotiated the first hurdle safely. She hadn't walked out on him yet.

On a success rating of nought to ten, the meal wouldn't have registered. Pilar pecked at her food, avoided his eyes and responded to his attempts at conversation in monosyllables. This was no more than Russell had expected, and he persevered. Once the last of the plates had been cleared away and their coffees were in front of them, the issue couldn't be ducked any longer. It was time for him to explain and he had to make it bloody good.

"I hated having to lie to you," he told her. "Unfortunately, I didn't have any choice."

Pilar didn't reply. She clearly didn't have any intention of making the confession any easier for him and this suited Russell down to the ground. If he was allowed control of the conversation, he could skirt around potential danger areas.

"I'm probably putting my job at risk right now," he continued.

"Why bother?" Pilar sounded bitter. "You already know how gullible I am. I believed everything you said about being a journalist."

"It's not just you," Russell assured her. "Everybody I've met on Madura thinks I work for a magazine."

"So you're a consistent liar." Pilar said this with a shrug. "Why am I suddenly worth special treatment?"

"I need your help and I need it fast. I think you're more likely to give it to me if you know the truth than if I continue with the deception."

"And that's the only reason for your change of heart?"

"No," Russell admitted. "There are personal motives as well but they're irrelevant for the moment."

This was a statement Russell made no attempt to amplify. He preferred to leave Pilar to read what she wanted into it. Although her defences were still firmly in place, her hostility was now tempered with curiosity.

"All right," she said. "So far we've established that you're not a journalist. What are you apart from a liar?"

"I'm a kind of policeman. That's not a precise description but it's near enough."

"Wrong. Going by your previous track record that could mean you're really a greengrocer or a brain surgeon."

The attempt at humour was definitely an encouraging sign and Russell's smile was genuine. He was making progress.

"O.K.," he conceded. "I'm attached to a special antiterrorist squad. Although it's an independent department, it works closely with official police forces. And before you start asking any more questions, I'll explain as much as I can later. For the moment I want to tell you why I contacted you in the first place."

"That should be interesting."

Despite the sarcasm, Russell knew Pilar was hooked. Once he had played his ace, the game would be won.

"It all relates to the Teresa Cavalcanti killing," he explained. "You never believed that your fiancé was the murderer, did you?"

"You know I didn't. I still don't, come to that."

"Nor do I. I'm pretty sure Raimundo was innocent."

"You are?"

He was mixing Pilar's emotions into a cocktail and it showed. She no longer knew quite what was happening.

"Teresa was raped and killed by her brother."

Russell made this a statement.

"You mean Raul?"

"He's the only brother I've heard of."

"But that's crazy."

"So is Raul. If I'm right, it wasn't simply a matter of raping and killing his own sister. He must have set your fiancé up as the scapegoat."

"How would he do that?"

"By forcing Raimundo to write out a confession and then killing him."

"I don't believe it."

Although Pilar was shaking her head, she was hanging on to every word.

"You will," Russell told her, "but this isn't the place to talk. Can we go back to your apartment?"

There was never any doubt about Pilar's answer.

Patience was one of Russell's greatest virtues. Although the actual Cavalcanti killing was no more than a starting point for him, he knew it was very real to Pilar. This was why he spent almost an hour explaining his reasoning and he answered all Pilar's questions without a hint of irritation. It was something he owed her. Besides, he was reestablishing trust and this was vital. By the time he had finished, Pilar was as convinced of Raul's guilt as he was himself.

"Do the local police know all this?" she asked.

"No. Even if they did, I doubt whether there is much they could do about it without a signed confession from Raul. There's very little hard evidence to back up what I've just told you."

"You mean Raul will get away with it?"

Fury battled with incredulity in her voice.

"I didn't say that. He certainly won't ever be convicted in a court of law. On the other hand, if you can provide me with the help I need, I'm probably going to kill Raul tomorrow."

As conversation stoppers went, this was a beauty. For several seconds, Pilar simply stared at him and it was impossible to tell what she was thinking. Russell had to hope he had judged her correctly.

"You really mean that, don't you?"

There was a note of wonder in Pilar's voice.

"Death isn't something you joke about."

"And you've killed people before?"

"A few. Does that worry you?"

"It should but I don't think it does. I want Raul dead. Part of me would like to be there to watch."

She spoke with a ferocity which suggested sincerity.

"How about me? How do you feel now you know what I am?"

"I'm not sure." Once again Russell suspected she was being sincere. "It's difficult to imagine you killing anybody."

"It's part and parcel of the job."

He could have said more but he managed to stop himself. He wasn't there to justify himself. He wasn't entirely sure this was possible.

"There's one thing I don't understand." Pilar spoke slowly, still trying to come to terms with what she had learned. "Why do you want Raul? I know why I hate him but you can't be in Madura because of Teresa's death."

"I'm not. Before I say any more, though, I need your word that what I tell you won't go any further. By rights I should make you sign the Official Secrets Act."

"That sounds heavy."

"It is. Do I have your word?"

"Of course you do."

"You won't repeat what I say to anybody?"

"I promise."

So Russell told her, just as he had intended to from the beginning. At least, he told Pilar most of it, about the kidnappings and the killings and the ransom demands. All he omitted were some of the most important parts.

"You're saying Raul did all this?" Pilar asked incredulously once he had finished.

Each new revelation was becoming more difficult for her to absorb.

"With help," Russell told her, "but Raul was the one in charge."

"Do you know who any of the others are?"

"Fernando Carreiro was one."

"But he was a policeman."

"So what?" Russell said this with a shrug. "Putting on a uniform doesn't make people any less human. Where large amounts of money are involved, almost everybody has their price."

"Do you?"

Pilar sounded genuinely curious. She was also striking very close to home.

"Probably."

"I don't believe you could ever do terrible things like Raul."

"I'd love to agree with you. Unfortunately, nobody knows what they're capable of until they're actually faced by temptation. Anyway, my weaknesses are immaterial. The important thing is that sometime tomorrow Raul will expect the ransom to be paid. Once it has been, he'll kill the remaining hostages."

"Are you sure?"

Once again Pilar was shocked.

"I'd put money on it. My only hope of saving them is to get to Raul before the ransom is handed over. That's where I'm hoping you can help."

"How?" Pilar was more bewildered than ever. "I haven't had any contact with Raul for years. Even when Teresa and I were friends, I didn't know him very well."

"But you did know Teresa very well."

"How does that help?"

"The hostages are being held somewhere in the mountains. Yesterday you told me that Teresa and Raul had their secret places in the interior, places they used to visit together. The chances are that Raul is holed up in one of them."

"I don't have any idea where they are." This was almost a wail. "They really were secret places. Teresa and Raul never allowed anybody else to go with them."

"Teresa didn't give you any clues as to where they went?"

"Not that I can remember."

"Nothing at all?"

"Not really. Once or twice she did mention an old cottage but it could be anywhere."

It was beginning to look like a wasted evening. Although Russell was disappointed, he wasn't unduly so. When you went for long shots, you had to accept the fact that you lost more often than you won.

"There isn't anything else that comes to mind?" he persisted.

"I'm afraid not." The regret was there in Pilar's voice. "Teresa and Raul were Cavalcantis, of course, but I don't see how that helps."

"What do you mean?"

"The Cavalcantis are a famous family on the island," Pilar explained. "They used to control most of the smuggling."

"I don't see how that can link up with a cottage in the interior. All the smuggled goods would have been brought in by boat."

"I suppose so." Pilar wasn't really sure. "Mind you, the Cavalcantis did have a big fight with another smuggling family in the 1930s or 1940s. We were taught about it at school. I seem to remember the Cavalcantis were driven right out of Viana for a while. They had to land their contraband on the east coast and bring it across the island on foot. I don't know any of the details, though."

"Who would know, then?"

Russell's interest had started to revive.

"It was old Senhor Rodrigues who told me. He used to teach history at school."

"Where can I find him?"

"I'm not sure. I haven't seen him for years. For all I know he's dead."

"If he isn't, he might be in the telephone directory."

"I can look and see."

It only took Pilar a few moments with the local directory to come up with the number. Although it was getting late, Russell didn't have any qualms about phoning Rodrigues straightaway. There was too much at stake for him to worry unduly about disturbing an old man's beauty sleep. In any case, the ex-teacher hadn't yet retired to bed. He was a trifle querulous at first, but his attitude changed once he learned what Russell wanted to talk about. Smuggling was evidently one of his pet hobbyhorses and he was quite happy to stay up a bit longer if Russell wanted to come over. Russell most certainly did and he was already on his way to the door when Pilar stopped him.

"I will be seeing you again, won't I?" she asked. "You will let me know what happens tomorrow?"

"Of course I will."

"Promise?"

"I promise."

Although Russell was almost certain that he was lying, this was the easy way out. He wanted to leave before it occurred to Pilar to ask him the names of any of Raul's other associates. It would be difficult to explain that he might have to kill her brother as well.

THIRTEEN

When Pilar first heard the knock at the door, she thought Russell must have returned and it was a shock to find Cesar standing outside, the familiar half-mocking smile on his face. Not that the manner of his arrival should have come as any surprise. For as long as Pilar could remember, her brother had drifted in and out of her life without prior warning and without any apparent sense of responsibility. On occasions she didn't see him for weeks on end. On others he would descend on her and take up residence in the flat as though it was his by right.

"This is a new venture for you, isn't it?" Cesar said, stepping over the threshold.

"What do you mean?"

"Picking up tourists and bringing them back to the flat. I was beginning to think your friend might stay the night."

"It wasn't like that." Although Pilar knew Cesar was joking, she couldn't stop herself from rising to the bait. There was an ambiguity about her feelings for the Englishman which made her sensitive. "He's an English journalist."

"Don't tell me you've suddenly become an international star."

Now Cesar was openly laughing at her. He had never taken her singing very seriously.

"Not yet. His magazine wants him to do an article on Teresa Cavalcanti."

"I thought that was all ancient history."

"So did I, but apparently I was wrong. Anyway, what brings you here?"

It was much simpler for Pilar to change the subject than to retail any more second-hand lies.

"I'm looking for a bed for the night."

"That is a surprise. You'd better take the spare room as usual—the bed is made up. Do you want something to eat?"

"I've eaten already, thanks, but I could manage a beer."

"I'll see if there's one left in the fridge."

When Pilar returned with the frosted bottle of Sagres, Cesar was by the window, peering out through the curtains. As he turned to take the beer from her, his face was unusually solemn.

"There's something I have to tell you, sis," he said. "After tomorrow you won't be seeing me for a while."

"That's nothing new."

"I'm not talking days or weeks, Pilar. Or even months, come to that. I'm leaving Madura for good."

"But why? Where are you going?"

"Portugal probably."

"What are you going to do there?" Pilar had already suffered her quota of surprises for the night and the new one had knocked her completely off balance. "Do you have a job to go to, Cesar?"

"You know work is a dirty word as far as I'm concerned. Besides, I don't need a job."

He was smiling at her, enjoying the effect of his news.

"Stop talking in riddles, Cesar. What on earth do you mean?"

"I mean that by this time tomorrow your brother will be a wealthy man. One of my little business ventures is going to pay off better than I expected. Much, much better."

It was as though a veil had been peeled away from Pilar's eyes.

Suddenly lots of little pieces had clicked into place and she knew exactly what Cesar was talking about. The shock must have registered on her face.

"Are you all right?" Cesar enquired anxiously. "I suppose it's very flattering but I didn't expect you to take the news this hard."

"I'm fine, thanks." This was an outright lie. Pilar felt physically ill and she had to sit down on the sofa before her legs gave way. "Does this business you mentioned have anything to do with Raul Cavalcanti?"

"It might have."

Cesar was watching her intently now, his eyes narrowed. For a moment it seemed as though it was no longer her brother standing there. It was a stranger, a menacing stranger, but Pilar didn't allow this to deter her.

"Tell me, Cesar," she insisted. "Yes or no."

"Yes, if you must know." Cesar was thinking furiously, wondering how much she knew or had guessed. "Raul has been working on this scheme with me, as it happens."

"Oh Christ."

She buried her face in her hands, feeling the wetness of the tears. Her entire world was collapsing in ruins around her and Pilar simply didn't know how to cope. She felt Cesar's weight settle on the sofa beside her and one of his hands rested lightly on her shoulder. There had been times in the past when this had been a comfort but not any longer.

"What do you know, Pilar?"

Although Cesar's voice was soft, there was no mistaking the tension. Or the underlying threat.

"Enough," she answered, lifting her face from her hands. "Please don't do it, Cesar. Please."

"Don't do what? I don't have the slightest idea what you're talking about, sis."

"Don't lie to me, Cesar." The sudden ferocity in his sister's voice made Cesar draw back slightly. "You have to get out of this while you can. Stay here with me tomorrow."

There was a brief, uncomfortable silence. For the moment, Cesar was as much in shock as his sister, unsure what he ought to do. The only thing he was certain of was that he had to discover just how much Pilar knew. Equally important, he needed to learn how she had come to know.

"It was the foreigner," Cesar decided at last, speaking his thoughts out loud. "He's been telling you things."

Although Pilar didn't respond, her silence was confirmation enough.

"So he's not a journalist after all," Cesar continued. "What is he? Some kind of policeman?"

Pilar still wasn't answering. He could read the contempt in her eyes as she stared at him and a cold anger began to replace his fear. Even so, he forced himself to be patient.

"Come on, sis," he cajoled. "It's me, Cesar. You've got to help me."

"Why?" The contempt was in her voice as well. "I don't owe anything to a kidnapper and a murderer."

"I've never murdered anybody."

"Raul has and you say you're helping him. That makes you as bad as he is."

It was getting worse by the moment and Cesar's head had started to ache. He made one final attempt to reestablish the old intimacy with his sister. As denial hadn't worked, he tried throwing himself on her mercy.

"O.K., O.K.," he conceded. "I've got myself into something which has gone way over my head. I admit it. Now everything has got out of hand and there's nothing I can do to put things right. Believe me, I didn't want it to finish like this."

"Nobody has ever made you do anything you didn't want to do."

Pilar's tone was icy.

"Maybe not." Like Russell before him, Cesar had decided that a degree of honesty was the only way to handle Pilar. "The kidnapping I went along with—I saw it as my big chance. If things went well, I'd be set up for life. The way it was planned, though, nobody was going to be hurt."

"That's rich." Pilar's laugh was devoid of all humour. "People have died because of you."

"Believe me, Pilar, it was none of my doing. It was that crazy bastard Raul. By the time I discovered what he was doing, it was too late to back out. Even though I didn't know about them, I'd have been an accessory to the killings."

Although Cesar paused, there was no sign of Pilar relenting at all. Not that this really surprised him. All he had left to work on was her sense of family.

"Listen, sis," he went on. "I know I've done terrible things, things which can't ever be forgiven, but I'm still your brother. You have to help me. Otherwise I'm going to spend the rest of my life in prison."

"Exactly what do you expect me to do?"

She sounded as inflexible as ever.

"I need to know what the Englishman told you."

"I'll repeat what I said before." Pilar was in no mood to give an inch. "Stay here with me tomorrow. After that you can get out and I never want to see you again."

"You don't mean that."

"Oh yes I do. Now I know what you are, the very sight of you makes me sick."

There was no doubt of her sincerity, so Cesar adopted the only other course open to him. Still sitting, he punched Pilar on the side of the jaw, t, chopping right which knocked her sprawling from the sofa. As she struggled to her hands and knees, he punched her again, harder this time, and she lay still. Cesar would have liked to leave things there but he couldn't. His very life might depend on Pilar telling him everything she knew. Taking hold of his sister's arms, he started to drag her into the bedroom.

Although Lopes hung on for as long as possible, his bladder inevitably won out in the end. He supposed this was yet another sign of advancing age. Until recently, nothing had ever disturbed him in the night apart from the occasional phone call from headquarters.

Wide awake now, Lopes went through into the bathroom and urinated noisily, admiring the stream as it splashed into the pan. Old man or not, he still maintained a pretty fair head of pressure. It was so long since he last used it for anything except pissing, it was a wonder the damn thing hadn't started to atrophy.

When he had finished, Lopes checked his watch. It was almost half past five, which meant going back to bed was a waste of time. Once he was awake, he was awake and that was that. Still in his bare feet, he padded downstairs to the kitchen to plug in the coffee percolator. Although there was only one bread roll left in the bin which was fit to eat, there was plenty of butter and cheese. This suited him fine. In Lopes's book, carbohydrates' sole function were as an easy means of transferring chloresterol to his mouth. It was one of the many characteristics which his wife had deplored. He sometimes thought her disapproval had been the main foundation of a very happy relationship. Lopes still missed Alfreda and couldn't visualize a time when this would change.

Once he had eaten and poured himself a second cup of coffee, Lopes pulled a notepad and pencil towards him. It was going to be the big day and he wanted to be sure his thoughts were in order. There wouldn't be any chance to redeem mistakes he made now. At the top of the page he wrote RAUL CAVALCANTI. After he had written the name, Lopes bordered it with a series of little daggers which he considered rather artistic, especially with the blood dripping from the points. They were also uncomfortably close to the truth. He had seriously underestimated the Cavalcanti boy and sometime during the day the remaining hostages would pay the price. As sure as eggs were eggs, there was going to be another bloodbath and he could do nothing to prevent it.

The second name Lopes wrote down was JAMES ANDERSON. The American merited a border of dollar signs. Anderson was his banker, the one fixed point in the whole sorry mess. The last name, written in much larger letters, was ALAN RUSSELL. He surrounded this with question marks. Lopes liked Russell a lot, had done from the first moment they had met. He respected him too, and this was why he wished the Englishman hadn't been sent to Madura. Russell was the unknown quantity in the equation, the one element which could make all Lopes's careful planning superfluous. He was well aware that Russell was playing an intricate game of his own. Lopes would have felt a lot easier in his own mind if he had been privy to how much Russell knew. And, far more significant, exactly what he intended to do with this knowledge.

Bewick had never been a morning person. It definitely wasn't the time of day when he was at his best. Seeing a spruce, wide-awake Russell standing outside his door did nothing to make him feel any better.

"I've ordered breakfast for two in your room," Russell announced as he pushed past.

"That should start the hotel staff talking."

"Let them. If you're up to it, we have a lot to sort out."

"Give me a chance to shower and shave and I'll be fit for anything."

Although this was something of an exaggeration, his morning ablutions did make Bewick feel considerably better. Dressed, and with the stubble gone from his chin, he felt he could face Russell on something approaching equal terms. It helped to discover breakfast had arrived while he was busy in the bathroom and Russell had already poured him a coffee.

"O.K.," he said, taking the other seat at the table. "What's on the agenda?"

"First of all, I want you to handle the ransom delivery."

"If it is today. Cavalcanti and company seem to be behaving as though they have all the time in the world."

"They're also keeping their promises. It will be today all right, probably this evening."

Russell spoke with absolute assurance.

"Presumably you'll be running interference for me when I hand over the money."

"No. We play it straight."

"What the hell do you mean?" Suddenly Bewick was fully alert. "Are you suggesting we simply hand over a million dollars?"

"You've got it in one."

"But that's crazy."

"We don't have any choice." Russell spoke in the authoritative tone which annoyed Bewick so much. "The kidnappers know the island. They've had plenty of time to work out the details of the transfer. Unless they're absolute idiots, which they most certainly aren't, they'll have made sure it's foolproof."

"They could still make mistakes." Bewick wasn't prepared to concede the point. "After all, they're only amateurs."

"It's a possibility, I suppose." Said in a dismissive tone. "And if the kidnappers do make a mess of the exchange, you'll be there on the spot. What we don't want is for you to clutch at straws which aren't there."

"O.K." Bewick was finding it difficult to contain his annoyance. "We hand over the money. What do we do then? Pack up and go home? I don't think that would make Dietrich very happy."

"Not to mention the PM and the Treasury." Russell was smiling now. "Come to that, it wouldn't do a great deal for my self-esteem."

"So what do we do?"

"I would have thought that was obvious." This wasn't the kind of remark which was likely to smooth ruffled feathers. "The kidnappers will be at their most vulnerable once the ransom has been paid. That's when they have to come down out of the mountains and try to leave the island. As none of them know that they've been identified, they'll think they're home and dry."

"How about the remaining hostages?"

"What about them? You know what Dietrich wants. The fewer loose ends, the better."

This was undeniably true but Bewick still had plenty of reservations about the proposed strategy. He had even more about Russell himself.

"Exactly what will you be doing while I'm handing over the money and not clutching at straws?"

"There's something I want to follow up."

Russell appeared to be absorbed in buttering a piece of toast.

"Care to tell me about it?"

"There's not a great deal to tell at the moment. Let's just say I may find where the hostages are being held if I'm lucky."

"I see." It was becoming increasingly difficult for Bewick to hold himself in check. "You've obviously been consulting your Ouija board again."

"It was something Pilar told me." Russell appeared to be oblivious to the sarcasm. "It may be nothing."

"How will you keep in touch?"

"By radio, but communication is likely to be patchy. I'll be up in the mountains."

"When do you expect to be back?"

"There again, I can't be sure. It may not be until after you've delivered the ransom."

"That's not good enough," Bewick said.

"What do you mean?"

Russell sat with the remains of his toast poised halfway to his mouth.

"I mean it's high time you remembered we're supposed to be working as a team. That involves pooling information. You don't go anywhere today unless I know exactly where you are and exactly what you're doing."

"There's something you ought to remember too, Mike." Despite the provocation, Russell's tone was mild. "I'm the person in charge of this operation."

"Let's just say the situation has changed. I'm taking over."

"And what gives you the right to do that?"

"I'd say this makes a pretty good start."

This was when Bewick showed Russell the gun he had been holding under the table.

"Put your hands on your head and push your chair away from the table."

Now Bewick had taken the plunge, he was wound up tight. He knew how dangerous Russell could be.

"Don't be so bloody silly."

"I mean it, Russell." It infuriated Bewick to discover Russell still wasn't taking him seriously. "Either you do as I say or I'll have to disable you."

"Disable me then." Russell remained unimpressed. "I'm going to finish my breakfast. If you're not too trigger-happy, you could try explaining the reason for all this melodrama while I'm eating."

"You know damn well." As Russell hadn't moved, Bewick had backed away from the table himself. It allowed him a safety margin. "You're the person who set up the kidnapping."

It wasn't very often that Russell laughed out loud, but he did so now, relishing the irony of the situation. Of all the possible reactions, this was the one Bewick had least expected. It was also the most disconcerting. Unless Russell was a consummate actor, his amusement was perfectly genuine. Bewick was already beginning to feel slightly foolish, but he didn't relax his vigilance.

"What's so funny?" he demanded.

"I'll tell you later. Presumably you have some basis for labelling me a criminal mastermind."

"Of course I do."

"Spell it out for me then. I'm intrigued."

This should have been Bewick's big moment. He had it all neatly laid out in his mind, but the facts didn't seem quite so damning with Russell sitting across the table from him. Although he didn't interrupt while Bewick was making his case, the cynical smile remained firmly in place. On a couple of occasions there were further snorts of laughter. They did nothing to bolster Bewick's confidence.

"I see," Russell commented once Bewick had finished. "It's all a bit circumstantial, isn't it?"

"Everything fits together."

"Sure," Russell conceded. "I'm not denying it, but that's the great drawback with circumstantial evidence. It can be arranged almost any

way you want. Don't you think your judgement might be a trifle clouded
by personal dislike of me?"

"No." This struck a raw nerve and the denial came out more force-
fully than Bewick had intended. "I've been as objective and professional
as possible and that still leaves the finger pointing in your direction. You
set up a situation here on Madura which was tailor-made for you and
you alone. I doubt whether Dietrich even considered using anybody
else."

"There is a certain convoluted logic to what you're saying," Russell
admitted. "I suppose I ought to be flattered to be credited with being so
clever. The trouble is, you're suffering from tunnel vision."

"In what way?"

The initiative had been wrested from Bewick's grasp and he wasn't
quite sure how to regain it.

"It's all there in front of you, Mike. The trouble is, you can't see the
wood for the trees. You've got the sense to realize this whole sorry
business stinks to high heaven. You've spotted most of the inconsisten-
cies. You even made the link with the Teresa Cavalcanti killing. Unfortunately, you don't like me very much. That's made you add up two and
two to make five."

"You'll have to convince me of that."

"I'll do my best." Although the Smith & Wesson was still pointing at
him, Russell remained completely relaxed. "As I see it, there are two
main counts against me. The first one is the mysterious tip-off which
brought the IRA to Viana. You're saying that at the time the only people
who knew we were coming to Madura were Dietrich, yourself and me."

"That's right."

"Wrong, Michael. The Maduran authorities knew as well. Dietrich
had already cleared it with them."

For a moment Bewick wavered. Then he recognized the speciousness
of what Russell was saying.

"Maybe he did," he said, "but nobody on Madura has a pipeline into
the IRA."

"Rubbish. Give me two or three hours and I could find a conduit
into any major terrorist group anywhere in the world. You could do it
yourself."

The trouble was, Bewick had. Almost all the large groups had associated front organizations which were perfectly legal and which included
the passing on of intelligence as one of their main functions. For the
moment, though, Bewick was sticking to his guns.

"We're professionals," he pointed out.

"The people here on Madura aren't complete amateurs and that
leads directly to my second point. You're worried about how easily I've
been turning up leads. Perhaps you ought to try turning everything
around. Hasn't it occurred to you that everything we've used is available

to the local police? Haven't you wondered why they've failed to come up with a single thing? After all, it's their island."

"What are you saying?"

"You know damn well." As Russell rose to his feet, Bewick's gun tracked him. "Rearrange the jigsaw a different way and the pieces fit even better."

The awful thing was that Bewick could see it now. At least, he could see most of it. There was one important piece which didn't yet have a home.

"Why complicate matters by involving the Provos?" he asked.

"I would have thought that was obvious. Somebody here on Madura didn't want me poking around."

"Superintendent Lopes."

The name was there in Bewick's mind without conscious thought.

"It's something to consider, isn't it? Anyway, we've wasted enough time. There's work to be done."

"I still don't know where you're going or why."

"Put that stupid gun away and I might tell you."

Bewick put it away. Later on, when he felt less of a fool, he might even apologize.

"Have you counted it?" Lopes asked.

"Twice," Bewick told him. "It's all there."

The attaché case containing the ransom money was on the desk between them. This made it the dominating presence in Lopes's office.

"You wouldn't think so much money would fit into such a small space."

"It's just as well it does if I've got to carry it around." Bewick looked at his watch. "What time do you make it?"

"Ten after twelve, but don't start getting excited. The kidnappers will probably keep us hanging around for hours. My guess is that they'll wait until after dark before they try to collect."

"That's what Russell expects too."

"It must be right then. Where is Alan, by the way?" Lopes deliberately kept the question casual. "I thought he'd be sweating it out at headquarters with us."

"I'm not sure where he is at the moment. Russell plays his cards pretty close to his chest."

"That doesn't surprise me," Lopes commented. "Anyway, my stomach is telling me it's lunchtime. What do you want to do? We can go out to eat one at a time or we can have some food brought in."

"Let's eat here. All I want is a sandwich."

"Me too. Do you have any preference?"

"Ham will do fine."

"And a beer too?"

"Two beers would be even better."

Lopes didn't have an opportunity to place the order. His hand was reaching out for the telephone when it started to ring.

"Superintendent Lopes speaking."

"There's an outside call for you, sir. I think it's the one you've been expecting."

"Put it through then, Sergeant."

Lopes was signalling for Bewick to pick up the other phone.

"Is that you, Lopes?"

The voice sounded curiously anonymous.

"It is."

"Do you have the money ready?"

"It's all here. How about the hostages?"

"They're fine. They'll be released once we have the ransom."

"That's no good. We want the hostages released at the same time as we hand over the money."

"You can want what you like. Either you play it our way or we'll deliver the hostages back to you piece by piece."

"At the very least we need some guarantee that they're alive and well."

"You have my word on it."

There was a finality about the kidnapper's tone which didn't suggest any likelihood of further concessions. Lopes looked helplessly across at Bewick and shrugged his shoulders. Neither of them had really expected anything more. They were negotiating from weakness and they knew it.

"O.K." Lopes conceded. "What are your instructions?"

"You'd better listen carefully because I shan't repeat myself. Take the money to your car and drive down to the harbour. Park by the public phone box outside the Tamariz. You'll be contacted there in fifteen minutes. Is that clear?"

On the other side of the desk Bewick was shaking his head. He was pointing at himself.

"It's clear," Lopes said. "There's just one minor snag. Senhor White insists that his representative delivers the ransom. Otherwise there's no deal."

There was a brief pause while the kidnapper digested this information. When he did speak, the suspicion was evident in his voice.

"Who is it?"

"An Englishman named Bewick."

Another, longer pause ensued.

"All right," the voice said at last, "but he drives your car and he comes alone. Any tricks and the whole deal is off."

"That's understood. When will the hostages be released?"

"Like I said, after we have the money. You have thirteen minutes to reach the phone box."

"But . . ."

There was no point in Lopes continuing because the line had gone dead. Bewick was already on his feet, the attaché case in his hand. The Rank 203 UHF transceiver was in his jacket pocket.

"Your men know what to do?"

"It's all arranged. They'll keep well away unless you request them to move in."

"Fine. In that case, all I need are the keys to your car."

Lopes handed them over, then accompanied Bewick downstairs. On the way, he couldn't stop wondering why the hand-over was being made so early. The superintendent was always worried by occurrences he couldn't explain.

It was a different Englishman who came down the steps of police head-quarters and climbed into Lopes's car. Even at a distance, Cesar could see it wasn't the man who had visited Pilar the previous night. For a moment he wondered whether his sister had been holding anything back. Then he cleared his mind of the suspicion. Pilar had told him everything she knew. Better still, he had hardly had to hurt her at all. Once she had realized he really meant business, Pilar hadn't been able to stop talking. And what she had had to tell him hadn't been nearly as bad as Cesar had feared. Moving the entire schedule forward a few hours was more of a precaution than a necessity. It was simply a matter of keeping his nerve and doing what he had planned to do all along.

No, Cesar decided, the second Englishman was probably exactly what Lopes had said he was. Not that it mattered anyway. He was alone in the car as he drove off and there were no signs of a police convoy setting off after him. In any case, the way the exchange had been planned, there was virtually no chance of a double cross. Raul might be a certifiable maniac but he was very clever with it. Treading out his cigarette, Cesar began walking, heading away from the harbour. The Tamariz was only the start of the Englishman's guided tour of Madura.

The doorbell was ringing again but Pilar didn't even bother to struggle. She had done all her struggling after Cesar had left her and it was no good. It hadn't taken her very long to appreciate that, unaided, she would never be able to free herself from the bed. With the gag in her mouth she couldn't even shout for help. She would simply have to stay where she was until help arrived.

After a while the doorbell stopped ringing and Pilar was left alone with her thoughts again. Although Cesar had promised he would send somebody around later to release her, there had been no mention of a time. Besides, there was no guarantee that Cesar would be in a position to keep his promise, because she hadn't told her brother quite everything. Pilar knew she might be in for a long, lonely wait. At the back of her mind was the fear that it might be too long.

Most of the public telephones in Viana were yellow plastic monstrosities, hideous mushrooms on little poles. The one opposite the Tamariz was an exception. It had been the first call box on the island and had been designed on the English model. Most residents of the island's capital thought it as shame that it hadn't served as the prototype for its successors.

Bewick, of course, knew nothing of this. He had arrived outside the Tamariz with almost five minutes to spare. After a quick visual check of the area, which told him nothing, he had gone straight into the phone box. While he waited, he pretended to study the directory and kept one eye on the attaché case at his feet. He wasn't used to having a million dollars in carrying-around money and it was making him nervous. When the phone finally did ring, it made him jump.

"Is that the Englishman?"

It was the same voice as before.

"It is."

"Good. You'll find further instructions at the Whites' villa. Look at the bottom of the right-hand gatepost at the end of the drive."

This was all before the line went dead. Bewick replaced the receiver, picked up the attaché case and returned to the car. Once he was clear of the harbour, he pulled the transceiver out of his pocket and thumbed it to transmit. If he was going to be taken on a magical mystery tour, he wanted Lopes to have some idea of the route. At least one of the men he was dealing with was a homicidal maniac.

"Bewick here," he said. "Telephone contact was made outside the Tamariz. My new destination is the Whites' villa."

"Message received."

Bewick dropped the radio on the seat beside him, where it kept company with a large-scale map of Madura. The case containing the ransom money was safely locked in the boot. As he steered Lopes's Datsun through the lunchtime traffic, Bewick wondered where Russell was. And how much of the truth he had been told earlier in the morning.

Russell was developing a grudging respect for the Cavalcantis of yesteryear. The present generation might be going to seed but Raul's forebears must have been a tougher breed. It was hard enough going for Russell without anything to carry. The smugglers would have followed the same route when they were laden down with heavy boxes. Always assuming that he was still on the right path, of course. Russell settled in the shade of a rock and swallowed a mouthful of water from his canteen before he took another look at the map. Although Rodrigues had marked the way in red pen, he had warned Russell that it might not be strictly accurate.

It was almost fifteen years since the history teacher had walked the northern route himself as he had had to rely on memory.

Provided he hadn't strayed from the track, it shouldn't be very far now. Difficult as it was to distinguish one mountain from another on Madura, the landmarks seemed to correspond with the directions Rodrigues had given him. It should simply be a matter of keeping the river to his right for the next couple of miles.

Ten minutes later, any lingering doubts Russell might have had were dispelled. The cigarette end on the path couldn't have been more than three or four days old and this wasn't a tourist area. Russell hunkered down beside it, looking around for any other signs. There weren't any he could see, but this was no real surprise. He was no tracker and the ground was too hard to retain footprints.

When Russell moved off again, he walked parallel to the path, keeping under cover of the trees. This was how he discovered the second, more substantial indication that he was on the right track. It was the buzzing of the flies which first attracted his attention and the smell as he approached which told him what he had found. Death had its own peculiar odour and it was particularly obtrusive up in the mountains. Like the cigarette end, the corpse was only a day or two old. Quite possibly the cigarette had been held between the same lips which were now crawling with flies. Russell would have very much liked to know exactly who the dead man was. And the how and why of his death. Unfortunately, the face was battered beyond recognition and there was no identification in any of the pockets. The body could belong to some unfortunate intruder, but Russell guessed it was more likely to be one of the kidnappers. The only flaw with this theory was that the build of the corpse didn't seem to match the descriptions Russell had been given of Raul or Cesar.

Whoever the body had once been, it was a reminder of how careful Russell needed to be. A lot of people had died already and he had no ambitions of adding to the total himself. At least, not as a victim. In the next twenty minutes Russell only covered half a mile but at the end of it he had reached his destination. The cottage was there in the hollow below, just as old Rodrigues had described it to him. The only question left to be answered was whether the hostages were there as well.

This was the end of the line. The mystery tour had taken him halfway around the island but now it was finally over. Although Viana was only a little over five miles away, Bewick couldn't have felt more alone if he had been on Mars. As per bloody usual, Russell had been right. Raul Cavalcanti and his merry band of kidnappers hadn't made any mistakes. There weren't going to be any straws for him to grasp at because the site chosen for the hand-over was damn nigh perfect.

For a moment or two Bewick simply sat in the Datsun, wondering whether to use the transceiver one last time. In the end, he decided there wasn't much point. For the last mile or so the road had been winding up out of the valley and it was safe to assume he had been under constant observation from the hills above. There had been no scope at all for any kind of chicanery and there wasn't now. He was parked on a miniature plateau at the top of the road with a spectacular panorama of the island spread out below. Bewick guessed that it was, or had been, an observation point, somewhere to bring the tourists on a day out. To his left was a ramshackle wooden building with the legend SOUVENIR above the door. It was closed and, judging by the dilapidated condition of the hut, hadn't been in use for some time. No doubt the local bus drivers had rebelled against bringing their coaches up the narrow, twisting road. It had been hair-raising enough driving up in the Datsun.

If there was no point in using the transceiver, there was even less in speculating where any watchers might be hidden. Wooded hills rose on three sides of the plateau and there were hundreds of places where an observer could conceal himself. Bewick only hoped that none of the kidnappers shared his own devious thought processes. It had occurred to him that a couple of well-placed bullets in his head would make the hand-over totally secure.

It was hot inside the car and even hotter outside. The simple act of opening the boot started him sweating. Walking was even worse, especially as the attaché case seemed to weigh a ton. The last note had instructed him to follow the path to the right of the souvenir shop and this he did. Basically Bewick was a city boy and he never felt completely at ease in the country. This had never been more true than now.

The further Bewick went along the path, the more uneasy he became. A steep, wooded slope rose up to his left and on his right there was an almost sheer drop to the valley, hundreds of feet below. Effectively, he was trapped on the path and, if somebody was planning to use a rifle, Bewick knew he wouldn't stand a chance. The extent of his ambitions was locked into handing over the ransom, getting the hell back to the Datsun and driving back to civilization as fast as he could. This didn't seem a lot to ask, but Bewick couldn't rid himself of the feeling that it might be too much.

The point where the two paths met was almost half a kilometre away, but the binoculars made it seem no more than a few metres. Cesar watched the Englishman place the attaché case in the middle of the intersection, then turn back the way he had come. He continued to watch him all the way back to the superintendent's car. It wasn't until he had actually started down the road into the valley that Cesar moved from his hiding place. When he did, Cesar moved fast, picking his way through the trees and boulders at almost reckless speed. Although he slipped and nearly lost his footing on a couple of occasions, he still didn't slow down. His instructions might have been followed to the letter, but it would be naïve to assume that the Englishman wasn't in contact with the police. Naïveté didn't happen to be one of Cesar's vices.

The going was much easier once he reached the path. Cesar settled into a steady lope and he hardly broke stride at the intersection, simply scooping the attaché case up. Although there was a comforting weight to it, Cesar wasn't tempted to stop and check the contents. The money would be no use to him if he was caught. His immediate priority was to put as much distance between himself and the site of the drop as possible.

It took him ten minutes to reach his car and another fifteen to strike the main coast road. Viana was to his left, no more than a few kilometres up the road, but Cesar turned right. The widow's garage was only two kilometres away and Cesar experienced a distinct feeling of relief as he pulled into the forecourt. He left the engine idling as he watched young Mario amble towards him. The poor kid had a few slates loose, but this wasn't something Cesar had ever commented upon. Mario was built like King Kong's big brother and he possessed a notoriously short temper.

"Hello, Cesar," he said. "What brings you here?"

As he spoke, Mario scratched his genitals affectionately.

"I came to see your mother," Cesar told him. "Is she about?"

"When does the old cow ever go anywhere? She's in the office."

"Fine. Ask her if I can use one of the lockups for a few hours, will you?"

"Sure."

Mario ambled off, one hand thrust deep in an overall pocket. Cesar lit himself a cigarette and puffed nervously at it while he waited. Everything he had ever wanted was almost within his grasp. Raul was safely isolated up in the mountains, thinking the payoff wasn't due until after dark. Anderson would have his boat fuelled up, ready for the night crossing to the Moroccan coast. Success was very close, but it just needed one nosey policeman to pull into the garage for everything to collapse in ruins. Cesar didn't think he could bear it if this happened. He'd probably burst into tears. Either that or blast the policeman away with the gun he had stuffed down the side of the seat. Although he had never killed a man before, a million dollars gave him all the incentive he would ever need.

After what seemed to be an eternity, the idiot reappeared, still walking as slowly as ever. Cesar flicked his cigarette out of the window and held out his hand for the keys Mario was carrying.

"Mum says you've got a bloody nerve," Mario told him as he handed the keys over.

"It's all part of my charm."

Mario's intelligence and looks had both been inherited from his mother. She was so goddamned ugly, there was almost a repulsive fascination about her. It was this which had got Cesar between her legs in the first place. After that, her chief source of sex appeal had been the six lockup garages behind the filling station. They had been useful to Cesar on more than one occasion.

Once the car was safely out of sight, the garage door locked behind him, Cesar sat in the front seat and pulled the crisp bundles of bank notes from the holdall which had been on the floor beside him. He had seen the money before, when he had transferred it from the attaché case on first reaching his car. Now he finally had a chance to count it. Even so, he didn't indulge himself for too long. As soon as he was satisfied that he hadn't been shortchanged, he carefully stacked the money in the special compartment he had had built in the boot. It wasn't until the screws had been replaced and the carpet smoothed out that Cesar lost the feeling there was somebody looking over his shoulder. He had the money and it was as safe as it was going to be until he deposited it in the bank in Rabat. He wasn't fool enough to believe he was home and dry but at least the hardest part was behind him.

Now the money was reasonably secure, it was time to pay the rent for the lockup. Once the garage door was locked and bolted, Cesar strolled across to the main building, going in through the rear door. Esmeralda was sitting behind the till, squat, bulbous and toadlike. Comparing her with the English bitch, it was like going from the sublime to the ridiculous. Cesar thought that if he did manage to get it up, it was going to be a triumph of mind over matter.

"You've got a bloody nerve, Cesar," Esmeralda welcomed him.

"So Mario told me."

"It must be at least a couple of months since I last saw you."

"They say absence makes the heart grow fonder."

As he spoke, Cesar was busy with the buttons on the bodice of her dress.

"I don't know why I put up with you."

"Don't you?"

Now he was cupping one of her pendulous breasts in his hand. It was rather like fondling a jelly with a nipple.

"Cesar, don't." The protest wasn't meant to be taken seriously. "A customer might come in."

"So let's go somewhere more private. I don't have to leave until after nightfall."

"All right. I'll tell Mario he's in charge."

Esmeralda sounded slightly breathless as she hoisted herself off her stool and waddled towards the door. The rear view wasn't any more appealing than the front, the cheeks of her buttocks hanging halfway down her thighs. For the money locked in the boot of his car, though, Cesar was prepared to make a hell of a lot of sacrifices.

* * *

Lopes had his feet up on the desk when Bewick entered the office. He was crumpling up pieces of paper from a scratch pad and throwing them at the wastepaper basket in the corner. Judging by the mess on the floor, his hand-eye coordination was way below par.

"Did you bring my car back safe and sound?" he enquired.

"Of course."

"What a shame. I was hoping you'd drive it over a cliff. Then I could use the insurance to buy a decent vehicle."

Bewick slumped down in the spare chair and wished there had been a can of beer available. Heat and nerves had combined to make his throat parched.

"I assume there's been no joy at this end."

"None at all." The superintendent flicked another crumpled piece of paper to join the growing collection on the floor. "The bastards chose the ideal place for the hand-over. Far enough out of Viana to buy themselves a breathing space and too big a choice of roads for us to monitor traffic. In any case, there's damn all we could do even if we saw one of the kidnappers strolling down the street with the attaché case. Now they have a million dollars and the hostages. I hope Russell knows what he's doing."

"So do I. Has there been any word from him?"

"Not a dicky bird. For all I know, he was the one who collected the ransom."

This came uncomfortably close to what Bewick had been thinking earlier in the day.

"So what do we do?"

"We wait," Lopes told him. "It wouldn't hurt to do a little praying as well. Unless Russell does come up with something, we're not likely to see the money or the hostages again."

Bewick could only nod his head in agreement. It could even be they wouldn't see Russell again either.

Perhaps Derek was right. Perhaps she really was frigid, because Raul didn't seem to be hitting the button either. Not that Deborah White really minded his visits. There were times when what he did felt quite pleasant and, in any case, she was grateful for the company. Opening her body to him was a trivial, unimportant price to pay. But surely there ought to be far more to it than "quite pleasant" and "grateful." In all the romantic novels she had read, the heroines experienced rapture, frenzy and ecstasy. Their sexual partners did things to them which made them melt inside. All Raul was doing to her insides was making them sore.

For a few seconds he was totally immobile, his whole weight pressing down on her. These were the moments Deborah enjoyed most, when Raul was at his most vulnerable. For a few instants, Deborah felt she was the one in charge. Unfortunately it never lasted long. All too soon Raul pushed himself up to sit on the edge of the bed.

For a minute Raul simply sat there, looking down at her. There were times when he frightened Deborah and this was one of them. She had long since decided that he wasn't completely sane. Since the incident with Paolo, she wasn't entirely sure about herself either.

"Are you afraid of dying?" Raul asked suddenly.

"I don't think so."

There wasn't much she really cared about at the moment.

"That's one of the things we share." Raul reached down to caress her cheek, then moved his hand to grip her throat. "I could kill you now."

"I know."

"All I have to do is squeeze."

As he spoke, Raul tightened his grip. Although he was hurting her, Deborah made no attempt to defend or protect herself. She lacked both the energy and the motivation. Although her head was beginning to swim, she could see that Raul was becoming aroused again. Instinctively she reached out to take hold of him.

"You really do understand, don't you?" Raul was laughing as he released her neck. "I knew you did."

Here we go again, Deborah thought. Perhaps this will be the time.

She had no way of knowing that Raul was thinking the same.

FOURTEEN

An hour was nothing. It wasn't even adequate. Done properly, surveillance should be measured in days and weeks, not minutes and hours. But this was a special case and Russell wasn't sure how much longer he could afford to lie among the trees. So far he had learned absolutely nothing. Apart from the odd lizard and one rabbit, nothing had moved in the area around the cottage. Although Russell was certain in his own mind that this was where the hostages had been held, he had no way of knowing whether they or the kidnappers were still there. Worse still, he was out of touch with Bewick in Viana. This meant he was functioning in a kind of limbo, which wasn't at all what Russell had intended when he had ventured into the mountains.

"It's Russell here," he said, trying the radio one last time. "Can you hear me?"

The burst of static told him that nobody could. It was no more than he had expected. Radio waves didn't bend over mountains and there were a hell of a lot of these between him and Viana.

Russell was back at square one. He had to do something and he had to do it soon, if only because almost anything was better than staying where he was. Unfortunately, the most obvious course of action was also the one which appealed to him least. Going into the cottage blind was as dangerous as playing Russian roulette. However, there was an alternative. It would involve some hard climbing and would temporarily take him out of sight of the cottage. On the credit side, though, it would enable him to use his radio. Once he knew what was happening in Viana, he could plan accordingly. Picking up his rucksack, Russell rose to his feet and started off through the trees.

A brief flicker of movement in the trees opposite made Raul duck down out of sight at the top of the cellar steps. It wasn't repeated and after a few seconds he began to think his eyes had been playing tricks.

"It's nerves," he told himself. "I've started seeing things."

Raul had actually started to straighten up when he caught another brief glimpse of the man, higher up the slope. Although he was only in view for an instant, there was no doubt at all this time. There were two more momentary sightings before the man reached the top of the ridge and vanished from view. He had been moving fast and, considering the lack of cover, very carefully indeed. Fingering the knife in his pocket, Raul decided he very much wanted to know who the intruder was and what it was he wanted.

"I read you," Bewick said. "Just about, anyway. Where the hell are you?"

"At the top of a bloody great mountain," Russell told him.

This wasn't strictly accurate because he was actually on a narrow ledge some two hundred feet below the summit. The sheer drop to his right did nothing to make him feel secure but he had saved time and energy by stopping where he had. More important, he was high enough to reestablish contact with Viana.

"Has your trip been worthwhile?" Bewick asked.

"That's the sixty-four-thousand-dollar question. When I know the answer to it, you'll be the first to know. What's been happening down there on the coast?"

"The ransom has been paid."

"Say that again."

Russell couldn't keep the incredulity out of his voice.

"You heard the first time. I handed over the ransom money about an hour ago."

"I didn't expect that to happen until tonight."

"Nor did anybody except the kidnappers. Perhaps they're cleverer than we gave them credit for. At the moment they have a million dollars of taxpayers' money and we have sod-all."

"What was the deal about the hostages?"

"There wasn't one. They're supposed to be released now that the money has been handed over, but I wouldn't bet on it."

Nor would Russell and suddenly there wasn't any time left at all. He would have to hit the cottage the moment he had climbed down the mountain again and Bewick would have to cover the bases in Viana. If he could.

"Are you still at police headquarters?" Russell asked.

"No. I'm back at the hotel."

This was what Russell had hoped.

"On your own?"

"Yes."

"Fine. Let's switch to the emergency frequency."

This only took Russell a second. Anybody who had been monitoring their conversation would take much longer to lock in again. By then Russell would have finished what he had to say.

"I'm ready," Bewick said.

"OK. I want you to stick to Lopes like a limpet until I can join you. Get onto him now and don't let him out of your sight. Equally important, don't let him know he's being followed. Lopes might take exception to that and he has an entire police force to back him up. Can you manage that?"

"I'll do my best. When can I expect you?"

"Hopefully by nightfall. Keep your radio on this channel and I'll contact you as soon as I have anything to report."

"I'll look forward to it. Be lucky."

At least, Russell thought as he stowed the radio away in his rucksack, the whole situation is clarified now. He didn't realize quite how clarified until Raul Cavalcanti stepped around the corner some ten feet away, holding the Savage automatic in both hands.

The sheer speed of the man amazed Raul. When he stepped out onto the ledge, the Englishman had been crouched over his rucksack. By the time Raul had taken in the slack on the trigger, his target had already dropped to the ground and begun to roll. The first shot was high, whining off into space. The second missed as well, spraying up splinters of rock from the ledge as the man continued his roll. The third bullet might have struck home or it could have been yet another miss but this didn't really matter. The Englishman had run out of ledge just as Raul had fired. He had rolled himself clear off the ledge and this meant he was as dead as anyone possibly could be whether he took a bullet down with him or not.

For a moment Raul remained where he was, feeling vaguely dissatisfied. It had been far too quick and far too impersonal for him to take any pleasure in the killing. But there was no other way it could have been done. And there were other things to be done now. Raul walked across to the rucksack, squatting down while he examined the contents. Apart from the walkie-talkie, there was a canteen of water, some bread and cheese, a map of the island and two grenades. Raul thought they might be stun grenades but he wasn't sure and he avoided tampering with them.

Picking the rucksack up by the straps, he went to the edge of the ledge. From where he stood there was a sheer drop of some hundred and fifty metres. The boulder-strewn scree slope at the bottom was almost equally precipitous, continuing for another three hundred metres downwards before it eventually reached the valley floor. Raul had no fear of heights and he stood there for a minute, totally secure despite the wind which was plucking at him. Then he threw the rucksack out into space, watching it tumble over and over before it hit the rocks far below. This was where the body would be too. Raul would have liked to examine it, to see exactly what the results of such a fall were, but there wasn't time to indulge himself.

Turning away, he retraced his footsteps down the mountain, moving easily and surely. It was only when he neared the bottom of the slope that he began to move more cautiously. Although he thought the man with the radio had been on his own, he couldn't be absolutely sure. For several minutes he hovered indecisively in the trees, looking towards the cottage and the cellars. It bothered him that the two women hostages were still alive. This wasn't at all how he had planned it. He felt particularly cheated at being denied the opportunity to share Deborah White's death with her. The way he had intended, it would have been even better than the last few moments with his sister.

Cesar was more important, though. Just thinking about his treachery started the blood pounding in Raul's temples. His English might not be perfect but it was good enough. If Cesar had already received the ransom money, if he had unilaterally moved the entire tightly planned schedule forward, this could only mean one thing. Cesar was striking out on his own. He was preparing a double cross and this wasn't something Raul could tolerate. Dealing with Cesar had to take precedence over everything else.

Even so, the hostages in the cellars were an almost irresistible temptation. The only thing which held Raul back was the awareness that the man with the radio might not have been on his own. His radio contact might have been in Viana but there might still be other men hunting him in the mountains. Being caught certainly hadn't featured in any of his plans. No, Cesar had to be dealt with first and, reluctantly, Raul started walking towards the track which would take him down to the coast. Although he had no idea where his prey might be hiding, Raul knew Cesar wouldn't be able to leave Madura before nightfall. And, better still, there was somebody in Viana who should be able to tell Raul exactly where her brother was.

* * *

He was beginning to hurt quite badly, muscles and joints protesting at the unreasonable demands he was making of them. Russell ignored the pain. Hurting was infinitely preferable to dying and this was the only alternative. This was why he had deliberately rolled off the ledge. There had been a much better chance of grabbing hold of the tree growing out from the rock face than there had been of avoiding the bullets Cavalcanti was pumping at him. At least, this was what he had thought at the time and nothing had happened to change his mind since. His hands were locked together in a grip which would last long after his shoulders had dislocated. Even without a foothold, he could hang on for hours.

Not that this was going to be necessary, because one of two things was going to happen very shortly. If Cavalcanti spotted him, he would shoot Russell at his leisure. If he didn't, he would go away. Russell very much hoped it would be the latter. The moment he had had a secure grip on the tree, Russell had started working himself inwards towards the cliff. The trunk was thicker there and the slight overhang in the cliff would do something to shield him from the ledge. However, this was the very best he could do. Everything else depended on what Cavalcanti did. Russell had watched his rucksack go sailing out into the void. He knew Cavalcanti was standing a mere twelve or thirteen feet above his head. And there was nobody to be seen at the bottom of the cliff. If it occurred to Cavalcanti that Russell might be in the tree, the overhang wouldn't be any protection at all. Raul merely had to lie down on the ledge and stick his head out over the edge.

After five tense, uncomfortable minutes, no mocking face had appeared above Russell. Although there was too much wind for him to have heard the sound of retreating footsteps, it was safe to assume that Cavalcanti must have gone. If he wasn't suspicious, there wasn't anything to keep him on the ledge apart from the view. It was a view Russell himself could have done without. Although he had never suffered from vertigo, there was simply too much space between the soles of his feet and terra firma. One mistake on his way back to the ledge and that would be the end of it. There wouldn't be any second chances.

Russell found this a great aid to concentration. In any case, the first step was straightforward enough. There was plenty of strength left in his arms to pull himself up onto the tree trunk. Once he was securely wedged into position, his back against the cliff, he had an opportunity to review the situation while he massaged his arms and shoulders. First impressions weren't particularly encouraging. O.K., the safety offered by the ledge was little more than twelve feet above his head, but this twelve feet included an overhang which wasn't going to help him at all. Nor was the structure of the cliff itself. On the credit side, it was hard volcanic rock which hadn't crumbled for thousands of years and wasn't likely to do so now. At the same time, it was depressingly smooth. There weren't any holds which were likely to help him at all.

He eased himself a little way out along the tree trunk and looked again. It was still no go. The twelve feet might as well have been fifty or a hundred because there was no way he could climb the rock face. This wasn't the kind of negative thinking Russell could afford. He had been trained to believe that every problem had a solution and it was simply a matter of finding it. Russell patiently began quartering the cliff face above him, examining it for anything which might help. After twenty minutes he had found one possible handhold some four feet below the ledge and midway up the overhang. In reality it was barely half a hand-hold but it should afford him some upward momentum if he could reach it.

By itself, this wasn't nearly enough. Russell went back to studying the surface of the cliff in minute detail and half an hour later he was almost ready to give up. Perhaps this was the problem which really didn't have a solution. Perhaps he really was meant to starve to death on a tree sticking out of a sheer cliff. Pushing such dark thoughts to the back of his mind, Russell started over again. Almost immediately he found the answer staring him in the face. The ferns were literally on a level with his eyes, but previously he hadn't attached any significance to them. Now he carefully pulled them free, dropping them into the void.

The crevice where they had been growing hardly qualified as a crack. Although it certainly wouldn't take a foot or a hand, it could still be used. Russell slipped his knife out of its sheath and began working at the crack. When he had finished, three inches of the blade were wedged into the cliff. This wasn't nearly as much as Russell would have liked and the knife wobbled alarmingly when he put some pressure on it. All the same, it was a hell of a sight better than what he had had before. At least he had a chance for the ledge. Maybe.

Esmeralda was snoring beside him, a bubbling, farting noise which was getting on Cesar's nerves. The covers were thrown back and she lay there like a beached whale, all fat and blubber. One pendulous breast hung to the side so it was almost in her armpit. She was more an object of revulsion than of desire. Even when he had shut his eyes and thought of the English bitch, it hadn't been easy. Mind you, thinking about the money in his car had been a great help. A million dollars was the kind of amount which gave him a permanent hard-on.

He lit himself a cigarette and looked over at the window. The afternoon was drawing on and it would soon be time to move. This would be the crucial moment, the last hurdle to negotiate. Raul he could forget about. He was safely out of it, up at the hideout and unaware that the ransom had been paid, but the police were a different matter. Cesar himself had almost certainly been identified as one of the kidnappers.

Although Pilar hadn't been entirely clear about this, there was no doubt at all in Cesar's mind. He had to assume the police were on the lookout for him and this was a complication he could have done without. He had to reach the *Amico* and this entailed driving into Viana. There just wasn't a way round it.

Or was there? The answer was so obvious Cesar was amazed it hadn't occurred to him before. No matter how many roadblocks the police had set up, he could get into Viana without any danger of being spotted. It might take a little longer but he was home and dry, if this wasn't a confusion in terms.

Cesar was smiling to himself as he eased himself out of bed and began dressing. Once he had finished, Cesar spared a last glance for Esmeralda. She was still snoring, worn out by the unaccustomed sexual activity. He hoped she had enjoyed herself because it would be a long time before the experience was repeated. Cesar certainly wouldn't be returning, and he couldn't imagine anybody else being fool enough to take her on. As he turned away, Cesar spared a fleeting thought for his sister, whom he had also left lying on a bed. Then he dismissed her from mind. If she hadn't been found already, somebody would be along soon to set her free.

The cottage still looked peaceful enough. Russell was almost convinced that Cavalcanti was, or had been, alone with the hostages. He was also aware that this was an opinion based on little more than guesswork. For all Russell knew there could be dozens of kidnappers involved. He didn't think there were, but it was a possibility he had to bear in mind. Then there was Cavalcanti himself. There was no telling where he might be. He could be taking a well-earned rest, thinking he had killed Russell on the ledge. He might be carving up the remaining hostages. Or he might be on his way down into Viana. Russell favoured the latter theory. Once again, though, this was little more than guesswork, based on the assumption that Cavalcanti had probably overheard his radio conversation with Bewick. There was only one way Russell was going to discover how good at guessing he was.

Russell pulled the Browning 9 mm out of its holster and slipped off the safety catch. Although he would be in the open all the way to the cottage, he wasn't afraid. His experiences at the cliff had nurtured an already strong streak of fatalism. If he was going to die, it should have happened there. There had been an instant, as the blade of the knife had snapped under his weight, when he was sure it had. He still couldn't fully comprehend how he had managed to survive, but he had. Momentum had seen him through, momentum and a hell of a lot of luck. Although he wasn't harbouring any delusions of immortality, Russell didn't think it was his day to die, certainly not at the hands of Raul

Cavalcanti. He had already taken his best shot at him and failed. Now it was Russell's turn to see if he could do any better.

He left the protection of the trees at a steady walk. If there was somebody in the cottage with a rifle, he was as good as dead. However, an antiquated Savage automatic posed no such threat. Unless it was being used by a marksman, the weapon's effective range was less than ten metres. Raul had already proved this, missing him three times at a range of less than ten feet. Russell was a marksman and he held the Browning down at his side as he walked forwards in the bright sunlight. He felt at peace with himself, clearheaded and alert. It was the way he always felt once the action started. He supposed it was something to do with the adrenaline.

Thirty metres from the cottage, Russell started to run, zigzagging over the uneven ground. If he had still had the stun grenades, the open doorway would have made an inviting target for one of them. As it was, Russell concentrated on keeping his zigs and zags as unpredictable as possible until he was safely pressed against the rough stone of the cottage wall, midway between the door and a window. He only paused for a moment. Although he was convinced the cottage was deserted, he went inside fast and low, moving from light to shade in a controlled roll which took him to the far side of the room. This was so much wasted effort. As he had thought, there was nobody there.

It didn't take him long to search the cottage. The most significant items were the three sleeping bags. Russell mentally allocated them to Raul Cavalcanti, Pilar's brother and the dead man in the woods. Apart from the sleeping bags, there were no personal items worth mentioning. At least, so Russell thought until he forced open the locked drawer of the table. There was no name on the exercise book, which was almost full of cramped, spidery writing. It wasn't necessary. Russell only had to skim through a couple of pages to know he was holding Raul Cavalcanti's personal diary.

The exercise book went into a pocket, to be read later at leisure. For the time being, Russell was finished with the cottage. Now it was time to discover if any of the hostages were still alive.

There were three doors. Only one of them was open and the cellar beyond was empty. The other two doors were locked but, as a large key was hanging on a nail in the wall, this was no great problem. Before he used it, Russell listened at both doors without learning anything. There was no way of telling whether the occupants were alive or not.

Deborah White certainly was. She was lying naked on the bed and she made no attempt to cover herself when Russell came in. There was an emptiness to her eyes which he found disturbing.

"Hello," she said. "Is Raul inviting his friends round now?"

"I'm no friend of his."

Russell's response was entirely automatic. He was trying to assess Deborah White's condition. For the moment he couldn't be sure whether she was suffering shock as a result of sexual abuse or whether it was something worse.

"So you don't want to screw, then?"

"Not at the moment, thank you."

"You can if you like. I really don't mind."

"I don't have the time at the moment."

There was a singsong quality to her voice which made the hairs at the back of Russell's neck prickle.

"You're not afraid of me, are you? I didn't mean to kill Paolo, you know."

"I'm sure you didn't, Mrs. White. I'll just check the other hostages, then I'll be back."

Once he was outside the cellar, Russell relocked the door. In Mrs. White's own best interests, he didn't think it was a good idea to let her wander around by herself.

He was very much hoping Janine Haywood was in better shape and first impressions were encouraging. She was not only dressed, she was quite presentably tidy. She too had been lying on the bed but as soon as the door opened, she jumped up.

"Who the hell are you?" she demanded. "I haven't seen you before."

"The name is Alan Russell."

"You're English." The alarm had given way to relief. "Does that mean I'm being rescued?"

"Something like that."

"Thank Christ for that. I was beginning to give up hope. What am I supposed to do? Throw my arms around your neck and call you my hero? Or aren't you allowed to do that to policemen?"

"I'm not a policeman."

"Let me guess." She had adapted to her change of circumstance with remarkable facility. "You're some kind of special agent."

"I'm not that special either."

"I bet you are. You have that look about you."

It was turning into quite an afternoon. The Haywood girl's approach might not be as blatant as Mrs. White's but the offer was basically the same. Despite the naughty-little-girl good looks and the flirtatiousness, Russell already had her classified as one very tough cookie. Perhaps she was a chip off the old block.

"I need to talk seriously," he said. "Can we forget the sexual innuendo for a bit?"

"We can, but it won't be nearly as much fun."

The little bitch was still at it. Russell decided it was high time he dampened her ardour a little.

"Perhaps I ought to explain something to you, Miss Haywood."

Now he was using his best official voice. "Earlier on you asked if you were being rescued. There are certain people, including your stepmother, who would prefer it if you weren't rescued alive. This was something which was made very plain to me."

"What do you mean?"

"Think about it."

It didn't take her very long. She was completely serious now and she obviously wasn't a fool.

"You're supposed to kill me."

She spoke slowly, almost forcing the words out.

"That was an important part of my job specification. The official thinking is that if you're dead, you'll be much less of an embarrassment to your stepmother."

"The bitch."

"I can't argue with that."

"You're not going to kill me, though, are you?" Although Janine's voice stayed firm, this was almost a plea. "If you were going to, you'd have done it without any warning."

"That's very astute of you, Miss Haywood. As it happens, I shall take great pleasure in delivering you home safe and sound."

"Why? What do you want from me in return?"

"It's not your body. Let's just say I shall enjoy seeing your step-mother embarrassed. I'm sure I can rely on you to make a good job of it."

"You can bank on it. Did she really say she wanted me dead?"

"That's how the message reached me."

"The bitch. Is there anything else I can do for you?"

"I could do with the answers to a few questions."

"If I know them, they're yours."

Russell took her through the kidnapping slowly and patiently, acutely aware of the pressure of time but refusing to rush. Even when Janine thought she had finished, he continued to push her, probing for the details which were buried in her subconscious. By the time he stopped, Russell was pretty sure he had it all. Putting together what Janine had told him and what he himself already knew or suspected, the jigsaw was virtually complete. It was up to him to go out and collect the remaining pieces.

Although there were a lot of questions Janine would have liked to ask herself, Russell told her they would have to wait. He also explained that he wouldn't be taking her down into Viana with him. As he said, he would be moving fast.

"I can keep up," Janine objected.

"Maybe you could but Mrs. White couldn't and she can't be left on her own."

"What about Rodney?"

"He's dead. Friend Raul killed him."

"Poor sod." Although Janine pulled a face, she didn't seem particularly upset. "He was a born loser."

"That's a beautiful epitaph. The thing is, Mrs. White is still alive but she's in pretty bad shape. She's going to need your help."

"What's wrong with her?"

"I'm not sure exactly. I'd say she's suffering some kind of nervous breakdown."

"You mean she's flipped her lid."

"That would be a less charitable way of putting it. I'd like you to get her dressed and tidied up. Then take her to the cottage."

"What then?"

"You wait. I'll send the police up to fetch you."

"They don't have a contract to kill me too?"

"No." Russell was smiling. "You'll be safe with them."

"And what happens if Raul or Cesar come back here first?"

"They won't. All they'll be thinking about is escaping from the island."

Although this wasn't strictly accurate, it was close enough to the truth to satisfy Russell's conscience and it kept Janine happy.

FIFTEEN

It was beginning to get dark now and the doorbell had started ringing again. Somebody had simply put a finger on the bell and was keeping it there. Although the incessant ringing was making Pilar's head ache, this was the least of her problems. The pain in her wrists and ankles, where the tights were cutting off the circulation, was far worse. And worst of all was the thirst. The handkerchief which had been used as a gag was like a ball of lead in her mouth. It had long since absorbed any moisture and swallowing had become increasingly painful. As the day had dragged on, water had become the single most precious thing in her life. If she had a life to look forward to. Her predicament had helped morbid fantasies to come easily. Pilar had long since realized that she might quite possibly die where she was, strapped helplessly to the bed. She couldn't remember how long humans were able to survive without liquids, but she knew it was only a matter of days. Nobody would be alarmed by her absence before then. The Ipanema would be annoyed because she hadn't contacted them and would try to telephone her. They probably had already, because the phone had rung twice during the day. Various friends and acquaintances would come and ring the doorbell for a while before they went away. But nobody would be particularly alarmed by her disappearance. Nobody was likely to suspect foul play until it was too late.

The doorbell abruptly stopped ringing. This was the same pattern which had already been repeated on several occasions during the day. At least, so Pilar thought, until she became aware of the scratching noise at the door of the flat. She thought it must be the neighbour's cat until she suddenly realized that somebody was trying to force the lock. Almost at the same time, she realized it must be Alan. He had always been her one hope. He was the one person who might suspect something was wrong if he didn't find her at home.

A great wave of relief washed over her as she listened to the door open and then quietly close again. Now Alan was actually in the flat with her. Pilar's hearing seemed to have become hypersensitive since Cesar had tied her to the bed and her ears tracked Alan as he moved quietly around the living room. When she heard him go through into the kitchen, she became afraid he might not think to look in the bedroom. Although shouting was out of the question, Pilar found she could manage a throaty gargle. This hurt her throat but it seemed worthwhile as she listened to the footsteps moving toward the bedroom. For a moment she closed her eyes to hold back the tears, thankful her ordeal was over. When she opened them again, it was as though a giant hand had squeezed her heart, making it miss a beat or two. It wasn't Alan standing inside the bedroom door. It was Raul and there was a pleased smile on his face.

"Hello, Pilar," he said. "I was hoping I'd find you at home."

"Any news?" Bewick asked.

"Not yet," Lopes told him, holding the receiver in place with his shoulder while he buttered a slice of bread. "I have every available man out on the streets and there hasn't been a single sighting. Like I told you before, it looks as though you've handed over a million dollars for nothing."

"It was the only way we could play it."

The Englishman sounded slightly defensive.

"That's what I thought at the time. Now I'm not so sure. If the hostages haven't been released by now, they're not going to be released. My guess is that they're already dead."

"That's one of the things I like most about you—your refreshing optimism."

Lopes laughed and reached out for the cheese.

"Optimism is something kids catch, along with measles and mumps. I'm too long in the tooth for it to affect me any longer. What's the word on friend Russell?"

"There isn't any."

This was something which had been bothering Bewick. It was several hours since Russell had last been in touch. None of the explanations Bewick could think of for this were good.

"Well, I'd say he's just about our only hope. Let me know if he does deign to contact you, will you?"

"Sure. I assume you'll be at home all night."

"Unless something unexpected crops up. If it does, you'll be the first to know."

After he had put the phone down, Lopes finished making his sandwich and went back into the living room. *Dynasty* was showing on the television, one of his least favourite programmes, but for once the banalities didn't irritate him. He was too busy thinking about the night ahead to pay any attention to what was happening on the screen. If he had realized that Bewick hadn't phoned him from the Méridien, Lopes would have had even more to think about. The Englishman had been using the phone box a hundred and fifty metres down the road. Now he was settled comfortably in the front seat of the hire car, eyes glued on the superintendent's house.

"Water," Pilar croaked. "Please get me some water."

"Sure," Raul agreed pleasantly. "Just hang on a second."

Pilar watched him walk out of the bedroom. Although Raul had tucked his gun into the waistband of his trousers at the back, she was more frightened now than she had been when she first saw him. She had had time to realize how completely at his mercy she was.

"Here you go," Raul said as he came back into the room. "You'll feel better for this."

The water was in a cup. Although Pilar would have liked to gulp it all straight down, Raul wouldn't permit this. Lifting her head with one hand, he dribbled the liquid into her mouth a few drops at a time, feeding her as though she was a baby. Water had never tasted quite so sweet before.

"Do you feel better for that?"

"Much but I could manage another cupful."

"Not yet." Raul was shaking his head. "You need to rehydrate slowly."

"In that case, perhaps you'll untie my arms and legs."

"In a minute. Let's have a chat first."

"What about?"

The terrible thing was, Pilar knew exactly what Raul wanted to talk about. This was one reason she was having great difficulty in controlling her bladder.

"Well, I don't like to be nosey, but you could explain why you're tied to the bed. I hadn't associated you with bondage before."

"It was a burglar." This was the best Pilar had been able to manage on the spur of the moment. "He must have been waiting inside the flat, because he hit me as soon as I opened the door. The next thing I knew I was tied up like this."

"So you didn't see who it was?"

"No. He left while I was unconscious."

There was no warning at all before Raul hit her. The friendly smile didn't waver and his hand moved so fast she didn't even see it coming. It felt as though every tooth in her head had been loosened.

"Let's try again," he suggested. "Who tied you to the bed?"

"I've told you already." Tears were running down her cheeks but she didn't dare tell Raul the truth. "It was a burglar."

Raul sighed as if in disappointment and reached into his trouser pocket. The blade on the flick knife glittered evilly in the lamplight as he waved it in front of her face. Although Pilar would have liked to scream, she didn't dare. With his free hand Raul took hold of her chin, holding her head immobile. Then he slowly moved the knife until the point was almost touching her left eyeball. It was so close Pilar was afraid to blink.

"There's something you have to understand about me, Pilar." Raul spoke softly, his voice almost a caress. "I enjoy hurting people. You could almost say it was a hobby of mine. When you lie to me, you're simply encouraging me to do what I like doing best. Do you follow?"

Although Pilar didn't speak, the answer was there in her terrified eyes. Raul smiled at her and raised the knife, the point still directed downwards at her face.

"The rules are simple," he explained. "If you lie to me, you have to pay. I'm going to hurt you worse than you believed it was possible to be hurt."

Then he stabbed down, aiming at her left eye. With his hand still gripping her chin, it was impossible for Pilar to avoid the knife. At the very last moment, Raul turned his wrist so that the blade brushed down her cheek and imbedded itself in the pillow beside her head. At the same instant, Raul bent down and kissed her, forcing his tongue between her lips. It was as though her mouth was suddenly filled with slime. Fortunately, the travesty of a kiss only lasted for a second before Raul pulled away again.

"I'm giving you one last chance," he said, stroking her cheek with the knife. "Was it really a burglar who tied you up?"

"No," Pilar whispered. "It was Cesar."

She knew she wouldn't be telling any more lies. Previously she had been afraid of dying. Now it was the manner of her death which concerned her.

"Why on earth would your brother want to do that?"

"We'd been arguing. I'd refused to answer some questions."

"So he hit you and tied you up like this."

"Yes."

"And then he persuaded you to answer him."

"That's right."

"They must have been very important questions. You'd better tell me what they were and what you told Cesar."

So Pilar did. As she couldn't be sure how much Raul knew already, she told him everything, trying to ignore what Raul was doing with the knife. All the time she was speaking, he was busy. First he cut through the shoulder straps, then he slit down the seam. When he had finished, it was like unwrapping a parcel. He pulled the material away and the entire front of her body was exposed. In her flimsy black underwear, Pilar was effectively naked. Although it was difficult to keep talking while this was happening, Pilar forced herself. The alternative was unthinkable.

"Where's your brother now?" Raul asked once she had finished.

"I don't know. Cesar didn't tell me where he was going."

"I see."

Raul used his knife again, carefully cutting through her bra in between her breasts. As the cups fell to the side, both breasts were bared. Raul bent down and started to kiss them, sucking and licking at the nipples. A numbed helplessness had settled on Pilar. She wasn't sure whether she wanted to scream or vomit until Raul suddenly used his teeth, biting savagely into her right nipple. The pain was agonizing and Pilar would have screamed then, regardless of consequences, if Raul hadn't already clamped a hand over her mouth. He kept it there until the pain had subsided to an ache.

"Are you absolutely positive you don't know where Cesar is?"

His voice was softer than ever. Pilar had the obscene notion that it was as though he was talking to a lover.

"I don't. I really don't." Pilar was crying in earnest now. "It's the truth. I swear it is."

Almost delicately, Raul cut through her knickers where they passed over her left hip.

"You're certain you don't have any idea where he might be?"

Now Raul had done the same over her other hip and the triangle of black lace fell free.

"None at all, honestly. Please don't hurt me any more."

Raul shook his head as though he was admonishing a backward child.

"Open your mouth wide," he said.

"Why?"

"Because I told you to. You wouldn't want to upset me, would you?"

This was the last thing Pilar wanted, so she did as he had instructed. When Raul replaced the gag, she suspected this might have been a mistake.

"I believe you, Pilar. I really do." For an instant hope flared in Pilar.

"I don't think you have any idea where Cesar is. There's only one little snag."

Although Raul only paused for a second, this was long enough for hope to die as quickly as it had been born. There was a feverish excitement about Raul now which told Pilar her ordeal had only just begun.

"You see," he went on, "I can't be absolutely sure. I could be wrong and there's only one way for me to find out. If you do decide there's something else you want to tell me, all you have to do is nod your head. I'll be only too glad to listen."

As Raul picked up the knife again, Pilar finally lost control of her bladder.

There was no light coming from Bewick's room. It was just another blank rectangle on the façade of the Méridien. Although Russell hadn't expected to find Bewick in his room, he would have loved to be proved wrong. Not for the first time, Russell cursed Raul Cavalcanti for the destruction of his personal radio. He had been out of touch with events in Viana for too long. The endgame was in process around him. Pieces were being moved and he had no idea of their position. He was losing control at the most delicate stage of the operation and this troubled Russell. Although there was one fixed point in the night ahead, this was still several hours away. Until then, unless Bewick was able to tell him the contrary, he would have to behave as though Viana was hostile territory.

There was one way he might be able to contact Bewick. Russell preferred to find out from a public telephone and the one he selected was a good quarter of a mile away from the hotel. He wanted to find people, not have them find him.

"Police headquarters," the desk sergeant said. "Can I help you?"

"I hope so. This is Alan Russell. Can you put me through to Superintendent Lopes?"

"I'm afraid he isn't here at the moment, Senhor Russell. He left several hours ago."

The sergeant sounded apologetic on behalf of his superior. And so he should be, Russell thought.

"In that case," he said out loud, "can you try his home number. The message is important."

"If you hold on a minute, sir, I'll put you through."

Russell held on but the link didn't materialize. When the sergeant spoke again, he sounded perplexed.

"There's no answer at the superintendent's house either, sir."

"Did he leave another number where he could be contacted?"

"He didn't, sir, and that surprises me." Now there was outright condemnation in the sergeant's voice. "He normally insists that all officers can be reached at all times of the day and night."

Although he didn't say so, the news didn't surprise Russell at all. What it did mean, though, was that Bewick was effectively out of reach as well. If Lopes had been at headquarters or at home, it would have been safe to assume Bewick was somewhere in the vicinity. Now he had no idea where to start looking.

Russell had the sergeant put him through to the senior ranking officer present at police headquarters. Once he was put through, he explained where the hostages could be found and outlined Deborah White's condition. He also extracted a promise that a relief expedition would be dispatched immediately. It wasn't something he wanted to be dependent on Lopes's authorization.

All this did nothing to solve Russell's own problem. Although the Méridien was the most likely place for Bewick to leave any messages, it was also a place where other people might come looking for him. On balance, Russell still preferred to steer well clear of the hotel. It would be easy enough to phone in regularly to check for messages. Better still, this course of action gave him the perfect excuse to see Pilar again before he left the island. The thought did something to cheer him up as he walked away from the phone box.

The lock on Pilar's door had been forced. The moment he saw the scratch marks, Russell knew they had been made by Raul Cavalcanti. There was no logical reason for this. Russell simply knew, beyond any shadow of a doubt, that it was Raul who had forced an entry into Pilar's flat.

There were only two questions in Russell's mind. Was Raul still inside? And, far more important, was Pilar still alive? He slipped the Browning out of its holster and listened, his ear right against the door. There might have been somebody talking quietly inside but Russell couldn't be sure. A radio was going full blast in one of the other apartments and it was impossible to blank the pop music out. He had to behave as though Raul was still there and had a live Pilar with him.

Very, very gently, he depressed the door handle, then pushed the door open. There was nobody in his line of vision and he slipped quietly inside. The living room was empty but there was no need to search the other rooms because now he knew where Raul was. He was in the main bedroom and Pilar was there with him. She was almost certainly alive, if not necessarily well. Otherwise there would have been no need for Raul's litany of obscenities, the graphic detailing of what he intended to do. The filth would have been wasted on a corpse.

Equally gently, Russell pushed the door closed behind him. He didn't want any interruptions because, whatever else happened, Raul wasn't going to leave the apartment alive. In Russell's mind, this was an established fact. Although killing had never given him any pleasure, there would be a great deal of satisfaction in dealing with the maniac on the other side of the wall.

Russell didn't make a sound as he moved swiftly across the carpet. Unfortunately, the gap between the door and the doorjamb gave him only a partial view of the bedroom beyond. Only the bottom half of the bed was in view. He could see how Pilar's ankles were tied to the bedposts and he could see what one of Raul's hands was doing between her spread legs. What he couldn't see was where the knife was.

"It's so sharp and you're so soft." Raul's voice was almost a croon. "I'm going to make such lovely patterns with your blood. When I've finished you'll be my masterpiece."

A cold, murderous rage had descended on Russell and he wasn't interested in hearing any more. Although he had no way of knowing what Raul had done to Pilar already, this was the end of it. He was going to step through the door and blow the top of the sick bastard's head away. Russell thought it was a great shame Raul wouldn't be around to appreciate the pretty patterns his brains made when they were splattered all over the wall.

But he didn't shoot. Although his finger was already squeezing the trigger as he stepped into the room, Russell eased the pressure almost immediately. Raul was drawing the knife lightly across Pilar's throat, leaving a crimson line behind the blade. To shoot would probably be to kill Pilar.

"I thought you were dead."

Raul had weathered the shock with remarkable aplomb. The knife had ceased its passage across Pilar's neck, the fingers of his other hand had stopped their pulling and prying between her legs but these were his only visible reactions. He was almost behaving as though he had expected Russell's arrival. Perhaps there were advantages to being deranged after all.

"You were wrong," Russell told him. "Throw the knife away."

"Why?" Raul sounded curious. "You're not going to shoot me. I can cut Pilar's throat before you pull the trigger."

He was right and Russell knew it.

"That won't help you," Russell told him. "Get rid of the knife."

"This is interesting." Now Raul's tone was conversational. "I'm not afraid to die. I wonder if you're afraid of what I'll do to Pilar. Let's see if you really will shoot me."

The knife began moving again. Raul was pressing slightly harder now and more blood was welling up to run down the side of Pilar's throat. Russell didn't dare look at her face.

"See, you do care." Raul sounded pleased with this confirmation of Russell's human frailty. "That means you ought to drop your gun."

"No."

This wasn't an option. Gun or not, Russell knew he could handle

Raul. He also knew that the moment he dropped the Browning, Raul would slit Pilar's throat. It was there in the maniac's eyes.

"If you don't, I'll kill Pilar now."

"And you'll be dead half a second afterwards."

"You're not listening to me." It was as though Raul was talking to a child. "I don't mind dying. It's the ultimate experience."

"Sure, but how do you feel about dying while I'm still living. And there's Cesar as well. He's double-crossed you and he's still alive."

"Ah, Cesar."

At last Russell had found a button to press. He had decided that shooting Raul now was the only chance Pilar had, but his finger relaxed on the trigger again. There had been no mistaking the sheer malevolence in Raul's voice as he breathed Cesar's name.

"Once you're dead, you lose any hope of revenge. You wouldn't want that, would you?"

"That's very true. Cesar definitely has to be punished. What do you suggest?"

"A straight trade, Pilar's life for yours. You leave Pilar alone and I let you walk out of the flat."

"You'll give me your word not to shoot me?"

Raul sounded amused.

"Something like that."

"You must be joking. You'd shoot me as soon as I moved away from the bed."

Too bloody right I would, Russell thought.

"OK," he said out loud. "I'll unload my gun."

Matching actions to words, Russell removed the clip of ammunition from the Browning, holding it up in his left hand. This still wasn't enough to convince Raul. Crazy he might be but he was no fool.

"It would only take you a second to reload," he pointed out. "I'd still end up shot."

"OK," Russell conceded. "How about if I drop the ammunition clip on the floor and kick it away from me? Does that give you enough of an edge?"

"It seems more than generous." Raul was looking for the catch. "What's to stop me coming for you with the knife while you're unarmed?"

"I'd kill you with my bare hands." Russell made this a simple statement of fact. "I'm going to kill you anyway but that can wait. At the moment I'm only concerned with Pilar. That's why I'm offering you a bonus."

"A bonus?"

This threw Raul completely off balance.

"That's what I said. Once you're at the bedroom door, I'll tell you where and when you can find Cesar."

"You know that?"

"I wouldn't be able to tell you otherwise."

"Why would you want to tell me?"

"It's my guarantee that you'll keep your end of the bargain. Besides, I'm hoping the two of you have a very convivial reunion. It might save me some work later."

For a moment or two Raul was silent. Russell knew the proposition must seem very tempting to him. The knife wasn't Raul's only weapon. He would be assuming this was something Russell had overlooked. Even so, he had one last objection.

"You're blocking my way to the door."

"So I'll move."

Russell stepped further into the room, keeping the bed between himself and Raul. Although he was aware of Pilar's imploring eyes looking up at him, he did his best to ignore them. He couldn't afford any distractions when he was dealing with somebody as unpredictable as Raul.

"Drop the ammunition on the floor."

Raul sounded very tense.

"It's a deal then?"

"It's a deal."

As he dropped the clip of bullets to the carpet and kicked them away from him, Russell knew they were at the moment of truth. This was the moment when Raul might still decide to slit Pilar's throat. But he didn't. Instead he walked quickly along the bed, not stopping until he was half concealed by the door. Russell guessed he would be easing the Savage out of the waistband of his trousers.

"Well?" Raul demanded. "Where do I find Cesar?"

"He'll be down at the harbour." Pilar was gurgling behind the gag but Russell didn't pay any attention. If it was an attempted warning, it was superfluous. He only intended to keep to the bargain as long as Raul did. "There's a boat there called the *Amico*. It belongs to an American named Anderson. Cesar should be going on board sometime after two tomorrow morning."

"The bastard. He told me it was arranged for twenty-four hours later."

"It all goes to show." Russell wasn't at all sympathetic. "You can't trust anybody nowadays."

"It's funny you should say that." Raul had undergone another mood swing. He was smiling again as he started to come back into the bedroom. "I think . . ."

Russell never did learn what Raul thought. Removing the clip from the Browning had simply been window dressing. The single round had been there in the chamber all the time, ready for the moment when Raul was well away from Pilar and offered a clear target. As Raul stepped out from behind the door, Russell finally had his opportunity and he shot

Raul in the heart. At least, that was where the bullet would have gone if Raul's left arm, the arm which had been concealed behind the door, hadn't been coming up and across as he tried to bring the Savage into play. Raul took the bullet in his biceps and fell backwards, out of sight behind the door again.

Empty gun or not, Russell was all for finishing it there and then. He had already started forward when he abruptly changed his mind. Raul must have squeezed the trigger of his own gun as he fell and the Savage blasted a jagged hole in the door. Russell was showered with splinters and a large chunk of plaster was removed from the wall behind him. It didn't matter a damn whether the shot had been aimed or not. When the bullets were flying, Russell went to ground. He was already hugging the carpet when a second hole appeared in the door. This time he was showered with glass as a Degas print suffered the worst of the damage. Antique or not, the Savage still packed one hell of a punch.

A quick roll took Russell to where the Browning's clip was lying. It only took a fraction of a second to reload, then Russell made a couple of holes of his own in the panels of the door, firing low at where Raul should have been. He wasn't, though. Raul was crashing through the living room on his way to the front door of the flat. Russell went after him, coming out of the bedroom as Raul exited through the front door. The light was bad, Raul was moving fast and Russell didn't have time to steady himself. Even so he clearly heard the soft thwack as the snap shot hit flesh. It was followed by a much louder thud as Raul went down a second time.

Russell didn't go after him immediately. He was listening and there was nothing to hear. This was worrying. The bullet had hit Raul in the right side, just above the hip, and there weren't any vital organs there. Unless Raul had dived headfirst into a wall and knocked himself out, he was lying in the corridor and waiting for Russell to come running through the door after him.

For the time being Russell wasn't running anywhere. Raul had left his knife behind in the bedroom, along with some of his blood. Russell used the knife to free Pilar's hands.

"Rub your wrists to get the circulation going again," he told her. "Then untie your legs."

"You're going after Raul."

"Yes."

Russell was already on his way to the kitchen, heading for the second exit from the flat.

"Will you be back?"

"I don't know."

Although it was a most unsatisfactory leave-taking, there wasn't time for any more. Russell didn't make a sound as he opened the kitchen door. It was only four steps to the junction with the main corridor and

Russell covered them on tiptoe. There was no sign of Raul when he peeped round the corner and for an instant the hairs on the back of his neck bristled as he considered the possibility that he might have been outmanoeuvred, that Raul had gone back into the apartment. Then he saw the bloody handprint on the wall at the top of the stairs and he knew Raul was on the run again. Russell started to run himself. Wounded or not, Raul was still dangerous and there was no question of allowing him to escape.

Raul was running pretty well for a man with two bullets in him. He was about twenty metres away when Russell hit the street looking strong. It was a long shot but not too long. Russell held the Browning in both hands, ignoring the hubbub in the building behind him as he sighted on Raul's back. What he couldn't ignore was the young couple who had stepped out onto the pavement on the far side of the street. They were near enough to the line of fire for him to lower the Browning again. Too many innocents had died already.

More people were coming out into the street all the time, some of them from the building he had just left. The brief paralysis caused by the spate of gunfire had worn off and now it was rent-a-crowd time. As he set off in pursuit of Raul, Russell hoped nobody would be stupid enough to interfere.

He had never been a sprinter. What Russell had was fitness and endurance. These were the qualities he called on now, settling into a steady lope he could maintain forever. Even if he hadn't been wounded, Raul would never have outlasted him. As it was, Russell was gaining with every stride, hauling him in like a fish on a line. They had lost their audience after they rounded the first corner and this was when Raul became aware of the inexorable presence behind him. A quick glance over his shoulder produced a brief burst of speed but it couldn't last. Then Russell was gaining again, running easily, knowing that very soon he would be within a range where he couldn't miss.

This time it was the woman in the yellow Metro who thwarted him. Raul had been running in the middle of the side street. When he reached the intersection, he just kept on running and the driver of the Metro couldn't have seen him until he was right on her bonnet. The best she could do was slam on her brakes and even then she caught Raul a glancing blow which knocked him sprawling. For a moment Russell was unsighted, but he distinctly heard the sound of the car door opening.

It all happened simultaneously. The woman started to ask Raul if he was all right, Russell shouted out a warning and Raul shot the woman. A second later he was using the car as a shield while he fired at Russell, the bullets coming close enough to send Russell diving into the doorway to his left. By the time Russell was ready to shoot back, Raul was already in the Metro, gunning the engine back to life. There was no real target for Russell to aim at, only an outline, but he put four shots into the car, aiming at where the driving seat ought to be, before the Metro was out of sight.

The woman was dead, sprawled at the side of the road. Raul had shot her full in the face and she must have died instantaneously. One quick check and Russell knew any number of ambulances and doctors would do her no good. He could leave her for some other Good Samaritan and concentrate on Raul. By now the Metro was already a hundred metres away and picking up speed. Russell needed transport of his own. Fortunately there were vehicles parked all along one side of the street and Viana wasn't like London or any other large city. Doors could be left unlocked, keys could be left in the ignition.

Russell struck lucky with the sixth car he tried, a Peugeot 505. Although it was bigger than he would have liked for the narrow streets, it started the first time and it gave him the edge in speed if not in manoeuvrability. As the Metro had long since vanished from sight, the question was where to speed to. If Raul was thinking clearly, he could lose himself forever in the maze of streets which comprised central Viana. If he was simply seeking to put distance between himself and Pilar's flat, he would follow the main road. This was the way Russell went, driving the Peugeot as fast as he dared.

As the seconds ticked by without any sign of his quarry, Russell began to think he must have guessed wrong. He would have to make a sweep of the back streets, hoping to pick Raul up there. At least, this was what he thought until he reached the intersection with the Pátria, the road which ran along the front. It was the longest stretch of straight road on the island and the yellow Metro was there, no more than two hundred metres ahead. Russell cut across the bow of an elderly Ford pickup, earning himself an indignant blast on the horn, then floored the accelerator pedal. Fortunately there was virtually no traffic and what little there was had the sense to make way for him. Once he had narrowed the gap to fifty metres, Russell slowed down. There was still one car between them, a maroon Fiat Uno, but this was an irrelevance. He was now in a position to cover any move Raul made.

At the end of the Pátria, Raul surprised Russell. Instead of turning left and following the road which wound up out of Viana, Raul carried straight on, heading into the dock area. The Uno had turned left and Russell doused his own lights as he followed the Metro between the warehouses, his foot suddenly heavy on the accelerator. There had been no conscious decision to act. It was merely a matter of seizing the opportunity. The red traffic lights were there a hundred metres ahead, flickering their warning. Russell could see the bulk of the diesel locomotive emerging from among the buildings to his left. As Raul slowed to a halt, Russell surged forward, slamming the Peugeot into the back of the Metro.

The impact sent the smaller, lighter vehicle spinning forward onto the track and a fraction of a second later the locomotive hit it broadside on. Although the train wasn't travelling particularly fast, its sheer weight flipped the Metro into the air. And when it came down, it landed rear first, ripping the petrol tank open. There must have been sparks too as the Metro rolled because the explosion was almost instantaneous. Russell only watched the miniature fireball for a moment before he put the Peugeot into reverse. There was still a lot of work left to be done.

SIXTEEN

For the life of him, Bewick couldn't work out what the hell Lopes was doing. When he had first come out of the house and climbed into the Datsun, there had seemed to be a sense of purpose about him. He had had the look of a man with somewhere to go and Bewick had experienced the first surge of adrenaline since he had been parked outside the house. It hadn't taken him very long to realize the adrenaline was wasted. Once he was behind the wheel, Lopes had appeared to lose all his urgency. He was driving the streets of Viana like a sightseer, travelling as though he had no particular destination in mind. At first Bewick had suspected the superintendent might be checking for a tag but this was an explanation he had discarded almost immediately. The way Lopes was behaving, the only way he was going to spot his tail was if Bewick held up a large sign saying I'M RIGHT HERE BEHIND YOU. Even then Lopes would probably have missed it.

"Russell, you bastard, are you out there?"

If he was, Russell still wasn't answering, just like he hadn't been since the early afternoon. A lot of old doubts were beginning to resurface. Although Russell's explanations had sounded awfully convincing in the morning, this was nothing to go by. He would have sounded equally convincing if he had been lying through his teeth. And he could well have been lying. Worse still, he could have been telling part of the truth. Lopes and Russell went back years. What if the two of them were in it together? What if Bewick had been pointed in Lopes's direction to keep him safely away from the real action? There were so many different permutations of possible deception Bewick was developing a headache thinking about them all. Not that it really made any difference. Lopes was all he had and he had to stick with him come what may.

It was pure self-indulgence, a farewell to the town he had lived in for most of his life. Almost every street he drove along had its own memories, most of them sweet, a few of them bitter. Viana had been his home and Lopes had been happy there. His roots were so deeply imbedded that until a few years ago leaving would have been unthinkable. He had had Alfreda and he had had the police force and they were all he had wanted from life. Lopes had loved them both but in the space of a few months they had both been taken from him. A large part of him had withered away when Alfreda had died but for a time Lopes had compensated by immersing himself in his work. Then Targa had been appointed to the post which should have been his by right and his second love had been taken from him as well. Although Lopes had tried to soldier on, he just didn't have the stomach for it. Early retirement had been one obvious answer but exactly what was he going to retire to? Apart from his memories there was nothing left for him on Madura.

Although the morality of what he had done bothered him a little, this wasn't going to keep Lopes awake at night. There was too much bitterness in him. He had lost everything which was rightfully his. His only reward for years of selfless dedication had been to be saddled with a useless prick like Targa. Wealth wouldn't replace the woman he had loved or make him chief of police but a few years of luxury were no more than his due. The only thing he regretted was the people who had died, something he had never intended. Unfortunately, it was too late to put the clock back. Russell would deal with Raul Cavalcanti. Lopes had a new life to start.

It was time to begin now. Self-indulgence was dead. Long live luxurious self-indulgence. Who knew? With money to burn, he might rediscover his taste for women.

After a quick check of his watch, Lopes turned up into the narrow streets of the old town. The house he stopped at on the 4 de Abril had originally belonged to his parents. When they had died, Lopes had rented it out but for the past two years it had stood empty. Lopes doubted whether more than a handful of people knew it was still in his possession and the VENDE-SE sign in the window was no more than a front, something to keep the neighbours from becoming curious. Nobody in their right mind was going to pay the price he was asking. He supposed it was going to stay empty for much longer now. Sorting out the legal implications could take forever.

For a while Lopes simply drifted around the house, wandering aimlessly from room to room. Nearly all of them were as his parents had left them. None of the furniture had been changed and where he had redecorated, the style and colour scheme remained the same. There was a comfortable familiarity about the place but, like his own house, Lopes would have no qualms about leaving it behind. His attachments were to people.

He was thinking about Alfreda again and this made him linger in his old bedroom. For the first two years of their married life, the metal-frame bed had been the one they had shared. It was the same bed where they had first made love one hot summer afternoon while his parents were at the market in Obidos. Sexually it had been a disaster, both of them too inexperienced and too eager to know what they were doing. All the same, it had been very sweet. Thinking about it brought the glimmer of a smile to Lopes's face and he patted the old brass bedstead before he turned away.

The suitcase he had come for was on top of the wardrobe and Lopes grunted with effort as he lifted it down. It contained all the possessions he would be taking with him. After he had switched off the light, Lopes took one last look out of the window. The street outside wasn't much of a view but it was the one he had grown up with.

The car parked round the corner of the Raimundo Alves was an intrusion. Although it was parked in shadow, Lopes was able to identify the vehicle as a Seat. More important, it shouldn't be there. He might have moved away from the area years before but Lopes had never completely lost touch. Very few people in the area could afford a car and of those who did have one, none Lopes knew of owned a Seat. More than likely there was a totally innocent explanation for the car's presence. On the other hand, Lopes couldn't afford to take anything for granted.

Once the house was locked up and his suitcase was in the boot of the Datsun, he drove off slowly, keeping a careful eye on the mirror. Five minutes and several corners later there was no doubt at all in his mind. He was definitely being followed. It seemed his departure from Madura wasn't going to be as trouble-free as he had imagined.

At the entrance to the fishing harbour, Cesar cut the outboard motor, drifting in silently with the tide. There were certain times of day when the harbour was a scene of frenetic activity, crowded with fishermen, their families and the buyers. This was early in the morning when the fishing boats returned home. Then, later on, the tourists would arrive, ready to be impressed by anybody who even vaguely resembled a fisherman. This was where most of the money was made nowadays. As the shoals of fish became smaller and the shoals of holidaymakers became larger, the nets on many of the boats were merely there for decoration or local colour. It was far easier and far more lucrative to run a two-hour pleasure trip than to spend all night looking for fish which might not be there.

All this was during the daytime, though. At night the fishing port was virtually deserted. The real fishermen were out at sea and the tourists were busy getting drunk in the bars. This was why Cesar had cut the outboard motor. The port was an obvious place for the police to be watching and he had no intention of advertising his arrival, especially in a stolen boat.

The *Amico* was moored at the west end of the port, in the lee of the mole. Cesar drifted in the opposite direction, losing himself among the small army of pleasure craft. The *Maduran Queen* was one of the largest and Cesar used the oars to steer himself alongside, tying on to the dinghy at the stern. Rope ladders were no strangers to him and Cesar went up fast, stopping three-quarters of the way up.

"It's all right," he whispered into the darkness. "It's me, Cesar."

"Bloody typical," a voice responded from the deck. "You never come quite far enough up for me to get a good crack at your head."

Cesar went up the last few rungs of the rope ladder and Pedro Filho stood up from where he had been crouched by the rail, the length of lead piping dangling from his right hand. Filho was the owner of the *Maduran Queen*. He had slept on board ever since his boat had been vandalized the previous year and any unannounced nighttime visitors were given short thrift.

"I didn't know you owned a boat of your own," he said.

"I don't," Cesar admitted. "I borrowed it from a friend."

This produced a derisive grunt of amusement from Filho.

"Let me guess," he said. "You forgot to tell your friend you were borrowing it."

"I didn't have the time." Cesar was grinning in the darkness. "Perhaps you can drop it off on your way past Cascais tomorrow morning."

"Why can't you return it yourself? I'm sure your 'friend' will be pleased to see you."

"I'm off to the mainland later tonight," Cesar explained. "At least, I hope I am. Have the police been poking around the port today?"

"No more than usual. What have you been up to apart from stealing boats?"

"Make me a cup of coffee and I'll tell you."

The *Maduran Queen* was as good a place as any to waste a couple of hours and Cesar was sure he could dream up some story which would satisfy Filho.

Bewick's thoughts about Viana were far from charitable. In the warren of back streets he didn't dare drop too far behind Lopes for fear of losing him and this was something he couldn't afford. Ever since the superintendent had come out of the house carrying a suitcase, Bewick had known that Russell's suspicions were correct. In all probability there was a million dollars inside and until he knew for sure he was sticking to Lopes like a limpet. At the same time, being spotted would be as disastrous as losing contact. It was exceedingly difficult to strike the right balance with no other traffic around to provide cover.

When the Datsun eventually turned off into the dock area, Bewick switched off the headlights of the Seat and moved even closer. Although he thought he knew where Lopes was heading, he had to be able to deal with any unexpected diversions. After a quarter of a mile of crawling along in the shadow of the warehouses, there was the flicker of the

Datsun's brake lights ahead. Bewick stopped immediately, pulling right up alongside the wall of one of the sheds. There was another brief flash of light as Lopes opened the door, then Bewick caught a glimpse of him at the boot of the Datsun. After this he was gone.

For a second or two Bewick stayed where he was, allowing his eyes to adjust to the dark. Although he hadn't been able to see where Lopes had gone, Bewick knew where he wasn't. He would have been visible if he had moved away from the warehouses.

Bewick removed the interior light and slipped out of the Seat, careful not to make any noise. For a moment he simply stood and listened. He could hear footsteps moving away ahead of him and Bewick started after them, keeping to the deepest of the shadows. When Bewick stopped again, level with the Datsun, he could still hear Lopes ahead of him. He appeared to be walking along the row of warehouses. It seemed sensible to Bewick to remove the gun from his shoulder holster before he started off again in pursuit. Although he didn't think Lopes knew he was there, it was silly to take risks.

The first hiccup didn't occur until they reached the last warehouse in the line. One moment Bewick could hear Lopes slip-slopping along ahead of him. The next the sound of his footsteps had ceased. To begin with, Bewick thought Lopes must have stopped to check the dimly lit area of quayside ahead of him. As the seconds dragged into half a minute, Bewick decided he must be wrong. He started inching forward again, eyes and ears straining to detect any hint of Lopes's presence. When he reached the open door, he knew where Lopes must be. For some reason Lopes had gone inside the warehouse.

This meant it was a hell of a sight more than a hiccup. Until this point Bewick had had a measure of control. He had been the hunter. He had thought he knew what Lopes was doing and where he was going. Better still, Bewick had been fairly confident that Lopes was unaware of his presence. Now everything had been thrown into question. The only certainty was that Bewick would have to go into the warehouse after Lopes, even if this entailed walking into a trap. There would be other exits and, whatever else happened, he still couldn't afford to lose his quarry.

Bewick ducked into the warehouse fast, sliding round the edge of the door so he wasn't backlit for more than an instant. Five quick steps along the wall, then he simply stood, absolutely motionless. It was pitch dark and he couldn't distinguish a thing. He would have to rely entirely upon his ears, filtering out all extraneous noises while he listened for Lopes. At least, this was what Bewick thought until the flashlight was switched on behind him.

All the while he had been driving, Lopes had been wondering how best to tackle the Englishman. Trying to lose him had never been a serious option. Although he could do it easily enough, he needed to talk to Bewick. He needed to find out how much was known and how much guessed. There was also the question of Russell. Lopes didn't underestimate Bewick, but he had no doubts at all about where the real danger lay.

In the end, the warehouse had seemed the obvious solution. The only nasty moment had come while he was waiting inside, wondering whether the bait would be accepted or not. Once the Englishman had followed him in, it was simply a matter of thumbing on the switch of the flashlight.

"Don't move a muscle," he said, putting every iota of urgency he could muster into his voice. "I really don't want to kill you."

For a moment it was still touch and go. He could see Bewick's shoulders tensing as he debated the odds for and against resistance. It was a relief when he reached the only sensible conclusion and relaxed.

"How long have you known I was tagging you?"

"Long enough," Lopes told him. "Transfer your gun to your left hand. Then throw it as far away as you can."

"I assume you really are pointing a weapon at me?"

"You'd better believe it."

Bewick did. He also knew he was in deep, deep trouble, but for the moment there was nothing he could do about it. As he listened to his gun skittering off across the warehouse floor, he hoped some opportunity would present itself later. Otherwise the warehouse was likely to be the last place he ever saw. In a detached way, he realized he was very frightened.

"That's good," Lopes said. "Now lean against the wall. Move your feet back and take your weight on your hands."

By the time he was positioned to Lopes's satisfaction, Bewick was pretty sure there weren't going to be any chances. Lopes wasn't going to come any closer and there was no way he could launch an attack from where he was. His life was going to depend on what Lopes had said about not wanting to kill him. Unfortunately, this wasn't something he had much faith in. From a practical point of view, he didn't see that the superintendent had any choice.

"Why were you following me?"

"I would have thought that was obvious." Bewick couldn't see any advantage in prevarication. "Tonight's the big night. It's when you skip Madura with your share of the ransom money."

"I see." Like Bewick, Lopes wasn't prevaricating. "How did you reach this conclusion?"

"Easily," Bewick told him. "You left a trail a mile wide."

"And who noticed this trail? Was it you or was it Alan?"

"It was a joint effort."

Although this was slightly stretching the truth, Bewick didn't feel any qualms at all.

"I see," Lopes said again. "How many other people have you told?"

"That's for you to find out."

There was no hesitation at all. Lopes shot Bewick in the fleshy part of his right thigh, hoping to miss the bone and artery but not really too bothered either way. To Bewick, it felt as though he had been punched very hard. Suddenly he found himself face down on the dirty concrete floor. When he tried to roll over, Lopes told him to stay where he was.

"Let's try again," Lopes suggested. "And please don't try to be clever. I don't have the time to waste and I assume you don't have too many parts of your body you want ruined."

"Too bloody true." The pain was just beginning to register and Bewick definitely didn't want to be shot anymore. "The answer is, we haven't told anybody at all."

"Not even Targa?"

"No."

"How about Dietrich?"

"Like I said, we haven't told anybody."

Although he was more frightened than ever, this wasn't the reason Bewick told the truth. There simply wasn't any point in lying. Not yet at any rate.

"What about Russell? Where is he now?"

"Would you believe me if I said I really didn't know?"

"That depends. You'll have to convince me."

"I'll do my best." The pain was really getting to Bewick now and he had to fight hard to concentrate. "Russell thought he had a line to the kidnapper's base. That's where he's been all day, trying to rescue the hostages. I haven't had any contact with him since early this afternoon. For all I know he's dead."

"Not Alan." Lopes said this with total confidence. "When were you last in contact? Was it after you'd handed over the ransom?"

"Yes."

"That must have come as a surprise to him."

"It did."

Bewick was quite happy to keep the conversation going. He knew it was likely to be very soon now and he still couldn't think of anything he could do about it.

"What alterations did he make to your arrangements?"

"We don't have any arrangements."

"I find that hard to believe."

"You shouldn't if you really know Russell. We have a great two-way partnership. The way it works is that he tells me what to do and I do it. In the meantime, he goes his own sweet way."

"What were his instructions to you?"

"I was to keep an eye on you."

"When were the two of you supposed to meet up again?"

"When Russell felt like it. He simply said he'd be in touch."

"How about the boat?"

"Which boat?"

"The *Amico,* the boat Cesar and I are using to leave Madura."

"This is the first I've heard of it. We knew you must have arranged some means of leaving the island after you'd collected the ransom money, but we weren't sure what it was. That's why I was supposed to follow you."

"I see," Lopes said for a third time. "So you have no idea at all where Russell is at the moment?"

"Your guess is as good as mine."

Lopes was reasonably satisfied that most of what the Englishman had told him was true. He was also certain that other things had been left unsaid, but there wasn't time to probe for them. He had already spent too long in the warehouse. Slowly he raised his gun, lining it up on the back of Bewick's head. He had really meant it when he said he didn't want to kill him. The trouble was, once you started along a path you had to follow it to the end.

"If you're really interested," Russell said. "I'm right here."

His voice came from the darkness behind the superintendent.

It was the shot which had brought Russell in through the back door of the warehouse. He had been on his way anyway but the sound of Lopes's gun had added a certain urgency. After he had heard the voices and realized Bewick wasn't badly injured, he had taken his time, staying back in the shadows while Lopes had conducted his rudimentary interrogation.

"What happens now?" Lopes asked.

"You should be able to work that out for yourself," Russell told him. "I hand you over to Targa."

"Do that and I'll spend the rest of my life in jail."

Lopes sounded aggrieved.

"Think yourself lucky. A lot of people have died because of you."

"It wasn't meant to happen that way."

"That's no defence and you know it. Incidentally, I'd appreciate it if you dropped your gun."

Lopes didn't obey immediately. Although he was no longer threatening Bewick, he kept the revolver in his hand.

"We go back a long way, Alan," he said. "Doesn't that count for anything?"

"You know it doesn't. We could have known each other from birth and it still wouldn't make any difference."

"I was afraid you'd say that."

For such a big man Lopes moved surprisingly fast, ducking and turning in the same motion. Even so, he never had a chance. Russell had shot him twice in the head before he was halfway round.

"Silly sod." Bewick was still on the floor, but he had heaved himself over onto his back. "He even forgot to switch off the torch."

"He didn't forget anything," Russell said. "He was making sure there was plenty of light for me to make a clean kill. Would you want to spend the rest of your life in prison surrounded by men you'd helped to lock up?"

"I suppose not."

It only took Russell a moment to check the superintendent's body. Then he went across to where Bewick had propped himself against the wall.

"How bad is it?" he enquired.

"Terrible," Bewick told him. "It's just that I'm being very brave."

Although he had tried to make a joke of it, the whole of his thigh was throbbing with pain. The wound might not be serious but it certainly wasn't pleasant.

"You're lucky." Russell had already finished his brief examination. "The bullet went straight through. As far as I can see, it didn't hit anything except flesh. You're not even bleeding too badly."

Bewick wasn't too happy about Russell's dismissive tone. In his book, lucky people were the ones who hadn't been shot at all.

"How did you know we were in here?" he asked.

"I saw the cars parked outside. Come on. Let's see how good you are at hopping. I'll take your weight provided you promise not to get any blood on my clothes."

With Russell to help him, moving wasn't too difficult. When they reached Lopes's Datsun, though, he signalled for a stop.

"There's a suitcase in the boot," he said. "The ransom money may be inside."

"I doubt it but I'd better check to make sure. Lean yourself against the car while I take a look."

The car keys were in Lopes's trouser pocket and Russell had to go back into the warehouse to collect them. It proved to be a wasted journey. All Lopes had intended to start his new life with was a change of underwear and a few shirts. After Russell had slammed the boot shut again, he helped Bewick to the hired car, half lifting him into the driver's seat.

"There you are," he said. "Can you manage to drive to police headquarters?"

"I think so."

"That's just as well. Otherwise I'd have to leave you here."

Although Russell was smiling as he spoke, Bewick didn't doubt him for a moment.

"What do you want me to say?"

"Tell Targa about Lopes. The hostages should be back by now."

"Both of them?"

"Both of them," Russell confirmed.

"I thought the Haywood girl was supposed to be expendable."

"That was Dietrich's thought, not mine. Let him do his own dirty work. Or you can do it for him if that's what you want."

These were no more than words. Now that Janine Haywood had been recovered, it would be very difficult to lose her again.

"So that's it then?"

"Just about."

"How about the ransom money?"

"Don't worry." Russell was grinning again. "I'll take good care of it."

Bewick was sure he would and he didn't give a damn. Having his life saved was worth a million any day of the week.

Anderson was somebody who paid attention to instinct. He had reason to because on occasion it had saved his life, like the time off Tampa in 1978. All the weather reports had been good but Anderson hadn't believed them. He had sensed the storm building up. This was why he had been safely anchored and battened down when it hit, sinking half the small craft off the west Florida coast. And it wasn't just storms either. Anderson had a nose for trouble in all its forms and he could smell something nasty now. The night had a bad feel to it.

"It's a bastard all right," he muttered, pouring himself another generous measure of Hennessy. "I ought to wring Cesar's neck."

Not that there was likely to be any need. Unless he was very much mistaken, Cesar would be lucky to last the night anyway. It was the other one who really bothered Anderson, the cold-eyed Englishman. There had been several occasions in the past few days when Anderson had been tempted to take a long vacation, to stay clear until it had all blown over. The trouble was, with bastards like Russell it never did blow over. His kind were like elephants. They never forgot and Anderson didn't want to spend the rest of his life looking back over his shoulder. No, he would do as Russell said. It went against the grain, but he would do it all the same. And he would pray he was still in one piece when it was all over.

Just then there was a movement on deck and Anderson pushed himself up off the deck, surprised to discover how drunk he was. It didn't matter, of course—he could do the run to Morocco in his sleep—but it was a shock to realize how unsteady he was on his feet. He must have downed the best part of a bottle while he had been brooding about the rotten cards life kept dealing him. Although the movement wasn't repeated, Anderson clambered up the aft companionway, the cool night air doing something to clear his head after the fug of the cabin. At the top of the steps he stopped. There were no lights on deck and it was too dark for him to see his visitor.

"Who is it?" he demanded, his voice only slightly slurred.

There was no answer and Anderson swore under his breath. He was in no mood to play silly buggers.

"Is that you, Cesar?"

There was still no reply and Anderson swore again. Perhaps he was so drunk he had been imagining things. One thing he wasn't imagining was the acrid smell of burning. There must be a fire somewhere on shore and Anderson was moving towards the rail to see if he could spot the flames when his feet slipped from under him. He went down hard, knocking his coccyx halfway up his spine, and he swore much longer this time. Something had been spilled on the deck—he could feel the dampness under his hand—but it was too dark to see what it was. Anderson hauled himself back to his feet and pulled his Zippo out of his pocket.

As soon as he saw the blood on his hand, he knew beyond any shadow of a doubt that all his instincts had been right. He was still incredulously examining his hand when he realized the smell of burning was behind him, on the boat. By then the knowledge was useless. The charred hand was already slipping over his shoulder to grip his chin, jerking his head back and to the side. The last thing Anderson ever saw was the faint glint of light on the shard of glass before it sliced across his exposed throat.

Raul knew he was very badly injured. Although he couldn't remember very clearly, as far as he could recall he'd been shot twice, run over by a car and then incinerated. This was without including any internal damage he might have suffered when the train had ploughed into the passenger side of the car. If he was honest with himself, he was pretty sure he was dying and it would be the burns which killed him. He'd only seen his hands and arms but it was safe to assume the rest of him was pretty much the same, which meant he didn't have a great deal of skin left. It was ironic really. The burns would kill him, but if the petrol tank hadn't exploded, he wouldn't have been blown clear. He'd have been ground into a pulp along with the car.

Only his hatred had kept him going this far, because he must have crawled half the way to the *Amico*. It was the certain knowledge that this was where he would find Cesar which had provided the motivation. O.K., it was all over for him but as sure as hell he wasn't going on his own. There was a score to be settled first.

Killing Anderson had been an irrelevance. In fact, Raul wasn't entirely certain why he had done it. The only real reason he could come up with was that it had seemed expedient. He simply hadn't been able to think of anything else to do with him. Now there was Cesar to wait for. This was Raul's sole *raison d'être* as he lay in the shadows of the wheelhouse, conserving his strength for one final effort.

The *Amico* was far too quiet for Russell's liking. Although he wouldn't have used the gangplank in any case, now he had an additional reason for going aboard over the stern. For a full minute he simply lay on the deck by the rail, more convinced than ever that there was something amiss. The last time he had visited the *Amico,* his mere weight on deck had been sufficient to alert Anderson. Now there was no response at all.

Speculation was useless and Russell began to crawl along the deck, keeping beside the rail on the seaward side. He didn't stand until he reached the short ladder leading to the roof of the cabin and wheelhouse. It was a situation where he wanted to dominate the high ground and Russell went up smoothly and quickly, keeping his body low as he rolled onto the roof. There was still no reaction from Anderson and Russell could still see no reason to alter his original opinion. The boat was too quiet and too dark, the only light coming from the open door at the head of the aft companionway. There was also a faint odour of burning in the air which made Russell uneasy without him quite knowing why.

Still flat on his stomach, Russell eased himself across the roof until he could see the gangplank leading to the quayside. He also had a view of the deck and as soon as he saw the body he froze. Although it was too dark for him to identify the victim, there was never any doubt in his mind about the man being dead. Corpses always had a special look about them. He was still debating what he ought to do when the sound of light footsteps coming along the quay towards the *Amico* made up his mind for him. He would wait and see what new surprises the night had to offer.

"It's all clear," Filho said.

"You're sure?"

"Of course I am. There isn't a policeman within half a mile."

This was good enough for Cesar. Filho might not be the brightest man on Madura—otherwise he would never have believed the cock-and-bull story about a scam at the casino—but he was reliable. If he said there were no police around, there weren't, and this was all Cesar needed to know. He himself had been keeping an eye on the *Amico* while Filho was taking his stroll, and there had been nothing there to alarm him either. O.K., there weren't any lights on deck, but this wasn't anything unusual. When this had happened before it had meant Anderson was down in his cabin with a bottle of Hennessy or Bushmills for company. Anderson was just about the heaviest drinker Cesar had ever met.

"Thanks, Pedro," he said. "I'll be off then."

"Good luck. I won't forget to return the boat for you in the morning."

"That's one I owe you. I'll be by to see you as soon as I get back to Madura."

"Sure."

There was a note of profound scepticism in Filho's voice, which suggested he might not be quite as dumb as he seemed. This wasn't something Cesar bothered to check out. Now the waiting was done with, he was eager to get it finished.

As Filho had promised, the dock area was deserted. Although Cesar kept his eyes open and one hand on the butt of the Savage, he didn't see a soul. At the bottom of the *Amico*'s gangplank he hesitated, wondering whether there was some little ceremony he ought to perform before leaving Maduran soil for the last time. Then he thought the hell with it and went aboard without a backward glance.

The deck was still in darkness, but light was spilling from the half-open door of the aft companionway. This was where Cesar headed, grinning to himself. In the doorway he stopped.

"Come on, you drunken sot," he said, careful not to raise his voice too loud. "Let's be having you."

There was no reply and Cesar smiled again. This had happened once before and on that occasion he had found Anderson fast asleep on his bunk, nursing an empty bottle in his arms. Although this was what he expected to find now, he didn't. The bottle of Hennessy was there all right, but it wasn't empty and Anderson wasn't holding it, asleep or otherwise. A couple of minutes later Cesar knew that Anderson wasn't anywhere belowdecks and he experienced the first prickle of unease.

After he had thought about it for a minute, Cesar decided it was a hell of a sight more than a prickle. Leaving the suitcase on the bunk, he slipped the Savage out of his belt before he started back up the steps. At the top he paused to switch on the deck lights. Then, taking a deep breath, he stepped outside.

The dead man was Anderson. Although this was something Russell had already guessed, it was always nice to know he was right. With the lights on he could see the smuggler hadn't died prettily. Somebody had cut his throat from ear to ear, which meant there was plenty of blood to stain the once spotless deck. As Cesar had only come aboard in the last five minutes, it was safe to assume he wasn't responsible. No, the killer was in the wheelhouse unless Russell was very much mistaken and for the moment he didn't have a clue to his identity. Not that this really mattered. Cesar would flush the killer out and then Russell could pick up the pieces. He edged a little nearer to the middle of the cabin roof and then lay still again. Unless somebody disturbed him or he had the oppor-

tunity to lay his hands on Cesar's suitcase, Russell was perfectly happy
to remain where he was.

Cesar's heart didn't quite make it to his mouth when he first saw the
body, but it came pretty damn close. His immediate thought was that
somebody else would have to ferry him to the mainland. Almost simultaneously he was acknowledging the corpse as Raul's handiwork. The
gaping wound in the neck, the killing for killing's sake, were hallmarks
he had come to recognize. Raul had been busy with his knife again,
which meant that somehow he must have learned about Cesar's private
arrangement with Anderson. And as sure as eggs were eggs, Raul
wouldn't just have walked away after murdering Anderson. He would be
lurking somewhere on board, waiting to collect the main prize.

As Cesar didn't want to be collected, he drew back against the cabin
wall while he thought things through. To his surprise, he wasn't at all
afraid. At the back of his mind he had always suspected there would
have to be a settling of accounts and now it had come he was ready.
More important, he had the edge. Simply shooting him wouldn't be
sufficient to satisfy Raul. If it had been, he could have gunned Cesar
down the moment he stepped aboard the *Amico*. No, the maniac would
almost certainly want to use his precious knife. He would want to make
Cesar bleed and suffer. He would enjoy gloating as he died.

Although the thought made Cesar shiver a little, this was what gave
him his edge. He was sane, whereas Raul was a complete nut case. Cesar
wasn't motivated by revenge and killing wasn't his main hobby. He
simply wanted Raul out of his face. This was why he intended to start
shooting the instant he saw the crazy bastard and keep on until Raul was
dead.

First he had to find him, though. As Raul hadn't been below, the two
most likely places for him to be were the wheelhouse or the roof of the
cabin. Cesar favoured the former. He had been around Raul long
enough to have some idea how his diseased mind worked. When it was
operating on a human wavelength, it went in straight lines. The wheelhouse was somewhere Cesar was sure to go. In that case, this was where
Raul would wait. Not that Cesar would have put money on it. If Raul
was having one of his off days, he could be hanging by his toes from the
anchor.

One thing was for sure, though. Leaving the body in full view on the
deck had been a kind of gruesome calling card, an announcement that
Raul was there. He had thrown down the gauntlet and it was for Cesar
to pick it up. This was something he intended to do quickly. With Anderson dead, Cesar had other arrangements to make.

His legs just weren't working anymore. They were useless appendages he
had to drag around with him. Raul had discovered this when he had

attempted to stand after he had heard Cesar come aboard. He hadn't even been able to make it to his knees. The best he could manage was to crawl into the corner of the wheelhouse, by the door, still clutching the shard of glass from the car window in his hand. Although it wasn't much compared with his knife, it had been good enough for Anderson and it would have to do for Cesar as well. Raul was still thinking this when he drifted off into unconsciousness.

It had taken Cesar a few moments to realize that Anderson must have died where he lay. This meant the blood which was spattering the deck all the way from the body to the wheelhouse must have come from somebody else. Cesar had followed the trail cautiously, ready for anything, but his caution was superfluous. One look at Raul, or what remained of him, had been sufficient to tell him there was no danger there. Although Raul was still breathing, this was obviously only a very temporary state of affairs. God alone knew what had happened to him, but it had clearly been drastic. Most of his clothing had been burned away and his body was either cooked medium rare or covered with blood. It was a miracle he had made it this far.

For a few moments Cesar kept the Savage pointing at Raul's head, his finger on the trigger. The temptation to pump a couple of bullets into him was very strong but there didn't seem to be much point. With Raul so close to death, shooting him would be a waste of ammunition. Besides, a shot would mean noise and Cesar didn't want to attract any attention.

Stuffing the gun back into the waistband of his trousers, Cesar left the wheelhouse and started back along the deck. Now Anderson was dead, somebody else would have to take him to the mainland and it would have to be done that night. It seemed Filho was elected. He would be reluctant and he would play hard to get, but he would do it all right if the money was right. Money was something Cesar had plenty of. At least so he thought until he reached Anderson's cabin. The suitcase was no longer on the bunk where Cesar had left it and suddenly the Savage was back in his hand. For the first time, it occurred to Cesar that there might be somebody other than Anderson and Raul on board.

Even though his eyes were closed, Raul had been aware of Cesar's presence in the wheelhouse. Although he had tried to will himself into action, to do what he had been waiting to do, there had been no response at all from his body. He hadn't been able to lift his eyelids, let alone his limbs. Raul had had to sit there, slumped against the wall, expecting the bullet which would end it.

But it hadn't come. Cesar had turned and walked away. It was this which had finally stirred Raul into one final effort. It was the disdain which infuriated him, magnified his hatred for Cesar a hundredfold. He,

Raul, wasn't somebody to be shrugged off like that. While there was breath left in his body, no enemy should ever make the mistake of turning their back on him. This was something Raul intended to demonstrate now. It was simply a question of mind over matter.

Only it wasn't simple at all. The mind Raul was relying on kept playing tricks, drifting in and out of focus, so there were long moments when he wasn't sure what he was doing or why. The matter wasn't too easy to control either, even when his mind was behaving itself. The low sill at the bottom of the wheelhouse doorway became an almost insuperable obstacle and it seemed to take forever before Raul could shift his centre of gravity far enough for him to tilt forwards onto the deck. Even then it took him almost as long to untangle his feet and legs.

Progress along the deck was equally slow. In one of his semi-lucid moments, Raul thought of himself as a snail, leaving his own trail of slime behind. Only in his case it wasn't slime, it was blood. Raul could see the marks of his passage to the wheelhouse staining the deck and he had no reason to think it was any different now.

The longer he continued, the more frequent the blackouts became. Raul guessed they lasted longer too, but he had no way of telling. Once when he resurfaced to find a body close behind him, he thought the job was done and Cesar was dead. He was on the point of letting go then until a brief spark of sanity reminded him it was Anderson he had killed, not Cesar. Somehow, dredging up the very last of his reserves, Raul managed to force himself forwards again, crawling inch by tortured inch towards his objective.

Cesar had virtually ripped the cabins apart in the search and there wasn't a sign of the suitcase anywhere. He had even managed to force open the hidey-hole, the secret place which Anderson hadn't realized anybody else knew about. Although there had been money inside, it amounted to little more than a couple of thousand dollars in assorted currencies. Cesar had pocketed this as a matter of course, but this did nothing to appease his fury. He had sweated blood for the ransom money. He had literally put his life on the line for it and this made the million dollars rightfully his. He wasn't about to let it go easily.

Once he was satisfied that the suitcase wasn't belowdecks, Cesar sat on the edge of Anderson's bunk and smoked a cigarette. He already knew who had stolen his money. In fact, there was only one person it could be with Raul in the wheelhouse and all the others dead. Pilar had contacted Anderson through Patricio and this would have made the bar owner curious. With his contacts and a few educated guesses it wouldn't have been difficult to piece it all together. Although Cesar had always considered Patricio to be a friend, he didn't harbour any illusions. In his book, no friend was worth a million dollars and he assumed that Patricio felt the same. Somehow Patricio must have become aware of how much money was involved and this had made him greedy. He must have bided his time, waiting to move in when the moment was right, and by now the money would be hidden away somewhere on the Gorgulho. This was where Cesar was going now. He intended to recover his property and if it had to be over Patricio's dead body, so be it.

At the same time, Cesar was aware that there was an outside chance he was wrong. Patricio and the money might still be on board. While he smoked, Cesar was listening, filtering out the normal sounds of a moored boat. There was nothing to alarm him but there were too many dead bodies around for Cesar to be anything but careful. Before he left, Cesar switched out all the lights belowdecks and spent another five minutes standing at the foot of the companionway. There was still no movement from the deck and Cesar started silently up the steps, the Savage in his right hand.

At first Raul wasn't sure what had dragged him back out of the deep, dark hole he had tumbled into. It took him several seconds to reorientate himself and realize he was lying beside the entrance to the aft companionway. Almost simultaneously Raul realized the lights had gone out below and that somebody was coming up the steps. This could only be Cesar and the knowledge was sufficient to snap Raul fully awake. It was now or never, and he began inching himself forward, the jagged piece of glass held in front of him.

Cesar stopped when he was nearly at the top of the steps and Raul knew exactly what he was doing. Cesar was standing there with his head at deck level, looking and listening. A great calm had descended on Raul. Although he couldn't actually see Cesar, Raul knew he could have reached out a hand to touch him if he had wanted to. Revenge was only a few seconds away. Then Cesar moved upwards again, the moment Raul had been waiting for.

"Cesar," he croaked, pushing himself forward. "I'm over here, you bastard."

As Cesar's head swung towards him, Raul used the last of his strength to slice the glass across Cesar's throat. It went into his neck like a hot knife into butter and blood from the severed artery drenched Raul's face and arm. For a brief moment, as Cesar tumbled backwards down the companionway, Raul experienced perfect contentment. The sensation might have lasted longer if Russell hadn't chosen this time to lean over from the cabin roof and blow away the top of Raul's head.

Three-quarters of an hour later the *Amico* was well out to sea and it was time for Russell to tidy up. Apart from Cesar's, none of the bodies was particularly difficult to shift to the rail. Even so, Russell was glad he stripped to his underpants before he had attempted to move them. The entire front of his body was caked with blood by the time he had finished and he had to wash himself thoroughly before he resumed steering towards the African coast. It had ended up very messy indeed, far messier than Russell had originally anticipated. He could only hope that his passport to anonymity, the suitcase which was keeping him company in the wheelhouse, would make it all worthwhile.